My Ex-Best Men

A Contemporary Reverse Harem Romance

Rebel Bloom

Copyright © 2025 by Rebel Bloom

All rights reserved.

No portion of this book may be reproduced in any form without written permission from the publisher or author, except as permitted by U.S. copyright law.

Contents

1. ***Claire***   1
2. ***Claire***   6
3. ***Claire***   13
4. ***Claire***   19
5. ***Claire***   24
6. ***Claire***   30
7. ***Claire***   35
8. ***Claire***   41
9. ***Will***   46
10. ***Claire***   51
11. ***Claire***   56
12. ***Claire***   61
13. ***Claire***   66
14. ***Claire***   71
15. ***Anthony***   75
16. ***Claire***   80

17.	***Claire***	86
18.	***Claire***	91
19.	***Claire***	96
20.	***Will***	101
21.	***Claire***	106
22.	***Claire***	111
23.	***Claire***	116
24.	***Zane***	121
25.	***Claire***	126
26.	***Claire***	131
27.	***Claire***	136
28.	***Anthony***	142
29.	***Anthony***	146
30.	***Claire***	151
31.	***Will***	156
32.	***Claire***	161
33.	***Claire***	166
34.	***Will***	171
35.	***Claire***	177
36.	***Claire***	182
37.	***Claire***	187
38.	***Will***	191

39. ***Anthony*** 196
40. ***Claire*** 202
41. ***Claire*** 207
42. ***Zane*** 211
43. ***Claire*** 215
44. ***Will*** 220
45. ***Claire*** 225
46. ***Claire*** 231
47. ***Claire*** 236
48. ***Claire*** 241
49. ***Claire*** 247
50. ***Claire*** 253
51. ***Claire*** 258
52. ***Will*** 263
53. ***Claire*** 268
54. ***Anthony*** 273
55. ***Zane*** 278
56. ***Claire*** 286
57. ***Claire*** 291
58. ***Claire*** 296
59. ***Claire*** 301
60. ***Will*** 306

61.	***Claire***	311
62.	***Anthony***	316
63.	Epilogue	322
64.	Free Preview of My Ex's Roommates	328

1

Claire

Sprinting across the JFK Airport in a four-year-old bra that I'd stitched back together a dozen times because I wasn't willing to lose my comfort bra wasn't a great idea. Between the boob sweat and bounce from my C-cup breasts the bra was having a lot asked of it. A lot, a lot. As much as it was shocking to feel my tits spring free in the middle of my mad dash, it shouldn't have been surprising. The bra was hanging on by a literal thread. I couldn't slow down. My connecting flight to Miami was leaving in minutes. So, sweat pouring, boobs bouncing, I dodged a slow-moving family and played a small game of Red Rover with a line of people doing their best to get their favorite chicken sandwich.

I wasn't a gym girlie. I wasn't even a long walks kind of girlie. I was more of a sit in my favorite chair and read a dozen manuscripts before moving again girlie. I couldn't remember the last time I'd had to run. Junior High, maybe? It wasn't for me. I couldn't catch my breath and I was sweating in a way that made me want to apologize to the people around me. When I got to my gate and saw that I'd made it I doubled over and struggled to take a deep breath. Wiping my forehead on the back of my arm I straightened and hurried to the desk.

My glasses were fogged over as I slapped my ticket down on the counter. "Sorry. I... Whew. I need to work out more. This is embarrassing."

The woman on the other side of the counter took my ticket with a slight curl of her nose. She tapped at her computer for a moment and frowned. "Your seat's been changed."

I let out a polite laugh, hoping she was joking. I didn't think it was all that great of a joke but I knew when to stroke someone's ego. As far as I was concerned, she was the next great comedian. "You got me."

"Ma'am?" She looked at me like she thought I was insane. "Your ticket was upgraded to first class."

"Are you still joking?"

She frowned and motioned for me to measure my carry-on to make sure it fit. "I'm not joking, ma'am. Please place your luggage here and- Great. It fits perfectly. You're the last passenger to arrive so just go up the ramp and a stewardess will be waiting to show you to your seat. Enjoy your flight, Ms. Morgan."

After a travel day from hell I felt like the flight gods were finally smiling down on me. Or maybe it was Sophia and Jake. Upgrading my flight to first class was something they'd do to spoil me. I went to move past her and she suddenly shot her arm out to stop me.

"Um... I think there's something wrong with your..." She gestured at her own chest and winced.

I looked down and saw that my bra was open in a way that made it look like I had four boobs. I groaned and did the only thing I could think of to make it better. I slipped my arms inside my shirt and took the poor, broken bra the rest of the way off. I shoved it into my carry-on, unwilling to leave it behind. I hunched forward in an attempt to hide that I wasn't wearing a bra and smiled awkwardly at the woman. "Thanks. I'm not normally like this."

She held up her hands. "You're going to miss the flight if you don't go."

I lifted my purse higher on my shoulder and juggled my laptop case and carry-on so I could wave at her. Groaning as I realized how weird I was being, I hurried up the small ramp and tried to put the morning's events behind me. I was still a sweaty mess, but at least I was a sweaty mess with a first-class seat.

The stewardess waiting at the top of the ramp for me smiled brightly and motioned me onto the plane. She was great at her job because she didn't react to the state I was in at all. "Here you are, ma'am. As soon as we're in the air we can get you something to drink."

My face burned as I felt everyone in the first-class cabin look up at me. If the stewardess was already offering me something to drink, I had to imagine I looked worse than I thought. I followed her a few feet down the aisle and thanked her when she opened the overhead compartment for me. I shoved my carry-on in first and then struggled to get my laptop bag to fit.

Wrestling with it, I shot an apologetic look over my shoulder at the stewardess and then glanced down to apologize to the person sitting next to me who was probably getting an eye full of tits with the way I was struggling. When my gaze collided with the familiar pale green eyes staring back at me, it took my brain a solid ten seconds to catch up. The flight gods were definitely not smiling down on me. They were smirking and probably letting out evil laughs.

Those pale green eyes slowly moved lower until they were focused on my chest. "Long time no see, Claire."

Zane Wilson. The ex who broke my heart. The lead singer in the massively successful band, Velvet Moon. The man who single-handedly ruined rock music for me. He was right there, lounging three inches from my personal space, that gravel-filled voice washing over me like a pot of boiling water. Painful. Scalding. And way too familiar. I could still hear that voice whispering dirty things in my ear like it was yesterday.

"Ma'am? If you'll have a seat I'll put your bag away for you." The stewardess was at my side, speaking to me, but she could've been an eight-feet tall dinosaur for all the attention I paid her.

"C'mere, babe. Let the nice lady put your bag away." Zane reached out and grabbed my waist, like he had any right to touch me, and pulled me past his knees to the window seat. He had to pry the computer bag from my fist to give it to the stewardess. "Thanks, ma'am."

"Oh, you're so welcome, Mr. Wilson."

I cut my eyes at the woman, disgusted by the breathy way she spoke to Zane. She should've saved her lust for a man who deserved it. Finally able to control my own motor functions again, I yanked my seatbelt on and rummaged through my purse for my earbuds.

Of course, in the chaos of traveling, I'd misplaced them. I never misplaced things. I was usually organized and put together. It was incredibly unfair that on the day that I ran into Zane for the first time in over half a decade I was a complete and total mess.

"So, Claire..." Zane turned his body toward mine. "Miss me?"

I slowly lifted my eyes to his and let all my hatred and anger show on my face. "About as much as I'd miss a fucking hammer to the head."

He didn't flinch at my coldness. Instead, he leaned in closer, his voice warm and low. "I know I deserved every word of that, and every dagger you have to throw. But if you're telling me you never missed what we had...?"

He smiled, gentle and sure. "Then you're the best liar I have ever known."

My heart slammed into my ribs. And every fiber of my being hated that he was right.

"Fuck off Zane."

2

Claire

"Ma'am!" The stewardess was still hanging around. "Please watch your language. There are children on board."

Zane didn't take his eyes off of me. "I guess I deserve that too. You want to get more out of your system, babe? I'm ready to take all the punches you can throw."

I apologized to the woman before she finally left and ran my hands over my hair. I felt the lopsided bun hanging limply and told myself it didn't matter. I pushed my glasses up my nose and sucked in a sharp breath when Zane leaned into my space.

"Come on, Claire. Fate brought us back together after all these years. Don't you think we owe it to fate to at least chat a little?" He gently touched my knee. "You look good."

I was going to end up in jail for murder. I swatted his hand away and let myself lean closer so I could whisper at him without the entire plane hearing. "Fuck fate and fuck you. You ghosted me. You- You were an asshole and that's all that matters. I don't want anything to do with you."

"Some part of you does..." He flicked his gaze down to my beaded nipples, then his tone turned serious. "I didn't know how to say goodbye the right way. I just... disappeared. And I've regretted it more times than I can count. I know that doesn't fix a damn thing, but I need you to hear it. I just hope one day you'll be able to give me some mercy."

The thing about Zane Wilson was that if you gave him a little mercy, he'd have you naked and bent over in two-point five seconds flat. "Leave me alone, Zane."

My dangerous tone worked on him for as long as it took the stewardess to go through her opening spiel about flight safety. As soon as she finished he was back in my space, his leather and citrus scent hitting me hard.

"You look really good. Despite what you think, there hasn't been a day that has gone by when I have not thought of you."

I narrowed my eyes at him and let out an angry breath through my nose. I hadn't been thrown so thoroughly by his presence to forget the situation with my bra and the sweat cooling on my face and neck. I didn't look good. I was pretty sure I hadn't looked worse in a very long time. "You're still a liar, I see."

The plane started taxiing down the runway but Zane didn't look away from me. If he felt any of the nerves I was feeling over the impending lift off, he didn't show them. "I was a lot of things, Claire, but I was never a liar."

I locked my hands together and squeezed them between my thighs as the plane took off. I hated the breathless feeling I got with every take-off and landing. Zane reached over and gently pulled my hands free so he could hold them both in his larger one. He stroked his thumb over my wrist and I felt a breathtaking moment of warmth towards him for the comforting gesture.

"Still nervous about the take-off, huh?" His eyes searched my face and for a moment it felt like time had reversed and we were back in my college dorm again.

Someone coughed across from us and I shook myself out of whatever trance he'd put me under. I pulled my hands free of his and scowled. Whatever warmth that I'd thought I'd felt had probably just been a warm breeze or something. Yeah. A warm breeze on a plane. That sounded right.

He moved away from me like the moment hadn't happened and the cocky smile was right back on his face. It made it easier for me to remember exactly who he was and what he'd done to me.

"To be fair, I haven't looked at much else since you shoved your tits in my face." He was unfairly beautiful. Messy black hair that made it look like he'd just crawled out of bed, tattoos crawling up his neck and down both of his arms, he was one hundred percent bad boy rockstar beautiful. The pale green eyes with envy-inducing eyelashes just added insult to injury. It made him saying crude things acceptable to most women. It was hard to be offended when you were swooning.

I wasn't swooning over Zane Wilson anymore, though. I narrowed my eyes at him and shook my head. "Go to hell."

"You wound me, babe."

"I would love to wound you but I have a wedding to get to and getting arrested wouldn't work with my timeline." I saw the stewardess stand and start prepping a drink cart. We'd reached altitude and could take our seatbelts off. As soon as I got a drink in me I was going to escape to the bathroom to fix myself up as best as I could and then I was going to beg someone to change seats with me.

"A wedding, huh?" Zane took his seatbelt off and leaned even closer. "Not yours, though. That ring finger is still bare."

"Do you *have* to talk to me?" I raised my hand to catch the stewardess' attention and she lifted a small bottle of liquor, the silent question clear. I raised two fingers and almost cried in relief when she left the cart and brought me two small bottles right away. I smiled at her as I took them. "Thank you so much. You're a lifesaver."

She could barely take her eyes off of Zane when she was that close to him but I couldn't blame her. He'd been wildly attractive to women before he became a famous rockstar. Add the fame and I was sure he had panties thrown at him hourly. She smiled at him like he was the center of her universe. "Mr. Wilson? Can I get you anything?"

I opened the tiny bottles and chugged them both. Coughing as the liquor burned my throat, I pressed my hand to my mouth and squeezed my eyes shut. Work had kept me so busy most of the past year or two that I hadn't had much time for drinks. Those two little bottles instantly went straight to my head.

Maybe I could handle a flight next to Zane. I was getting to fly first class after all. Surely, I could put aside my hate for long enough to enjoy the extra leg room and free booze.

"Cold, babe?" Zane smiled down at my chest and raised his eyebrows. "Need a blanket?"

Never mind. The flight was going to suck. I couldn't handle it. Not even a little bit. Especially not when I was so unprepared. I normally went into battles at work fully put together and organized. It was how I preferred to live my life. He'd caught me completely off guard and out of sorts. My defenses were down. And my nipples were hard. So that was great.

"One. I'm not your babe. Two. No, I don't need a blanket. If I did, though, I could ask for one myself." I crossed my arms over my chest and frowned at the seat in front of me. I needed a few minutes to figure out my battle plan. "I'm going to the bathroom."

He stood up when I did, shifting like he was letting me pass. When I was caught between his body and the seat in front of his he leaned into my space, though. His hands went to my hips and he dropped his face until his mouth was against my ear, his lips brushing the sensitive lobe. "Careful, Claire. If you're not cold I might start to think your nipples are trying to tell me something."

My breath caught and I stupidly froze. It'd been a few months since I'd had sex and even then it hadn't been good. It'd been years since I had *good* sex. Having a man with Zane's raw sex appeal whisper into my ear while his all-man scent flooded my senses was dangerous.

Zane's fingers pressed harder into my flesh and he let out a low growl. "If you keep looking up at me with those fuck-me eyes, I'm not going to be responsible for how I react."

I couldn't be sure but I might've yelped. That threat sent me stumbling up the aisle to the tiny bathroom, my purse banging into each seat I passed. I rushed through half a dozen apologies before I was able to slip inside the bathroom and lock the door. I dropped my purse in the sink and silently swore when the water automatically came on.

I moved it to the floor and then gripped the counter and stared at myself in the mirror. I looked like shit. There was no other way to put it. I was still blotchy and red from my run across the airport, my hair was sticking out in every direction, the baby hairs around my face doing their best to make me look like a puffer fish. The dark bags under my eyes made me look older than my twenty-eight years and there were multiple stains on my t-shirt from my awful morning.

I'd run into my rockstar ex-boyfriend while looking like I'd just gone through some sort of apocalyptic event. Wasn't that just my luck? Bending down to grab my makeup bag from my purse, I smacked my forehead on the counter and stumbled backwards onto the toilet. Groaning, I didn't let it slow me down more than that. I got back up and began working on my face.

Some concealer and bronzer brought me back to life and a quick swipe of my hairbrush made my bun more cute messy bun and less horrific messy bun. There was nothing I could do about the stains on my shirt but I finished off with a pop of cherry lip-gloss and felt at least slightly more presentable.

I couldn't do much about preparing mentally for facing an hours-long flight next to Zane so I took a deep breath and opened the bathroom door, as ready as I was ever going to be. I gasped when

I looked up and on the other side of the door was Zane, his hands gripping the frame as he stared at me with hunger in his bedroom eyes.

    I told myself to step out of the bathroom and go back to my seat. When Zane stepped forward, though, I stepped backwards, deeper into the bathroom.

3

Claire

Zane shut the door behind him and the sound of the lock clicking into place was loud in the small space. His scent was thicker as he slid his arms around my waist and tugged me into his chest. His eyes were smoldering as he slid one hand down to cup my ass through my thin leggings and the other one up to grip the back of my neck.

The next moment in time seemed to stretch on and on as we stared at each other, neither of us moving. Our eyes saying the things we never said. The air even seemed frozen between us. I waited for my brain to snap me out of the trance but before it did, Zane moved. I felt the puff of his breath against my mouth just before his lips. Then time exploded around us as I sucked in a sharp inhale and reached for him.

He held me tighter while I tangled my hands in his silky hair the same way I always had. I loved it but I knew his scalp was sensitive and I wanted him to feel the same burning need that I did. He responded by nipping my lip and forcing his tongue into my mouth. He tasted like spearmint on my tongue.

I raked my nails over his scalp and whimpered as he gripped my ass harder and then slid his hand down to pull my leg up around his waist. He was hard against my middle and I felt dizzy knowing that he wanted me that badly. He gripped my bun and yanked it free so my hair spilled down around our faces. My chest pressed against his and my nipples ached painfully. Like he had all the right to do it, he slipped his hand under my shirt and cupped my breast, raking his thumb over my nipple until I gasped.

Zane groaned and pulled back enough to yank my shirt over my head. "Fuck, Claire."

I pulled his mouth back to mine and tugged at his hair. "Don't stop."

He dropped both hands to my ass and picked me up so he could put me on the counter. The sink came on and I felt the cold water on my ass but I just scooted forward and wrapped my legs around his waist. He kissed me hard and cupped my breasts with his hands. His fingers were rough from his guitar and the feel of them on my skin was enough to make me want to beg.

"Zane." Running my hands over his shoulders and across his back, I tried to feel all of him that I could. Down to his tight ass and around to the hard cock pressing into me. I cupped him through his pants and we both groaned.

"Goddammit, Claire. Can you be quiet?" When I didn't answer right away, too focused on kissing my way across his strong jaw, he gripped the back of my hair and tightened his hold until I looked up. "I'm about to sink nine inches deep into you, baby, and I need to know if you can keep quiet. You never were very good at that before."

Shivers went up and down my spine at the promise in his voice. My entire body felt like one giant nerve ending, throbbing for more of his touch. Before I could fully process what he was saying, there was a firm knock at the door.

"Excuse me? I'm sorry but you both need to leave the lavatory and return to your seats."

I shoved Zane away from me and covered my face with my hands. I was mortified and I suddenly remembered very well what went along with hooking up with Zane. It was far from the first time we'd been caught in a compromising position but I was way too close to thirty to feel anything other than horrified by it.

"Just a minute." Zane pressed his palms to the tops of my thighs and growled my name in his gravel-filled voice. "Look at me."

I needed my shirt. Jesus, where was it? I pushed him away again and slid off the counter, which just put me right in Zane's arms again. Still, I refused to look at him.

"Stop freaking out, C. I'll tip the flight staff and buy everyone a drink or three." He gripped my face and tilted it up to his. "It's fine. We're both adults."

"I don't do this kind of stuff anymore, Zane. Just...find my shirt and let me get back to my seat." I tore my gaze from his and saw my worst-case scenario. My shirt was in the toilet. I groaned and sank back into the sink. "Shit."

Zane was quick to react. He pulled his t-shirt off and didn't wait for my permission before he pulled it over my head. It left him in a simple white tank top that showed off what felt like miles and miles of beautiful ink. "I'll buy you another shirt."

With his warmth and scent surrounding me, my nipples didn't get the memo that we were putting the brakes on. I hastily pulled my hair back into a bun and spun around so I could make sure I didn't have lip-gloss smeared all over my face. "I don't need your money, Zane. I can buy a new shirt all on my own."

"I know. I also know you could've flown first class today but didn't upgrade your seat yourself. You're still a prepper, aren't you, baby?" He leaned in, pressing his still erect dick against my ass. The new position was one of my favorites and it had me gripping the counter with white knuckles.

I bit my lip to stifle a moan and then his words penetrated my lust-fueled fog. "How did you...? You didn't. Zane, tell me that you weren't the one who upgraded my seat."

He pressed a kiss to the back of my neck and smirked when I shivered. "I wanted you closer."

Warning sirens blared in my brain. "Why are you flying into Miami, Zane?"

"I'm playing a gig." He sighed when there was another knock on the door. "Coming."

I had a million more questions. How did he know I was going to be on the flight? Why did he want me closer? What the hell was wrong with me that I'd let him get me half naked within five minutes of seeing him again? Instead of asking them, though, I pushed him out of the way, grabbed my forgotten purse, and shoved open the door.

Coming face to face with an annoyed stewardess, I winced and kept my gaze down as I hurried back to my seat. Did Zane? Of course, not. He was all smiles and confident ease on his walk back, like a big peacock. I was bright red with shame, which was a much more appropriate response than Zane's smirk.

He sat next to me and leaned into my space. "Come on, C. Don't be mad at me."

I curled into my seat facing the window and shifted as far from him as I could get. "Don't talk to me, Zane."

He sighed. "If that's really what you want, I'll back off."

His voice dropped, raw. "But just so you know—I'm proud to be seen with you again. I don't care if the whole world knows I wanted to fuck you in that airplane bathroom."

He glanced at me, then away. "I want to spend every damn minute of this flight trying to make up for how badly I fucked up. Not because I expect forgiveness—I probably don't deserve it—but because you deserve to know I still care."

He leaned back slightly. "But if silence's what you need... I'll give you that too."

I pressed the call button for the stewardess and asked for earbuds. After I had them, I put one in and then looked at Zane. "You broke my heart, Zane. You left me and didn't even have the decency to end it like a man. Whatever just happened? Forget it. It was a mistake and it won't happen again."

I shoved the other earbud in and tapped aggressively at my phone screen to start a podcast about a woman murdering her partner. I didn't read into why I'd chosen that episode and I didn't look back at Zane once. No matter how many times I wanted to.

4

Claire

"Mr. Wilson? I'm so sorry to bother you but I was hoping to get your autograph and maybe a picture with you?" It was the third time someone had come up to Zane.

I stared even harder out of my window as he greeted each fan with his signature bad boy charm and took pictures with them. I was sure I was in the background of each one, looking like I'd been sucking on a lemon. If I could've managed to get the window open, I would've taken my chances jumping from the plane.

I tried to read a new book I'd been wanting to read in my free time but I lost focus every other line because of something Zane did or said. He was driving me insane. The plane honestly couldn't have landed fast enough.

I opened my purse and took the time to go through the contents on my tray table. I was usually so organized that having the purse to put back together was almost calming. I had everything lined up on the table in order of size and then color and was just about to start putting it all away when Zane spoke up.

"You never said whose wedding you're going to." Zane had shifted in his seat again, turning to face me completely. He reached over and gently moved my makeup bag out of order. "Or if you have a date."

I silently seethed as I put the bag back where it belonged. I still had the earbuds in so I pretended like I hadn't heard him. Of course, Zane was a determined asshole, though. He plucked the earbud from my ear closest to him and laughed when he listened to it and heard nothing.

"Tricky, Claire. Now that I know you heard me, answer the question before I combust from curiosity."

I tried to take the earbud back from him but he just grabbed my hand and held it to his thigh. "Dammit, Zane."

"Dammit, Claire."

"Sophia's getting married! There. Happy now? Can I have my hand back?" I glared at him and instantly remembered why I'd been facing away from him for so long. Looking at him was dangerous. He was too interesting with all the tattoos on display and those pale green eyes filled with interest.

"Yes and no." He leaned even closer. "I'm happy but you can't have your hand back. You didn't answer the question about having a date."

My cheeks flared with anger. "Do you think I would've found myself in the bathroom with you if I was taking a date to Soph's wedding? Despite the damage you did I'm still the same monogamous woman, Zane. I don't cheat."

He grew grimly serious for the first time, outside of when he'd had his tongue down my throat. "I didn't cheat, Claire."

I hated that I needed to hear those words so desperately. It was a wound from years earlier. It shouldn't have mattered. I had no reason to believe him. "Well, considering how you never officially broke up with me, I'd say you've probably cheated."

His hand tightened on mine and he pulled me closer. His eyes were intense as he drew close enough that our breaths mingled in the air between us. "I didn't cheat on you. Never. I fucked up more than enough without that so it's not like a huge badge of honor, but I never cheated on you. I didn't touch another woman the entire first six months I lived in LA."

Meaning he had after the first six months. I swallowed back a wave of hurt and yanked away from him. "Wow, Zane. How loyal of you. I'm so touched by the obvious love you continued to carry for me after leaving me and refusing to answer my calls. I'm flattered."

"Oh, my gosh. Zane Wilson! Can you sign my shirt?"

I didn't bother looking back at him or the woman fanning out over him. I kept my gaze on the window seal and wondered if a swift headbutt would get it to open or just knock me out. Either way, I wouldn't have to consciously deal with Zane anymore.

Before I had to do any serious damage to myself, though, a stewardess came over the intercom and informed us that we'd be landing soon. Still not soon enough, if you'd asked me. I clicked my seat belt back on and meticulously put away everything from my tray table. My purse being perfectly organized should've made me feel better but it didn't.

While the plane began its descent Zane watched me. "Some men might not be into the chip on your shoulder, babe, but I love a challenge. Especially since I was the one who put it there."

Just as the plane touched down I yanked my belt off and shoved my phone in the tiny pocket in my leggings. "You were hardly the only man in my life who disappointed me, Zane. Nice ego trip, though."

His scowl was vindicating. "Who else?"

I laughed and jumped up before I was technically supposed to. "That's none of your business."

If I was expecting him to get up and chase after me once the plane doors opened and I made my escape I would've been disappointed. Luckily for me, I was done with my trip down memory lane. I didn't want, or need, Zane Wilson chasing after me.

I did, however, need my luggage. My carry-on held only my bridesmaid gown because I was being especially type-A and cautious while packing. I'd wanted to be sure nothing happened to the dress but I should've been a little more worried about the rest of my things because as I stood there watching the luggage carousel, I slowly realized my suitcase was nowhere to be seen.

Twenty minutes and two frustrating conversations with annoyed airport staff later I knew I was screwed. Somewhere between London to New York and New York to Miami, my suitcase had been lost. With my current luck I was willing to bet it'd fallen out of the plane over the ocean. I was dismissed with a promise that they'd call me as soon as they found my luggage, but it could be up to seventy-two hours before I heard anything.

I was standing there wondering what I'd done to deserve the day I was having when my phone rang. I checked and saw it was Sophia calling. She was a bright spot in my day, at least. "Soph. I have so many things to tell you. Are you here?"

Sophia had been my best friend since I was ten-years-old and I knew every one of her quirks and tells. I knew the moment she let out her guilty laugh that something was wrong. "I'm not there, no. But only because Will was already going to Miami today to pick something up so he volunteered to drive you back from the airport. Surprise?"

I stopped walking and got shouldered by someone from behind for it. Hurrying out of the way, I pushed my glasses up on my nose and bit back a sigh. Sophia had no reason to think Will picking me up would be an issue. It just proved that I'd been cursed. There was no other explanation for my day.

"I told him not to force you to listen to his shitty music and that if he bores you to death before you get here that I'll never forgive him." She rushed on, unaware of the panic growing in me. "I figured it'd be okay. Is it? I mean, it's a few hours we won't have together but-"

"It's completely fine! Don't worry, Soph. You're dealing with wedding stress. I'm glad you had the morning off from driving duty." I swallowed down my reservations. "Um. Does Will have my number to let me know he's here, or-"

"He's already outside waiting for you. He got there like an hour ago. I told him he was coming off a little desperate."

5

Claire

Will Callahan desperate? Not a chance in the world. The fact that he was outside waiting on me made my glasses fog up as my breathing kicked up. I took them off with a sigh and cleaned them, not sure that I shouldn't just shove them in my purse so I wouldn't be able to see anything or anyone for the rest of the day. Not being able to see Sophia's big brother was about the only way I was going to relax.

"Earth to Claire? I know you're still there. I can hear your breathing."

I scoffed. "I'm not a mouth breather, Sophia Callahan. Don't start that again."

Sophia had managed to convince me that I was a mouth breather when I was eleven and I'd spent an entire summer so focused on my breathing that I started having anxiety about whether I was still breathing or not. She'd felt horrible and had just meant to play a joke but she was too good at lying back then. Or I just wasn't as good at reading her.

"You know how when something bad happens and you start praying like you haven't skipped the past decade of church and you start bargaining with god? Every single time I have one of those moments I apologize for that stunt. I figure if god can forgive me for making you think you weren't breathing and for the way you started gulping with every breath you took that maybe I'll be worth saving." She groaned. "Everyone called you Guppy that year at school."

"What are we doing here? Is this supposed to be making me feel better about the day from hell that I'm having?" I started walking towards the pick up area, dragging my feet as I went to put off what was surely going to be an awkward time.

"Tell me everything, Guppy."

"I'd love to, asshole, but it's a long story and I have to find your brother." I bit my lip and promised myself a book store shopping day when I got back to London. "Are you going to be at the hotel when we get in?"

"Are you kidding? Of course. I'll be the woman by the pool with the alcohol, waiting on you." She let out an excited breath. "I'm so glad you're going to be in hugging reach soon, Claire. I've missed you."

I squeezed my eyes shut and forced down a wave of emotion. So many things were changing and I'd be a liar if I said change didn't scare me. She was getting married. I'd broken up with another boyfriend just a few weeks earlier. I was getting left behind. "I've missed you, too, Soph."

After hanging up with her, I walked out of the airport's arctic air-conditioning and straight into the pits of hell. My body immediately broke out in a sweat and I could feel my hair growing larger from the humidity. Of course I was going to look like a damp, frizzy disaster the moment I saw Will for the first time in years. Right on cue, my glasses fogged up completely, just in time for me to trip over someone's suitcase. As I piched forward, all I could think was: *Did I piss off a witch or something?*

I landed mostly on top of my carry-on but my knee took the brunt of my weight. I felt my leggings rip and the sting of torn skin but mostly I felt horrified that I'd just eaten shit in front of a ton of people, none of whom stopped and helped me up. Just as I was considering rolling onto my back and waiting for a car to run me over a big shadow fell over me.

"I hate to say this, Claire, but you aren't getting more graceful with age." Will Callahan. The first man I loved. The man who took my virginity and made me see stars with every stolen kiss. His face appeared over mine as he grinned down at me, brilliant blue eyes crinkling in the corners from years of laughter. "Hey."

I shoved my glasses to the top of my head to stop myself from checking him out. "Any chance you could pretend like this didn't happen?"

His hands were bigger and rougher than I remembered as he wrapped them around my upper arms and pulled me to my feet. "That'd be kind of hard since I need to check out your leg before we get on the road. You're bleeding."

I waved my hand in the air like I was trying to brush everything away. "It's fine. I'm fine."

"I'm a firefighter and a paramedic on the weekends, Claire. What kind of asshole would I be if I didn't check you out?" He took my bags from me and kept his hand wrapped around my upper arm. "Come on. I'm not parked too far away. You feel up for walking or do I need to carry you?"

Without seeing where I was going I immediately stepped off the curb without noticing it and stumbled. With a groan I put my glasses back on but kept my gaze away from Will. "I can walk, despite what current circumstances may imply."

If anything, he held me tighter. "How was your trip?"

I laughed. "I've been wondering if I'm cursed."

He led me to a large pickup truck and dropped the tailgate. He picked me up and put me down on it as if I weighed nothing. "Hold that thought while I grab my bag."

I made my first mistake when I looked up as he walked away. The man had a nice ass. He filled out the worn denim in the most delicious way, from his ass to his thick, muscular thighs and beyond. I made my second mistake when he turned and came back at me. Will Callahan was still so painfully good looking that he took my breath away. He'd been the all-American football star in high school, with sunkissed hair and the prettiest blue eyes, and he'd just grown into an even hotter man. It wasn't fair.

Dropping a heavy leather bag next to me, he rested his hands on my thighs and dipped his head so we were eye to eye. "How have you been, Claire?"

I wanted to laugh. "If you'd asked me that question first thing this morning I would've told you that things were fine."

"And now?" He slid his focus to my knee and I took the chance to study him. He was still so sunkissed that he made the perfect image of a man from an island, even if it was a Florida island. Tan with light brown hair full of natural blonde highlights, he would've looked right at home on the beach with a surfboard in his hands, even though I was pretty sure he'd never surfed. Nope. Not Will Callahan. He was too busy saving people.

I looked away and frowned when I saw a hooded man walking towards us with purpose. Instead of shifting or redirecting to go around us, he came right at us. I was just about to lose my cool when the hood shifted backwards enough for me to see it was Zane. I stammered and then hissed when Will rubbed something over my knee.

He looked up at me through his lashes as he pursed his lips and blew on my knee to stop the sting. "Sorry, Claire. I should've warned you."

"What happened? You were fine when you stormed away from me on the plane."

Will stood up straight and turned a hard look on Zane. "You two were on the same plane?"

"Yep. We even got to sit next to each other. We go back a lot farther than that, though. Isn't that right, Claire?" Zane ignored the wary look Will was giving him and dropped his bag at his feet so he could come up right next to me. He ran his hand up my arm to cup the back of my neck. "You okay?"

Will's eyes missed nothing. He shook his head and pressed closer to me, edging Zane out. "She fell. I'm taking care of it."

Zane's hand fell away from my neck and he turned to fully face Will. "I'm guessing you're the brother."

"Will Callahan. Go ahead and throw your shit in the back." Will applied a cream to my knee and then carefully applied a bandage through my ripped leggings. "I'll check it out again later tonight to make sure it's healing okay."

I looked between the two of them. "Why would Zane be throwing his shit in the back of your truck, Will?"

Zane's mouth twisted into a wicked smirk. "I didn't mention that I'm one of Jake's groomsmen? Huh. It must've slipped my mind."

6

Claire

The backseat of Will's truck was full of things he'd picked up for the firehouse so the three of us rode in the front seat. The bench seat would've been plenty roomy if the two men I was sandwiched between weren't huge and if they weren't both exes of mine. I clutched my purse to my chest and once again wondered what I'd done to get so unlucky.

"You've always been organized, Claire, but I'm impressed you fit everything you needed into one small suitcase. I remember that trip we all took to Georgia your junior year. You and Soph both packed so much that we had to take two cars." Will glanced over at me and he let out a quiet laugh at the blush taking over my face.

I remembered that trip, too, but I didn't remember the luggage situation. I remembered the way Will had snuck me out of my room and into his private one. Losing my virginity in Savannah, Georgia after doing a ghost tour had been oddly romantic and idyllic. Will had managed to slide right past the awkward first-time stage and straight into giving me multiple orgasms.

I also remembered the sneaking around behind Soph's back and guilt over secretly dating her big brother. Looking down at my lap, I forced my mind back to the present. "Oh, um... They lost my suitcase. I gave them the address to the hotel and they're supposed to contact me as soon as they find it. The only thing in that suitcase in the back is my dress for the wedding."

"Do you want me to have some clothing options available for you? I know a personal shopper in Miami who would-"

I cut Zane off and shook my head. "No, that's too much. Thanks, though. Uncle Sal will probably have a few of my old things still. I'm just going to stop by his trailer tomorrow and grab a few things to make work until my suitcase arrives."

"How is Uncle Sal?" Zane stretched his legs out and let his thigh rest against mine.

"You know Uncle Sal?" Will casually gripped the steering wheel with his left hand and rested his right arm behind my head on the seat. The scent of his deodorant and his body heat was basically an aphrodisiac.

"Yeah. Claire and I dated for over a year. I met everyone important to her." Zane raised his eyebrows as he looked at Will. "I never met you, though."

Will noticeably stiffened beside me. "Oh. You're the ex who ran off to make it big. Huh. I thought you'd be bigger."

I cringed between them. I was still desperate for a window to open so I could dive out of it. It wouldn't have the same impact as diving out of a plane but if I was lucky I'd get run over by a semi-truck. Considering my luck, I figured I'd better rethink that whole plan.

Zane shot me a hurt look, as if I'd betrayed him by telling anyone about how he'd left me. "So you've heard about me. I've still never heard anything about you, Will. You're the best friend's older brother?"

I felt Will glance at me and I could feel the blame coming off of him, as well. I kept my eyes on my lap but I was freaking out inside. Did Will really think I was supposed to tell people about him? He was still my biggest secret.

"Claire and I go way back." Will dropped his arm so it was around me. "I've known her since she showed up at my door in pigtails and a Hooters t-shirt."

I groaned, thrown back down memory lane far enough that the tension was momentarily forgotten. "Oh god. That was so inappropriate for a ten-year-old to be wearing. Uncle Sal thought it was hilarious, though. I thought your mom was going to lose her mind."

"She did. She accused Sal of trying to get you kidnapped and handed off to a pervert ring. Her words. That was the one and only time I've ever seen Sal look even remotely apologetic." Lightly squeezing my shoulder, Will glanced down at me and smiled. "As a twelve-year-old, I didn't understand why everyone was so up in arms about a shirt about owls."

Zane rested his hand on my thigh. "That wasn't the same shirt you-"

I squeaked, the memory of surprising Zane on Halloween in a Hooters costume coming hot and fast. We'd gotten drunk and had sex in a Hooters bathroom that night. I'd come just as an angry manager banged on the bathroom door, demanding I get back to work. "Nope! Not the same shirt."

A tense silence fell over the truck and I sat between the two of them feeling like my body was on fire. They were both touching me and I was so embarrassed that I wasn't sure I'd ever recover.

It was a two-hour drive from Miami to Manatee Key. One hundred and twenty minutes. That was a lot of time to sit there wishing for a sudden coma. I was going to kill Sophia. She might not have known about my relationship with Will but she knew all about my relationship with Zane. How could she have put me in the position I was sitting in? It was a cruel and unusual punishment.

"I owe Jake big time for asking me to be in the wedding." Zane squeezed my thigh and looked past me, to Will. "I'm looking forward to this week."

"I didn't realize you were so close with Jake." Will put the truck on cruise once we were on the open highway and then his thigh was pressing into mine, too.

I looked at Zane and nodded. "Will's right. I knew you met him when we were together but I had no idea you two were groomsmen close."

He just shrugged. "We've kept up with each other through the years."

"That's cryptic." Will leaned forward and jabbed at the radio until old country music filled the air.

If I thought not speaking would ease the awkwardness, I was wrong. It was the drive from hell. I almost felt like a fire hydrant that two dogs were fighting over. It made no sense. It'd been years since

I'd been with either of them, but they were both acting territorial in a way that somehow both made my skin crawl and my downstairs damp.

7

Claire

"I'll grab your stuff, Claire. Soph got you checked in earlier." Will shot a look at Zane and nodded towards the front of the impressive hotel. "The office is that way."

I looked anywhere but at Zane or Will. There was plenty to see with the beautiful hotel spread out before me. Just two stories, it almost looked like a beautiful old home in New Orleans, with wrought iron detailed balconies and a massive wrap around porch. There were plants everywhere and I found myself stepping slightly closer to Will. It'd been a long time since I was in Florida but I hadn't forgotten the way the local wildlife liked to hide in plants.

"I'll find you later, Claire." Zane winked and then strolled away, his leather scent going with him.

Will brought a softer scent with him as he moved even closer, the salty scent of the ocean breeze. I inhaled as deep as I dared and looked up at him. He was staring back at me with a curious expression on his face.

With my bags in one hand he wrapped his other arm around my waist to guide me towards my room. "Interesting. He must've been less of a dick when you dated him."

A lizard skittered out from a bush and shot across the sidewalk in front of us. I stopped walking and practically formed my body around his. "You know what I've never seen on a sidewalk in London? A fucking lizard."

Will's arm tightened around me and his hand settled low on my hip. The hold was intimate and it brought back a thousand memories of him holding me the same way when we were both so much younger. We'd both made it a point to not ever be alone the few times we'd been in the same place over the years and I wondered if the tension had always been there, lurking just beneath the surface, waiting for a moment when it was just the two of us.

"Claire?" Will's thumb inched under the bottom of my shirt to brush against my bare skin. "About Zane?"

I ducked my head and blew out a long breath. What in the world was happening to me? "Um... Yeah. I guess. I don't really know anymore. He was my first serious relationship after..."

"Me." Will stopped outside of room one-oh-five and put my bags down at our feet. "I guess not having to hide everything was a lot more exciting and fun for you."

Staring up at the absolute hunk of a man, hearing what sounded suspiciously like self-doubt, I knew I'd fallen down a hole and was in some other universe. I had to laugh, because while dating Zane had been exciting and fun, dating Will had been thrilling and invigorating in a whole different way. "I think we both know that you and

I shared plenty of exciting and fun times, Will Callahan. If you're fishing for compliments, though, here's one for you. You look even more like a Greek god now than you did a decade ago and I think I hate you a little for it."

His smile stretched wide as he planted his hands on the wall behind my head and leaned into me. "If you knew what I was thinking you'd slap the shit out of me, Claire. You've grown up since the last time I let myself look at you."

My heart hammered away in my chest and the idea of tipping my head back and offering myself up to him was blaring in my head but I knew better. I wasn't a kid anymore. I couldn't do stupid things and excuse them anymore. I wrapped my arms around myself to keep my hands off of his body and pressed my forehead to his chest for a stolen moment. "Where's your sister?"

He groaned and stepped away. "I'm guessing the pool."

"I'm going to find her and rip her a new one for not telling me that my ex was coming to the wedding." I saw his mouth twist in annoyance and sighed. "Two of my exes. But it's not like she knows about you."

He looked out across the porch to the beach and ocean beyond. I'd been so caught up in looking at him that I hadn't even noticed the view. "Have dinner with me tonight, Claire."

I'd been weak to nineteen and twenty-year-old Will. Thirty-year-old Will Callahan was a nuclear weapon. The way he tipped his head down just slightly and smiled while flashing those bright blue eyes at me? It was a knockout. I bit my bottom lip for a moment to try and hide my smile but it was useless. "Sure."

He slid a key card from his pocket into my hand and stepped back. "Seven?"

I nodded and then my conscience kicked in. "Dinner as two old friends catching up, though. Okay?"

He quirked an eyebrow at me and shrugged. "Sure."

I watched him walk away because I was a masochist and liked torturing myself via my ex's tight ass. He'd grown up in ways that made all of my lady parts sing. It wasn't good. Not with the way he was looking at me and my documented lack of self-control when it came to him.

I rushed inside my room and hung up my dress before slathering myself in sunscreen and heading out to find my soon to be murdered best friend. She had a whole world of hurt coming her way for surprising me with Zane. Zane, whose shirt I was still wearing. "Shit."

Like Will had guessed, his sister was at the pool, sunbathing on a lounger in a pristine white bikini. Her tan skin glowed and her long blonde hair was tied up in a bun that looked like a bow. She was the picture of relaxed beauty but as soon as she heard movement and looked up to see that it was me she turned into the same nut she'd always been.

"Claire!" Jumping up, she stumbled over her towel and I had to catch her before she went headfirst into the pool. She didn't even react, she just threw herself into my arms and hugged me so tight that I struggle to breathe. "You're here! You're here and I'm losing my mind! I'm getting married!"

I laughed with her and took in the moment with her. She really was like a sister to me. She'd been my best friend since I was ten and my parents died, leaving me to move to Florida to live with my Grandma Bertie and her insane brother, Uncle Sal. Soph had been there for me the day I stepped onto Florida soil and I owed so much of my sanity to her. I held her back just as tightly and inhaled her cherry blossom scent.

"Where's your bathing suit? You need to be in the sun immediately. London has turned you pale, babe." She pulled back to look at me and her eyes filled with tears. "Dammit, Claire. You're too far away. I miss you."

I groaned as my own eyes burned. "Don't make me cry. I've just had the day from hell. My luggage is missing so I have no bathing suit. And as much as I love you, I also am so angry at you right now. Zane Wilson, Sophia? Really? You didn't think to mention that my ex was going to be in the wedding?"

"I swear that I didn't know until today, C. Jake planned it as a surprise. He was just going to have Zane play a surprise song for me at the end of the ceremony but I guess two of his groomsmen ended up having to bail. Zane volunteered. If I'd known he was coming I would've warned you." She dragged me with her towards a private bungalow on the other side of the pool. "I have extra suits. After finding out Zane's coming you definitely need some sun to cheer you up."

"Not coming, Soph. He's here. We flew in on the same flight from London and I just spent two hours in the truck wedged between him and Will. Also, he changed my seat to first class so I had to sit next to him." I groaned and felt like stomping my foot. "It wasn't good."

She didn't reply until she had me in her honeymoon suite with a bikini in her hand. "Okay, first of all, I'm going to need a minute to freak out over the fact that *Zane Wilson* made you sit with him on the flight. Second of all, you have so much to tell me. Put this on."

I looked at the bikini and scowled. "Over which boob?"

"Don't be dramatic. Just put it on. And explain to me why you're wearing a man's shirt."

I just groaned.

8

Claire

Time had gotten away from me and before I realized it, it was seven and I was still in the miniscule bikini. I was red from the sun, my hair was frizzed out in every direction from the pool water, and I smelled like sunscreen and chlorine. I wasn't exactly at my best but Will was as prompt as he'd always been. I grabbed a throw blanket from the bed and wrapped it around myself so I could open the door for him.

He stood on the other side of the door in a fresh t-shirt and jeans, his hair still damp from a shower. His ocean scent was stronger than earlier and he looked perfectly put together.

"I'm running late. I'm so sorry. I just need to change and brush my hair and I'll be ready." I let him step inside and then I noticed that he was carrying a couple of bags. "What's that?"

He let the door shut behind him and held up the first bag. "Clothes. Just a few things I grabbed from my bag for you. And this bag has our dinner. I figured you'd feel more comfortable eating in once you saw the clothes I brought you."

My shoulders sank from around my ears as my nerves calmed. "You're amazing. Thank you so much, Will. Eating in sounds perfect. I was just going to throw my travel clothes back on and hope you took me somewhere dark."

He handed me the bag of clothes and shook his head. "Not a chance. I want to see you."

I flushed as our fingertips brushed and his words sank in. I had to clear my throat and take a big step backwards. "I'll just get changed really quick... Actually. Would you mind waiting while I take the world's fastest shower? I smell like the pool."

"Go ahead. I'll get everything set up." He paused. "What'd you swim in, by the way?"

I stopped at the bathroom door and pulled the blanket off. Tossing it back on the bed, I forced myself to let him look. Then I made a humiliating squeaky noise and locked myself in the bathroom. I took the world's fastest shower while berating myself. Showing Will the tiny bikini was wrong. I was going to give him the wrong message when all I really wanted was to be a good friend to Sophia. I had no business even having dinner alone with Will. I was breaking so many rules.

That didn't stop me from taking a few extra minutes after my shower to make sure I didn't look awful. My makeup bag had thankfully been packed in my carryon so I put on some mascara and lip gloss before putting my wet hair up in a bun and opening the bag of clothing Will brought me.

Instantly I felt like I'd been punched in the chest. I dropped the bag on the counter and pressed my hand over my heart in an attempt to alleviate some of the ache. There were three things in the bag. A pair of massive socks, a pair of black boxer briefs, and the t-shirt I'd always stolen from him on the rare occasions we got to spend the night together. Worn and filled with holes around the neck and sleeves from years of wear and tear, it was one of his senior year t-shirts from school.

I knew it had to be too small for him with the way he'd filled out, but he hadn't gotten rid of it and he'd brought it for me. When we'd dated, I hadn't been able to keep things of his for fear of Sophia finding it. Every chance I'd gotten to wear his shirt, I'd taken it, though.

I brought it to my nose and inhaled his scent, feeling a growing desire in my gut and lower to show the man in the other room how much I appreciated his thought. I dressed in his clothes and stared at myself in the mirror, trying to find my moral compass. Jumping Will was not a good idea.

My hands shook as I opened the bathroom door and stepped into the bedroom. Will was standing on the other side of the room, the remote in his hand as he scanned the TV. He looked up and the temperature in the room went up ten degrees.

"Still looks good on you, sweetheart." He dropped the remote and slowly moved towards me. "Hungry?"

I didn't know. I couldn't feel anything but my racing heart and my throbbing core. I made an unintelligent sound and fisted the hem of the shirt.

"Shit, Claire." He stopped toe to toe with me and licked his lips. "We have a problem."

I watched his tongue and then his throat as he swallowed and his adam's apple moved up and down. "We do?"

"This whole 'old friends catching up' thing. We were never friends, Claire. From the moment I saw you in that Hooters shirt, I was crazy about you." He watched me gasp and balled his hands into fists at his sides. "Fuck, sweetheart. I don't think I can sit here and keep my hands to myself. If that's not what you want, I need to leave."

The idea of him walking away from me again filled me with dread and I reacted without thought. As soon as I reached for him he was there, grabbing me up.

I lost my breath when he yanked me into his hard chest and slammed his mouth over mine. I felt every moment of time between our last kiss and that one in the way he devoured me. I gripped his thick shoulders hard and opened my mouth when his tongue stroked the seam of my lips.

The first taste of Will Callahan after so many years was as delicious as it was wrong. He tasted minty with a slight hint of vanilla. That was a secret of his. Tough guy Will had always secretly used a vanilla chapstick. His lips were soft and warm against mine, a harsh contrast against the sharp hardness of his teeth as he nipped my tongue.

Once the cork popped, it felt impossible to stop the reaction between us. He kissed down my throat and ran his hands down my back, straight into the boxer briefs. His big hands on my ass made me go up on my toes and gasp. He'd always been an ass man and he proved then that nothing had changed. His fingers dug into my flesh as he squeezed and his mouth came back to mine for another earth-shattering kiss.

"God, Will, what are you doing to me?" I muttered the words even as I gripped his hair and directed his mouth back to my throat.

Will tightened his grip on my ass and picked me up, groaning when I wrapped my thighs around his waist. He turned around and lowered me to the bed with his body over mine. "So fucking pretty."

I whimpered when he lowered his hips and ground his denim clad erection into my core. Planting my feet on the bed, I pushed my hips back at him, needing more. I kissed across his jaw and shivered as his short beard tickled my mouth. That was new. I wondered what else was new and tugged at his shirt.

He got the hint and yanked his shirt off with one hand. His chest was covered in a dusting of pale hair that thinned to just a trail leading into his jeans. There were also tattoos. Not as many as Zane had but more than I'd expected, especially considering I was expecting none. I wanted to explore them but he was impatient. He lifted his hips enough to reach between us and he expertly slid his hand into my underwear. "You're so wet, Claire. Jesus."

Just as his fingers touched my clit I made eye contact with one of his tattoos. It was a picture of Sophia as a little kid. Knowing their relationship, I immediately knew he'd either lost a bet or had done it to mess with his sister since it wasn't the most flattering picture. There she was, though. My sweet best friend. My sweet, trusting best friend.

9

Will

Claire stiffened under me and I was already pulling my fingers away from her wet sex when she planted her hands on my chest and pushed. My dick throbbed painfully in my jeans, hoping against reason that she just wanted to switch positions. Once I sat back on my heels and saw her face, though, I knew the moment was over.

"We can't." Crawling backwards, she didn't stop until she was pressed against the headboard with her arms wrapped around her knees. "Your tattoo… She was just staring back at me."

I looked down at the tattoo of Soph and scrubbed my hands down my face. It was the result of a drunken bet but I'd never regretted it until that moment. "Claire…"

"Nothing's changed." She looked away from me and ran her hand through her mussed hair. "Shit. I'm sorry, Will. I… I don't know what to say to make this better."

Frustration bit at me. "Everything's changed, Claire. We're both adults who can do what we want."

"We can't betray Soph again. We lied to her for almost two years before, Will. I don't want to do that to her. I hated lying to her then and I don't want to go back there. I know you don't, either."

"No, I don't. I was willing to date you openly back then and I'd do it now, too. Soph wouldn't love it at first but she'd get over it."

I let out a groan when I heard myself. I was arguing for the same thing I had a decade earlier. It didn't feel good to know I was still in the same place with the woman in front of me.

"She means too much to me to chance it."

I stood up and dragged my shirt back on. "Alright. I didn't mean to jump you. I wanted to have dinner and catch up. Let's just both take a breather and eat."

Looking up at me with honey-brown eyes and enough pout to her lips to make me want to yank my hair out, Claire shook her head. "I think we both know that being alone next to a bed is a bad idea."

"You want me to leave?"

She looked so sad that my anger immediately faded. Instead of making her answer I walked around the bed and grabbed her into a tight hug. She clung to me tight enough that I knew she didn't really want me to leave. It didn't matter, though. She wasn't willing to chance hurting Soph and I respected her for taking care of my sister, even if it sucked for me.

"Alright, I'll go. Promise me you'll eat." I pulled back enough to look down at her crestfallen face. Her glasses were sliding down her nose but she didn't reach to fix them. I reached up to do it myself and forced a smile. "Don't look so sad, sweetheart. If you think I'm leaving for good, you're sorely mistaken."

"What do you mean?"

I dropped a kiss to the corner of her mouth and backed away. "You want the PG version or the TV-MA version?"

She watched me closely. "I've always been a masochist. TV-MA."

"I have the feel of your ass on my palms and the scent of your pussy on my fingertips, baby. Sex with you was fucking amazing when we were both teenagers and I'm hungry to find out just how good it would be now. Because it would be. You and me? We've got unfinished business."

I watched her thighs clench as she shifted from foot to foot. Her cheeks darkened but she didn't look away from me. "The PG version?"

"I made a mistake all those years ago, sweetheart. Walking away from you is still my biggest regret. I may not be a rocket scientist but I'm smart enough to not make the same mistakes more than once, not when they hurt so much." I reached out and gently pressed up on her chin to close her mouth. I still got a thrill from seeing her shocked by something I did or said.

For most of my time knowing Claire Morgan she'd been a vault, a beacon of keeping her shit together. She was hardly ever caught off guard. I liked being the person who'd always been able to surprise her.

"You want me to go back to the TV-MA version?" I grinned and tapped the end of her nose. "Get some rest, sweetheart. You've got a big week ahead of you."

She followed me to the door and before I could open it she was there, pressing her body into my back. She took a deep breath and then was gone again. "Night, Will."

A fiend for the woman, I spun around and grabbed her up again. Pulling her to my chest, I kissed her hard once more and then left the room before it got even harder. I stood on the other side of her door, chest heaving as I fought for control. Every part of my being ached to go back inside and be with Claire. It felt unnatural to walk away.

I breathed in the thick night air and shook my head. I couldn't push Claire. I'd made that mistake once before and I'd shot myself in the foot.

I heard a sound from a few rooms down and glanced over to see Zane fucking Wilson standing there watching me. I wanted to punch the asshole for even daring to exist so close to Claire. I was beyond annoyed at my future brother-in-law for inviting one of Claire's exes. He didn't know I was interested in Claire but still. The rockstar shit stain had abandoned Claire for a chance at fame. He didn't deserve to be near her.

He was sitting against the porch railing with a guitar in his arms and I just knew he was going to start dramatically strumming it at any moment to get Claire out of her room. Not on my watch.

I walked in his direction and sat in one of the rocking chairs lining the porch. I shot him a smirk and crossed my arms over my chest. "Go ahead and play me something, big shot."

He smirked back at me but I could see the anger behind his mask. "Your sister know you're sneaking around her best friend's room?"

I narrowed my eyes at him. "Does your girlfriend know you're wearing her jeans?"

"So the muscles haven't cut off all oxygen to your brain? Good to know." He stood up with his guitar and shook his head at me. "You won't always be around, fire boy."

"I wouldn't count on that if I were you."

10

Claire

Bright and early the next morning I caught one of the three cabs working Manatee Key and headed over to the premier trailer park on the island. The Golden Coast was a mix of new and old RVs and trailers, each with its own wildly differing owner. Growing up I'd lived with Grandma and Uncle Sal in a single wide trailer at the back of the park, next to an African woman who sang me to sleep without knowing it for the first two years of my life in Florida and a giant Russian man who'd scared the hell out of me. When Grandma passed and it was just me and Uncle Sal he'd moved us into a fancier trailer, one of the silver bullet ones, at the front of the park, right on the beach.

Uncle Sal was still in the same trailer, though he'd made some upgrades. When I got out of the taxi and took a long look at it I couldn't help but laugh out loud. There was a mural of Uncle Sal painted on the side of the trailer. In a Taylor Swift *Blank Space* move, there were names painted and crossed out all over the spots not taken up by his face. Hot pink lawn furniture and human sized statues of tropical birds filled his small yard and there was a radio somewhere playing techno a little too loud.

The trailer door swung open and Uncle Sal stood in the doorway in all his glory, pausing to give me time to appreciate his dramatics. The man was closing in on seventy-years-old but he got around better than most men in their forties. He'd been to visit me in London more than Sophia had, just to sample the locals, according to him. He stood there in a floor length pink silk robe trimmed in hot pink feathers. His balding head was covered in a platinum blonde wig cut into a sharp bob and he had a long cigarette holder between his lips, smoking an ultra slim cigarette.

Happy with his purposeful pause he stepped out of the trailer in a pair of kitten heels and a leopard print speedo. The robe didn't hide enough for my liking but I'd learned a long, long time ago that no one changed Uncle Sal.

"What in the hell are you wearing, child? You look like one of those lesbians down at The Flamingo on ladies night. Are you gay now? Oh, lord, did I give it to you? Anita Bryant was right! It is catching!" He waved his hand at me and shuddered. "I am turning over in my grave, honey. I taught you better than this. I couldn't do much for your grandmother, god rest her boring soul, but I thought I'd made an impact on you."

I rolled my eyes and wrapped him in a tight hug. He was a tiny man, barely over five-feet tall, and I felt massive next to him. "Turn down the theatrics, Uncle Sal. You are not turning over in your grave, seeing as how you're still alive and kicking. And I'm not a lesbian, even though I wish I was. Especially right now."

"Boy troubles?" He eyed my outfit again. "God, honey. Let's get you inside before someone sees us together. Where is that cute little red number I bought for you when I was in London last month?"

"Men. I'm a little too old for boys now." I followed him into his vintage themed hot pink home that had once been ours to share. It'd just gotten more pink over the years. I could see a poodle skirt hanging on a garment rack waiting for him. "That red number is safely in the back of my closet at home. The airline lost my luggage, though. I was hoping you had a few things of mine still. And that crack about Grandma being boring was rude. I hope she haunts you tonight."

"Oh, honey, if your grandma poked her head into this trailer at night, she'd throw her ghostly back out trying to get away from all the debauchery. You're not the only one with *men* troubles. Although my troubles are more along the lines of who I'm going to bring home tonight. They do get jealous, my lovers." In a twirl of feathers and silk Uncle Sal led the way to what had once been my room. "I would never keep anything in this trailer that could offend my delicate sensibilities but I do have a collection of clothing that just so happens to be in your size and correct coloring."

"Uncle Sal..."

"Well? Aren't you going to ask me about my current lovers?" He draped himself over a chaise lounge and pointed to the closet. "Take your pick, honey."

"Please, Uncle Sal, tell me all about your current lovers. I'm just dying to know." I couldn't have sounded more sarcastic if I'd tried but he was never one to care about nuance.

"I was dating a young man named Paul the last time I saw you in London, right? Well, I broke up with him when he suggested we stay in on a Friday night and watch some dating show. Do I look like I'm ready to curl up and die like that? Ugh. After him there was a man named Donnie. He liked the color orange. Then there was Mark, Damon, and a beautiful ginger straight from Scotland. They were just a little dull for me. Oh, then I dated a guy from Arkansas. He had all of his teeth and the cutest little accent but when he called out to god, he was actually praying and that just threw me. I'm used to my men calling out to god in a lot of other ways, but never that."

I'd stopped trying to count Uncle Sal's lovers a long, long time ago. "Are you being safe?"

He cackled. "I'm too goddamn old to catch an STI, honey. I wrap it up each and every time. I keep a cabinet full of condoms in there if you need some. I've got them in every flavor and size. If you're like me, you'll want to grab them from the right side of the cabinet. We're size queens in this trailer."

I closed my eyes and told myself that I could hear every traumatizing thing he said without letting it leave me shaking in the corner. "Uncle Sal..."

"I'm not finished with my list yet, honey." He jabbed his perfectly manicured fingertip at the closet. "You can look while you listen, surely?"

I cut my eyes at him. "Alright, old man. Watch the sass."

His blue eyes were still as bright as in the photos I'd seen of him when he was a young man. He grinned at me and crossed his legs. "You're the only person I let boss me around, Claire. Your grandma never understood it but I tried telling her over and over again that you're my other half. You're a chip off of this beautiful block."

I scoffed. "Me? You think *I'm* a chip off the block? *Your* block?"

"Yep." His laughter was musical. "You're going to surprise yourself one of these days, honey, and when you do, I'm going to be right there watching and cheering you on. I just hope you choose to do it soon because I can't expect to be in this fine form for another thirty years."

A deep, rumbled laugh from the bedroom doorway signaled the arrival of a man so beautiful that he took my breath away. He looked like an oiled up Latin soap opera star. "You'll be in that fine form for longer than that if you keep going the way you do now, Sal. You wear me out and I'm hardly old."

11

Claire

Uncle Sal ran his eyes over the barely dressed man and fanned himself. "Claire, this is my current beau, Cassius. Cassius, meet my grand-niece, Claire. She's in town for a wedding and lost all her clothes. That's the only reason she looks like that."

Cassius walked over to me and ran his hands around my shoulders as he circled me. "You've shown her the closet?"

I let myself ogle Cassius' muscles because they were completely safe. No attached baggage in any way. "Wow. Just…wow."

He suddenly gripped my waist and squeezed before doing the same to my ass. "Oh, yes, the clothes you chose will fit her perfectly, Sal. Your body is beautiful, Claire. Why would you hide it in such…interesting clothing?"

I danced away from his wandering hands and looked to Uncle Sal. "Is he always so handsy?"

"Oh, so much more, honey." He puffed at his cigarette but it'd gone out minutes earlier. "Be a dear and let Cassius dress you while I finish updating you about my lovers."

If Cassius minded hearing details about Uncle Sal's previous lovers, he didn't show it. He kept focused on his task of pulling and shoving my body into so many different clothing items that I stopped paying attention.

"And before Cassius there was Bruno. Such a feisty lover but he didn't want to share me with Cassius so I waved him goodbye." Uncle Sal watched Cassius and smiled. "For now, Cassius is holding my attention nicely."

"You hold mine just as well, Sal." The younger man plucked at a few strands of my hair and winced. "Does it always do...that?"

I scowled at him then, tired of being insulted. "My hair doesn't like Florida, thank you very much."

"It's just that your hair is distracting from the clothes." He looked me over. "And the body. Stay right there. I'll be right back."

I looked down at myself and gaped. "No. Freaking. Way. Is this...? Uncle Sal! Are you kidding me? Did your boyfriend really just dress me up like *Pretty Woman* Barbie?!"

"You can't go wrong with a short skirt, honey. And you need to show off your stomach while you still can. As soon as you decide to join the herd and pop out a couple of kids, it'll never be the same." He studied me closer and wagged his finger. "Once Cassius is done with your hair, I'll have him add a bit of makeup. You can't go out looking like your face just came home from the office when your body looks like it's heading out for sin."

The two men were a force that I couldn't fight, especially when Cassius used a hellish amount of hairspray to tame my hair and Uncle Sal kept poking at my boobs while talking about how he didn't get them. I felt like I'd fought ten rounds with Mike Tyson by the time they finished with me. The two of them looked thrilled with my finished look but I was too scared to look. I didn't want to know.

"What are you doing today? We should've asked that before finishing the look." Cassius slapped my hand away from where I'd been pulling at the dress hem. "Stop it. You have long, sexy legs. One look at you and men are going to imagine them wrapped around their heads."

I choked on a breath mint and he had to touch up my eyeliner after I cried part of it away. Still wheezing, I went over the plan I had burned into my brain. "Most of the wedding bridal party is arriving today. Once everyone gets settled in we'll get together for dinner. The real events don't start until tomorrow. I'll need something tamer to wear for tomorrow if my suitcase doesn't arrive. I'm hosting a luncheon for the other ladies in the wedding. This would not be appropriate for a luncheon. Can we agree on that?"

Cassius waved me off but Uncle Sal shrugged his elegant shoulders. "We'll see. Now that you're dressed to hang out with me let's go sit outside and enjoy the sun. You're looking a little London pale. Cassius, put together a bag for my beautiful niece, please. She needs night clothing and something to wear tomorrow morning on her way over here."

"If my suitcase doesn't arrive." I realized when I was being ignored and rolled my eyes. When Uncle Sal and I were sitting outside, I glanced back at the trailer and kept my voice quiet. "Are you serious about him?"

That earned me another twinkling laugh. "Have you ever known me to be serious about anything other than fashion and having a good time?"

"How did I turn out to be a serial monogamist?" I tilted my head to the side as I thought about my last few years of dating. "Well. I don't know if you'd call the last few years monogamy when none of the relationships lasted more than a few months each."

"If you were only with one dick at a time, it was monogamy, honey. *Boring.*" Lighting his cigarette again, Uncle Sal waved it at me. "What happened to that last bag of dust you were seeing?"

"Jordan?" I snorted. "I caught him cheating on me with the woman he'd introduced as his sister. She wasn't actually his sister, but I'm not sure that makes *me* feel any better about the whole thing."

"Good riddance." He got a twinkle in his eye that made me nervous. "You know who I see around all the time that is one fine hunk of man meat?"

I groaned, knowing where he was going.

"That Will Callahan. I saw him coming out of a burning building a few months ago and I swear to you I felt the holy spirit move through me, honey. That man could melt panties and impregnate ladies with a single glance."

I was saved from having to answer by my phone ringing. I jumped to grab it from my purse and ignored the knowing look Uncle Sal sent me. Seeing that it was Soph calling I answered it with a twinge of guilt burning in my gut. "Soph? What's up?"

"You might want to get back to the hotel, babe. There's been a few…developments."

I immediately imagined her dress in shreds or the hotel on fire. "Are you okay? I'll be right there. I'm at Uncle Sal's."

"I'm good. I'll send Jake to get you." She hung up before I could refuse.

"I've got to go. Apparently, something's happening at the hotel." I glanced down at myself once more and sighed. "You'd tell me if I looked like a street walker, wouldn't you?"

Cassius stepped out of the trailer with a hot pink leather duffle bag. "Cassius doesn't do that kind of street wear, Claire. If you're too afraid to look hot, just say so."

I shot a look at Uncle Sal. "I don't remember any of the others being so mouthy at me."

He threw back his head and laughed. "Maybe I'll keep him around then. I do love to see you challenged, honey. Now go handle your straight people wedding problems."

12

Claire

Jake shot me another look and I swear I heard him muffle a giggle. I reached over and smacked his arm. "Shut up, Jake. You know Uncle Sal."

He cleared his throat and nodded. "Sorry. I'm just... I didn't expect you to look so... Well..."

"Spit it out, Jake."

"I wasn't prepared for you to look like you're heading out for a date with Richard Gere..." He snorted and then gave into his laughter.

"It's not funny!" I flipped down the visor and looked at myself in the small mirror. "Oh, my god. Tell me that this mirror is a circus mirror and I don't actually look like a carbon copy of Julia Roberts in a movie where she played a *hooker*."

"I don't want to lie to you, Claire. I think Uncle Sal is trying to tell you something." He turned into the parking lot for the hotel and suddenly winced. "Oh, hell. I was supposed to be telling you about the current situation happening here. I was too distracted by your...everything."

"What is it? Just spit it out really fast while I try to take off some of this eyeliner."

"Your ex showed up." He saw my deadpan expression and winced even harder. "Okay, I messed up about Zane. I don't mean him, though. I mean the one who was also invited to the wedding as your plus one. He showed up."

My jaw dropped and I forgot all about how I looked. "Are you kidding me?"

"Nope. He's probably still in the lobby, trying to check in." Jake parked the car and patted the top of my head. "Wow. Your hair just kind of...bounces."

I slapped his hand away and managed to get out of the car without showing my entire vagina. I wobbled in the heels Uncle Sal had forced me into and then strutted across the lot to get to the front office. I heard a car honk and heard a man yell out of his window and turned to glare at Jake. "He better have been honking at you."

Jake was bright red from laughing. "I think he asked how much..."

I growled and had to catch myself as the front door was opened for me before I could grab it. Jake helped steady me and then he had to push me inside once I saw what was waiting for me. The cold air felt frigid compared to the heat outside and I could feel my nipples pebble inside the thin white top I wore. Just like that, Uncle Sal and Cassius had turned me into a sideshow to Soph's wedding.

Sophia rushed over to me and stared at me with her mouth hanging open. "Holy shit."

I groaned. "I'm going to kill Uncle Sal."

"Add him to the list. Look who decided to show up." She stepped aside and I had to look at the horror show in front of me once more. My most recent ex, Jordan Welsh, editor at the publication house I worked at, was standing with a suitcase and a grin within fifteen feet of Zane and Will. And they were all looking right at me. Sophia grabbed my hand. "How do you want to handle this?"

Jordan answered that question for me. He came towards me with that same stupid grin on his face and a pair of roaming eyes that I wanted to stab out. "Well, darling, if I'd known this is how you dress in Florida, I would've had us make the trip ages ago."

Not wanting to put on a show in front of everyone, I grabbed his arm and tried to tug him to the side of the lobby. We moved but so did everyone else. If anything, Zane and Will were closer than ever.

I suppressed my groan of embarrassment and focused on the first problem at hand. "What the hell are you doing here, Jordan?"

He held his hands out to gesture around us at the hotel. "We may have broken up but if you think I'm giving up a vacation, you're nuts. Things went sideways with Mary and I needed to get away for a while. This happened at the perfect time."

Taking a deep breath, I shook my head. "No. Sorry. This isn't a vacation. It's my best friend's wedding. You need to leave."

"No can do, Claire. Don't you remember that we booked the room in my name with *my* credit card?"

"I already changed the card on file, Jordan. I'm paying for it."

He smiled. "It's my room, babe, and I'm taking it. If you want to stay with me, you're more than welcome. We always did share a bed pretty well. Just so we're clear, though, I'm not trying to double dip in the Claire dating pie. I'm here for a vacation, not you. If you're open to a little open fun, though..."

Will stepped forward. "Do you need help getting rid of this asshole, Claire?"

"I'm not staying in a room with you! You cheated on me and I dumped you! That means you don't come on the trip we planned together!" I was going to lose my mind. "Oh, my god. This is not happening. I left you in London for a reason."

"Oh, shit. What's he doing here, Jake?!" Sophia's panicked voice stole my attention and I followed her gaze to the entrance of the hotel.

My stomach bottomed out and I swayed. Standing there, staring back at me with such an intense focus that I couldn't catch my breath, was Anthony Carter. He was Anthony, but he wasn't. The man I'd dated the year before I moved to London had been the exact opposite of Zane. He'd been safe and sweet and everything comforting that I needed. The man striding towards me looked dangerous and hard, like the billionaire CEO that he now was.

The few times I'd allowed myself to stalk my exes online, I'd never spent much time looking at pictures of them. That was a mistake, clearly, because the man coming at me was so damn hot that I was going to need Will to put the fire out.

Anthony wrapped his arms around me and squeezed me to his chest, lifting me off my feet as he did. His scent had changed. He no longer smelled like clean soap but something much, much more expensive. There was an edge of spice to it that made me want to inhale more to figure it out. I was so shocked that I just let him hold me while I breathed him in.

"Long time, no see, Claire."

13

Claire

Anthony's voice was deeper, even. He had to be my sweet Anthony's dark twin. "London's been good to you. You look good."

I finally managed to suck in a full breath and shift back enough to look up at him. "Anthony?"

His lips tipped up at the corner as if my stupidity amused him. "So you haven't forgotten me. That'll make the rest of this easier."

"The rest of what?" I sounded about as vapid as I ever wanted to.

He leaned down and pressed his mouth to the corner of mine. He lingered there, letting his trim beard tickle me. I was so aware of his large body against mine but I could still feel everyone staring at us and it made me want to hide. Anthony pulled back slightly and opened his mouth like he had more to say but Jordan cut him off.

"Look, Claire! It's perfect. You can stay with whoever the hell this is while I take my room."

I pulled free of Anthony's embrace, because no matter how good it felt, it was a dangerous game to cuddle your exes. "It's not yours, Jordan. You don't belong here. The entire hotel is full of family and friends of the bride and groom this weekend. You are none of those things. You need to leave."

"I'm telling you, Claire, I can't go back to London yet. Mary didn't take me cheating as well as you did. You were an angel compared to her. She threatened my manhood. So, I'm sorry that you didn't remember to change the name on the room, but it's mine and I'm staying." Jordan patted my cheek and laughed. "You really do look like a good time, Claire. I would never have cheated on you if this was how you looked."

Will grabbed Jordan by the back of the shirt and yanked him away from me. "No touching."

"Will!" Sophia smacked her brother's arm. "Do not get us kicked out of this hotel. If you want to kick his ass, do it somewhere else on the island."

"Why would you want to kick my ass?" Jordan straightened his shirt and moved to stand behind Sophia, like she'd save him. "I've done nothing but show up to a vacation."

"Jesus, Claire. The way you acted over seeing me again, I'd assumed I was the biggest asshole you'd ever dated but I'm looking pretty good right now, aren't I?" Zane raised a single brow and tilted his head to examine my outfit. "I might like this probably more than I should. Even more than I liked the sight of you in my shirt yesterday."

Anthony's hand came up to grip the back of my neck. When I looked up at him, he lifted his thumb to trail it over my bottom lip. "If you need anything, you come to me."

"Oh, my god. This is so exciting!" Sophia bounced in place and grinned like a fool. "Jake, isn't this so exciting?"

"Who is this guy?" Will crossed his arms and stepped forward, putting himself nearly toe to toe with Anthony. "You're coming off a little pushy, brother."

"He isn't the only one." Zane glared at Anthony's hand and then at Will. "I saw you coming out of Cl-"

"Well, this is cute. I'm going to head to my room, though. They deactivated your room keys for me, Claire. If you need in, come see me, babe."

As grateful as I was for Jordan cutting Zane off, I still wanted to throttle him. I moved away from the men closing in on me and shot Sophia a panicked look. I needed help but I didn't even know where to begin. Well. I needed to change rooms first because there was no way in hell that I was bunking with Jordan. "All of my things are in there, Jordan! Just let me figure out where I'm going and I'll get everything."

"You'll stay with me. Since I was a last-minute addition to the wedding and the hotel was full I rented the house next door." Anthony followed me. "There's plenty of room for you. I'll help you get your stuff."

I froze. Anthony wasn't just any ex, like Jordan was. He was my last serious boyfriend and he was the man I'd been sure I was going to marry until he told me I needed to chase my dreams all the way to London. He'd broken my heart and what made it worse was just how kind he'd been the whole time. I couldn't even hate him. I definitely didn't want to become his roommate for a week, though.

Especially not when he was acting like the dominant twin I knew he didn't have.

"You can always room with me, Claire." Zane ran his hand through his hair while biting his lip, a move that I was sure made his fans melt at his feet into puddles. "I won't even complain if you get a little handsy."

"Wow. This is something else, huh?" Jake grinned but as soon as he saw the look I gave him, the grin died. "Shit. I didn't mean to bring in your exes, Claire. I swear. You just dated some really cool dudes who I happen to really like."

He was lucky Sophia loved him so much. I looked towards the front desk and saw that the two staff members standing behind it were both watching everything that was happening. The older woman wagged her finger at me.

"Sorry, honey. There ain't a single room available. Not here or anywhere else on the island, either. It's wedding season." Her larger than life hairdo wobbled as she spoke. I found myself wondering if mine would do the same.

"Come on, C. Stay with Anthony. There's no way you can stay with Jordan. The house next door is massive. You could have your own bed. And your own shower." Sophia wrapped her arm around me and leaned closer to whisper in my ear. "I have no idea why half of Jake's groomsmen are your exes but I'm going to find out. This is wild!"

"Find out and let me know so I can decide if I love you enough to not murder him." I took a deep breath and kept my eyes anywhere but on my three exes. "Fine. I'm going to get my things from Jordan before he touches anything and then you and I are going to escape to the pool for the rest of the day."

She didn't argue as I pulled her with me towards my room. She did, however, look back and giggle. "They're following us."

"Thank god I don't have many things. As soon as I get them I'm going to throw them in the general direction of the house next door and then you and I are getting drunk by the pool. No men allowed." I stopped outside of Jordan's room and frowned. "Wait... No, I'm sorry, Soph. Of course, you want to spend time with Jake and everyone else. I don't want to ruin the week for you. Even though I've already turned today into a circus... What do *you* want to do today?"

She threw her head back and laughed. "I'm about to marry Jake and promise him the next fifty to seventy years of my life. One day at the pool without him sounds great."

14

Claire

I tiptoed through the house Anthony rented, unsure of where I was supposed to be staying. It was late. I'd avoided every male on the island for as long as possible, until I was burned and just past drunk. It was after dinner, I knew, but I wasn't sure what time it really was. It was dark out and that was adding to my difficulty in finding a bed to sleep in. I didn't want to face Anthony while drunk, still in shock at seeing him, and in another one of Sophia's tiny bathing suits.

"Claire?" Anthony's voice called down from upstairs and I froze.

I'd been thinking about him all day long and I didn't want to come face to face with the man and have to be mature about everything. In my panic I shook myself out of my stupor and slipped into the closest room. Thankfully, it was a guest room with a lock on the door. I silently turned that lock and backed away. I just wasn't ready to face Anthony. I wasn't sure I ever would be.

"Claire? Where'd you go?"

My thighs hit the bed behind me and I tumbled back onto it gracelessly. It was luckily a silent fall and I was just drunk and tired enough to roll the rest of the way into the bed and tuck myself in under a throw blanket. Even with the panic at the idea of facing Anthony, I passed out in seconds.

I wasn't sure how long I'd been asleep but I woke up shivering and clutching the thin blanket to my chest. I thought the cold air conditioning had woken me up until I heard a commotion coming from outside the bedroom door. Sitting up, I strained to make out the voices and when I couldn't, I climbed out of bed and walked over to pull the door open. I was still a little tipsy and I wanted the noise to stop so I could go back to sleep.

Someone had turned the lights on in the house and I realized I was in a guest room just off the main living room. Across the room, standing just inside the front door, were my three exes. They'd all stopped talking and had turned to stare at me.

I clutched the throw tighter with one hand and rubbed at my eye with the other. Surely, I was dreaming. Then I noticed the luggage sitting at the feet of the three men. "What's happening?"

"My room had to be given to Jake's uncle who showed up last minute." Will shrugged like it was nothing.

"And my room is flooding. Weird, huh?" Zane ran his eyes over my body and even from across the massive room, I felt the heat of his gaze. "We came by to see if Anthony was still feeling generous about letting people stay with him."

Anthony was still in his suit, with just the jacket missing. He'd rolled his shirt sleeves up to his elbows and when he crossed his arms, the veins in his hands and forearms stood out. I'd always been a sucker for a sexy pair of veiny forearms. "Stay wherever you want."

Zane slapped him on the back and went to move past him, towards me.

"As long as it's on the first floor." Anthony crossed the room and swung me into his arms bridal style. I gasped and clung to him and it seemed to please him. He shot me a burning look before moving towards the stairs. "Your room is upstairs. Your stuff's waiting for you, along with a few things your uncle sent over."

"She has legs. She can walk." Will had managed to cross the room in the blink of an eye. He stared moodily at Anthony. "Maybe she should stay down here on the first floor."

"Not going to happen." Without waiting for an answer Anthony climbed the stairs two at a time and carried me to a room with double doors. "This is your room. There's a door connecting it to mine if you need anything."

I couldn't take my eyes off of the man who'd once been a little dorky in the most endearing way. There was no sign of that dorky guy. Not even a single crooked grin. I wanted to know what'd happened to him to turn into the hard looking man holding me.

He put me down next to a massive four-poster bed and held me with his arm around my waist while he turned down the plush bedding. "You need pajamas."

I sank down on the side of the bed as he stepped back and swiftly unbuttoned his shirt. Button by button, he revealed more and more muscular chest. My mouth watered and my liquor soggy brain shut off as he shrugged out of the shirt and pulled me to my feet to wrap it around me. I realized quickly that Anthony was the kind of rich that allowed him to wear professional, button-down shirts that were softer than anything I owned.

"Arms out, Claire." He wasn't shy about looking at my body when the throw dropped to my feet. He didn't hesitate for too long before helping me into the shirt and buttoning it, though. Just when I thought the feel of his knuckles brushing against my stomach would kill me, he took it a step farther and reached inside to tug the strings loose at my back.

I gasped. "Anthony?"

That earned me my first slightly crooked smile. "I'm just making sure you're comfortable, Claire."

He pulled the small bikini top the rest of the way off, keeping his hands away from my most private spots. I was still a heavily panting mess by the time he finished, though. I licked my lips and sank heavily onto the bed when he let me go.

"We'll talk tomorrow when you're sober and rested. I want you clear-headed for the conversation I want to have." He waited for me to settle fully in the bed and then he tucked me in. He stared down at me for a few seconds, his eyes flicking between my mouth and eyes. "You're even prettier now. I didn't think it'd be possible, but you are."

Anthony leaned down and lightly pressed his lips to my forehead before walking through the door that connected our rooms. I noticed he left it slightly parted before he shut out the lights.

I was in big trouble.

15

ANTHONY

"Send my calls and emails to Mark or Nevayah. I don't want anything with work bothering me this week. Understand?" I waited for my assistant, Paul, to agree before continuing. "As for the house, have breakfast sent over daily and be sure there are snacks available all day long. Dinner might be-"

"Look, Will, it's a CEO in the wild. See how he bosses his employees around and stands as stiff as stone?"

I glared at the pretty boy rockstar who'd somehow ended up in my way. "I'll call you back, Paul."

Zane smirked at me as he grabbed a glass of fresh juice. "You do all of this for us? How sweet."

Will grunted. "It's fucking seven o'clock in the morning and he's already in a suit. You couldn't pay me enough."

I glanced down at my suit and then at the pair of them. Will was in a firehouse t-shirt and Zane looked like his henley had been through a few world tours since it'd last been washed. "Seems as if no one does."

I heard soft footsteps coming down the stairs and looked up just as Claire walked into the kitchen and froze. She was dressed in another one of her Uncle Sal's outfits and every curve was on full display in the tight little pink dress. Even with her feet bare, her legs looked a mile long. Her hair was in a pile on top of her head and her black-framed glasses were sliding down her nose. She was an intoxicating mix of sexy and innocent.

After a few seconds of staring at us, she focused in on Zane and her eyes widened. "You're awake this early in the morning?"

I bristled at the familiarity between them. Of course I knew that she'd dated before me and after me, but she'd always been everything to me. There'd never been another woman who came close to capturing me the way she did. Maybe it was greedy to want that same devotion from her but I fucking wanted it.

"Cut me some slack, Claire. I was a stupid kid when we dated. I'm a grown man who recognizes the benefit of an early morning now." The prick winked at Claire. "Especially when he knows you're an early riser."

I leaned against the cabinet and lifted my mug to my mouth. "You two dated? I didn't know."

Zane cut me an annoyed look. "Yeah, we dated. You must've come before me if you didn't know that."

Claire's face turned red and she quickly turned, opened the fridge door, and leaned inside. "Um... I dated Anthony after you, Zane."

Zane scowled at me. "And you didn't tell him that we'd dated?"

I smiled back at him, something cold and cutting. "Must not have made much of an impression."

"I doubt that, rich boy. What Claire and I had was special. Still is. Some things just don't fade. That much was made obvious by the moment we shared on the plane ride here." Zane's smirk made me want to punch his lights out.

"I've always heard about the drugs you rockstar guys do and now I'm seeing the effects. You're delusional." I looked at Will. "Are you hearing this shit?"

Will, the guy I knew only as Jake's soon to be brother-in-law, rested his elbows on the table and narrowed his eyes at me. "I hate to give Zane credit in any way at all but I was Claire's first in every way and she kept that secret tight, I'm willing to bet. The woman's a vault when she wants to be. As for shared moments... You saw me coming out of Claire's room, Zane."

Claire spun around, face and neck blood red, and glared at Will. "You... You can't just announce that! All of you need to stop talking!"

Zane and I were suddenly drawn closer by a common enemy. I studied Will in a new way and decided I wouldn't hate destroying the asshole. Zane's face said that he agreed.

"What? It seemed like we were all raising our legs like a bunch of dogs and I didn't want to be left out." Will cut his eyes at me and I got the feeling he'd be a worthy opponent. It'd been a while since I'd gone up against anyone who felt that way.

"This is... I... I'm going back to my room." Claire shut the fridge door hard enough to rattle its contents and stomped out of the kitchen. "If everyone could just stop talking about special moments and first times, I'd love that, thank you very much."

Zane sighed after we heard the bedroom door upstairs slam. "Well, that went well. So much for spending the morning with her."

Will groaned. "That was fucking embarrassing. I think I just blacked out."

I looked at both men and shook my head. "I have work to do."

"Thought you took the week off." Zane raised his eyebrows. "You wouldn't happen to be plotting to get your own special moment with Claire, would you?"

I tapped my knuckles on the counter and let a cold smile twist my lips. "I didn't get to where I am by exposing my hand."

I stayed downstairs for the next hour as I waited and watched. Zane wasn't wrong. I refused to let Claire be taken in by a smarmy rockstar or her best friend's big brother. Not when I'd never stopped wanting her. I knew the morning schedule for the groomsmen and smiled as I heard both Will and Zane leave the house to report for their duties. Maybe I should've gone with them but I was a backup groomsman for Jake and as his friend and boss, I was giving myself a little leeway.

I shrugged out of my jacket and rolled up my sleeves on the way upstairs. I could hear Claire inside her room, talking to herself as she paced. I had no plans on making things easy for her. I'd done that once and it'd been the wrong choice. If she wanted to get away from me again, she was going to have to work for it.

I opened the door and strode inside. She looked up and went still as she watched me coming at her. Her lips parted and I felt her soft exhale a moment before I slid my mouth over hers. Wrapping my arms around her I held her tight and proved to her that I'd forgotten nothing.

16

Claire

I wrapped my arms around Anthony's neck and held on as he gripped my ass and lifted me off my feet. I'd just been debating running away from the wedding seconds before, out of shame and embarrassment, but it seemed Anthony had other things on his mind. He forced my legs around his waist and nipped my bottom lip before kissing down my jaw. That was the thing about Anthony. He'd always consumed me. He kissed me and touched me like he wanted to own me. And he had.

He'd never kissed anyone before me. I was his first in every way and he'd spent an obscene amount of time learning everything he could about my body. He'd never stopped watching me so he'd know every inch of my body and how it responded to his fingers, lips, tongue. He'd been an obsessed lover. He proved that morning that his memory ran deep.

His lips grazed the skin under my ear and his teeth tugged at my earlobe. His hands bit into my ass as he held me tight. What was new was the ragged growl to his voice as he spoke. "I need to see your face when I make you come, baby."

I was coming? That was a surprise to me but it shouldn't have been, not with Anthony. He'd only taken a few nights of studying my body to perfect his art. I hadn't been with anyone since him who'd expertly worked my body as well. Still, I'd just been panicking so the idea of an orgasm coming so soon after was a shock.

Anthony walked us backwards and pinned me to the wall while sliding his hand under my thigh to reach my core. The short dress allowed him easy access and the miniscule panties offered no resistance when he tugged them to the side. He brought his mouth back to mine and kissed me hungrily while teasing me with the tip of his finger. He ran it up and down my lower lips, never quite touching where I needed him to touch. Not until I locked my hands in his hair and tugged.

He pressed his forehead against mine and watched me as he pushed two fingers deep inside me and curled his thumb over my clit. His fingers curled as well, almost as if he was trying to rub them against his thumb, and I made a sound I hadn't made in years. A mix between a pant and a scream, I dug my heels into his back and my head dropped back against the wall.

"Oh, god. Anthony..."

He watched me as he fingered me with a precision that should've been illegal. Within seconds my head was rolling from side to side and I was making a mess on his fingers as I came. Seconds. He'd taken seconds to get me off.

"You're still the most beautiful woman I've ever seen come, Claire. The way your nose pinches and your skin flushes... Your glasses always fog up when you forget to take them off and when the fog clears and I see those pretty brown eyes rolling in pleasure... Fuck. I want to nail you to the wall right now, baby. I want to fuck you so hard you forget any other man who's ever touched you."

As he spoke his fingers continued to curl and fuck me. His thumb moved in softer circles but he never stopped. His body was tense and he seemed larger than ever as he pressed into me. Then he shifted his pinky finger lower to tease my ass and I thought I'd die right then and there.

"You've always gotten so wet for me. Nothing's changed, has it? Does this pussy leak for anyone else the way it does for me?" He rocked his hips against mine and lowered his mouth so he spoke against my lips. "I shouldn't have let you go. I should've tied you to my desk and fucked you until you realized that was exactly where you belonged. I was too nice, Claire. Not anymore."

I sank my teeth into his bottom lip, so lost in the new side of him that I couldn't think beyond the feel of his thick fingers punishing my core. He'd added a third finger and was relentless in his possession of my body.

"Come for me again, pretty girl. Let me feel this pussy weep for me before I fuck it raw." Anthony's voice was dark and low as he ordered me to come and it worked. It triggered an orgasm and the smile on his face as I came for him was diabolical. It told me that he knew he owned me.

I didn't even realize I was talking until he pressed his lips to mine and the gasping sound filling the room went away.

"You beg so pretty." Pulling his fingers out of me and running them down the inside of my thigh, he let me feel just how wet I was for him. He let me watch as he lifted his hand and made a show out of licking my come off his fingers. "You still taste so fucking good, Claire. I'm going to need you spread out on my desk all day long so I can lean over and taste you whenever I need to."

I whimpered and offered my mouth to him but before he could kiss me the bedroom door swung open and I realized that what I'd always thought was my worst nightmare was nothing compared to having two of my exes walk in on me hooking up with another ex. With just one shocked look at Will and Zane's furious expressions, and I scrambled to get away from Anthony.

He was in a much more relaxed mood as he slowly moved away from me and made a display out of reaching between my thighs and fixing my panties before he let me step away from him. "It's customary to knock, I believe."

I shimmied along the wall until I was as far from the three of them as I could get. Zane and Will kept looking at me and then back at Anthony in a way that made me think I really should've jumped out of the plane.

"Are you fucking kidding, asshole? You're up here manhandling her? You have no right to touch her like that. You're-" Will was cut off by Zane, who seemed just as angry.

"This is a joke. *You're* a fucking joke. You just swoop in here and start grabbing all over Claire? Keep your hands to yourself, asshole."

In all the time I'd known Anthony, I'd never seen him lose his cool. He was a collected guy. Until that moment. "She's *mine*. Whatever moments you think you had before I arrived, they're over. If you have an issue with hearing her scream for me, maybe go back to your rooms. I have every right to touch her and I'm going to keep touching her. Both of you can fucking see yourselves out unless you're ready to sit there and watch me-"

"Watch what you fucking say." Will grew even larger as he puffed out his chest. "She's not-

"Both of you watch what you-" Zane cut Will off just to have Anthony cut him off.

"You heard her coming for me. Take it as your sign and walk away."

It was too much for me to handle. I was dying. I couldn't even process what all I was mortified by but I was sure if I was given a few weeks, I could make a pretty comprehensive list. I couldn't stand there and listen to them for another second. I looked around, desperate to escape a mess of my own making, and made a go for the sliding door to a small, personal balcony.

Fortunately for me the three men were so focused on shouting at each other that they didn't notice me slip out onto the balcony. I looked over the edge and decided it was worth risking a broken leg if it meant I could run away from my problems. Climbing over the balcony railing, I hung on the side for a few moments and shut my eyes. The drop was only a few feet but I was barefoot in another of Uncle Sal's sex worker dresses.

"Claire? What are you-" Jake let out a grunt of pain as I crashed into him. He'd chosen the wrong balcony to be passing beneath that morning.

We landed in a pile on the pathway between the house and the hotel's garden. Jake had caught me, mostly by accident, but he'd cushioned my drop enough that I could easily roll off of him and climb to my feet. He stayed on the ground like a flattened starfish, his limbs spread out in every direction.

"I'm sorry! I had to escape. You okay? Should I get someone?"

He grunted again. "This is karma for inviting your exes, isn't it?"

I leaned over and patted his chest. "Maybe. I have to go. Sorry, buddy. Feel better."

I left him there groaning and made a run for it. I hadn't decided just yet if I was running for the hotel to find Sophia or the ocean to walk into the waves...

17

Claire

I walked next to Sophia and thought about pushing her into one of the blackhead plants. She was so busy cackling at my predicament that she probably wouldn't have noticed she was no longer standing for a solid thirty seconds. She was having too good of a time at my expense. We were heading to a dress fitting for the bridal party and while the bride should've been more concerned about her dress, she was instead completely focused on me telling her every detail about my morning. For the third time.

"I'm not telling you again. You're supposed to be supportive and give me ideas about how to fix this." I pouted and crossed my arms. When a passing car honked I looked down and saw my cleavage was pushed about as high as the heavens. Groaning, I let my arms fall back to my sides and glared at Sophia. "Uncle Sal is on my shit list, too. He's trying his best to make me look like a sex worker."

Rolling her eyes, Sophia finally caught her breath and wiped her eyes. Her mascara was ruined and I made a note to make sure she had waterproof for the wedding day. "He's trying to make you look your age. Every time he comes home from visiting you, he acts more and more traumatized by your wardrobe. This last visit he described things as dire and in need of Jesus."

"There's nothing wrong with my wardrobe. I dress like a professional." I sputtered. "A *business* professional."

Up ahead I saw a group of women standing around in a parking lot and knew we'd almost reached our destination. Shine was an overpriced dress shop that happened to get Sophia's business because her wedding planner's sister owned it. I'd had quite the time getting them to ship my dress to me in London so I could have a seamstress work on it for me. I had a feeling it was because of who the wedding planner was.

"What was Will doing during all of this? I can't imagine how awkward he was." Sophia stopped, her focus fully on me. "And tell me just one more time about how Anthony pushed you against a wall and fingerbanged you. Since you might've broken my future husband's dick this morning, I need the lady spank bank material."

"Okay, first of all, don't say lady spank bank. Gross. Second of all, I didn't break Jake's penis. He's fine.... Probably. And third of all, don't say fingerbang." I could feel my face flushing. "And don't say anything about any of this to anyone. But especially don't say anything about it to Mad-"

"Madeline!" Sophia grinned over my shoulder and squeezed my hand. "Hi! You two remember each other, of course!"

I squeezed her hand a little tighter. "Of course. Good to see you again, Madeline."

Madeline Moore was the last person I wanted to spend my week with. She might've been an amazing wedding planner but she was still the mean girl who'd been determined to stake her claim on Will in high school. No one had ever known that Will and I were together but Madeline must've had some sort of sixth sense because she'd hated me. When she hadn't been able to force Will into going out with her, she'd turned her attention on Sophia and struck up a friendship that left me wanting to pull my hair out. Madeline had never managed to edge me out of Sophia's life but she'd managed to get her claws in deep enough that it'd been natural for Soph to choose her as the wedding planner.

Madeline batted her lashes at me and gave me a smile that was more nose curl than anything. "Were you able to get things sorted with your dress, Claire? I heard that it was too small. Hopefully you were able to find someone to sort that out for you?"

Having the dress shipped to me finally two sizes too small had been diabolical but it had Madeline written all over it. Luckily, I knew a seamstress who worked miracles. "Oh, yeah, I found someone. I can't imagine if I'd waited until arriving home to work out my dress alterations. If I hadn't found out the store ordered the wrong size so early, I might've been walking down the aisle in my underwear."

Sophia frowned. "You didn't mention the dress came in the wrong size. You should've said something and I would've made them fix it, C."

"Oh, I think our friend here just got her sizes mixed up. Those European sizes are just so different." Madeline leaned in like she was sharing a secret. "Or maybe you remember being a smaller size? We've all been there!"

Bless her heart, Sophia came to my rescue just like she always did. "Madeline, don't be silly. Claire knows her sizes. As does her Uncle Sal, because look at this body! It's no wonder she's got men lining up to be her date to the wedding."

I cut my eyes at her. "Soph, let's go ahead and get your dress on. I'm dying to see it on you. The pictures just don't cut it. I need to see you glowing in person."

"Don't say glowing! One hint of that word and my parents are going to assume I'm pregnant. That's the last thing I need. They're already emotional enough as it is." Wrapping her arm around my waist, Sophia led me past Madeline and towards the rest of the waiting women. "Let me introduce you to everyone else and then we'll get this over with so we can get to the food. I'm starving!"

I knew a few of the other bridesmaids but only by name. There was Lizzie Crowder and Katelyn Banks, both women who worked with Sophia at the realtor office she managed. I knew Fiona James and Kinsley Hendrix in passing from college. The only other bridesmaid was Madeline. I was the maid of honor but I had a feeling Madeline had made a play for the title, since she was actually present for everything Soph might've needed.

It was hard not to feel like a bad best friend while watching Madeline swan around the bridal shop, meeting every one of Sophia's needs before she had them. She *had* been present through all the planning and preparation, not just as a planner but as a friend. I'd been an ocean away, working all the time so I could leave for my one-week vacation without falling behind.

I'd planned the week before the wedding and I'd tried my best to take care of Sophia, but I was starting to doubt myself. Especially with all the drama I'd already caused. All I wanted in the world was to make things perfect for Sophia and in the face of Madeline's stomach-turning perfection, I felt like I was coming up short.

That just meant I had to make sure everything else went perfectly. I could do it. I was a Type A woman who suffered from imposter syndrome. That meant I had an anal level of drive to be the best at anything I did. I'd use that for Sophia's benefit.

After leaving the dress shop, we all headed back to the hotel for a bruncheon I'd planned. I'd been so explicit in my directions to the hotel manager and wedding coordinator, but I was still nervous up until the second I saw that they'd set up the venue perfectly. On the eastern patio overlooking the ocean, the hotel staff had set up a beautiful table in Soph's wedding colors, piled high with delicious looking food. Mimosas were bottomless, of course, and the atmosphere was fun with a playlist of Sophia's favorite dance songs playing in the background.

Sophia looked at me with real tears in her eyes and hugged me tight. "You even had them cut the french toast crust off for me!"

Madeline frowned at me over Soph's shoulder and turned up her nose. "It's a little buggy out here, isn't it?"

18

Claire

Two mimosas in and Madeline's sly critiques stopped bothering me. I'd eaten a troubling amount of bacon and had practically turned up a syrup bottle to get the last drop of the sticky goodness in my mouth and I was feeling good about the morning. Soph was next to me, her hand over her belly as she continued to push bite after bite of french toast into her mouth.

"And then Sophia looked at me and we both nearly died laughing. Mr. Billingsly was so angry but we couldn't help it! The woman was farting in every room of the house we were showing her like she was marking it as her own!" Lizzie wiped tears from her eyes and finished her third mimosa. "I've never seen anything like it and I pray to god I never do again."

I laughed along, happy to finally be around people who weren't so serious all the time. Working in a publishing house in London meant I didn't get many chances to hear a woman snort while telling a story about farting. It was refreshing in a way I hadn't known I needed and I could feel layers of tension falling away.

"Oh, no, Claire. It looks like we're out of drinks. What a bummer!" Madeline flipped her perfectly styled blonde hair over her shoulder and pouted. "If you're not used to planning events, it's so hard to get everything perfect."

I waved her off. "There's more in the kitchen. I'll just go ask them to bring more out."

I had a little more pep to my step after seeing the gleeful light in her eyes dim just slightly. I wasn't going to let her ruin things. I was just going to ignore her and make sure Sophia had the time of her life. It seemed like two mimosas was the perfect amount of alcohol for me to be laid back about Madeline's shitty attitude towards me. Turns out it still wasn't enough for me to be laid back about my temporary roommates, though.

I made it back to the patio and saw that all the women had migrated to the edge closest to the beach. They were all leaning forward, watching something. When I got close enough to see what they were staring at, I stumbled and landed on my hands and knees in the sand.

Madeline giggled. "Wow. You might want to cut back on the drinks, Claire."

Okay, so I learned quickly that besides alcohol, the sight of my three exes running shirtless down the beach towards me was also a good way to forget about Madeline. They looked like the cast of *Baywatch* as they jogged with the rest of the groomsmen. Muscles flexed, skin shined like it'd been oiled, and things swayed inside swim trunks that had the women around me fanning themselves.

I was sure Jake and his other groomsmen were just as hot but I couldn't look beyond Will, Zane, and Anthony. The three of them looked like gods kicking up sand as they jogged our way. I was so blown away by all the skin on display that I hadn't even realized I was still in the sand. I struggled to my feet but by that time the other bridesmaids had recognized Zane Wilson as the rockstar he was and they were all so focused on getting closer to him that I was knocked over again.

Sophia pulled me up, a laugh bubbling out of her. "You okay? You got in the way of those women getting closer to muscles. They ran you right over."

I tore my eyes away from the men and faced Sophia. "I'm guessing Zane is a surprise to them, too?"

She nodded. "Oh, I found out about Anthony being here, too. I'll tell you later."

Jake swooped in and picked up his soon to be wife. "Consider your girly lunch crashed! Feed us women! We've been playing volleyball all morning and we demand sustenance!"

I rolled my eyes at him and peeked back to see that Zane wasn't the only man being swarmed. Madeline was hanging onto Will's arm as she gazed up at him like he was a superhero. Lizzie was grinning up at Anthony with her breasts squeezed together in the tank top she wore but he was staring blatantly at me. When I looked closer, I realized that all three of them were staring at me.

I squeaked and spun around. That was too much attention. No matter the bolt of jealousy I felt threatening to burn through me, I couldn't handle that much attention in front of the whole bridal party. I quickly sat back down in my seat and shoved another piece of bacon in my mouth.

The hotel staff was painfully efficient and had more chairs at the table before anyone could even ask. It was silently decided that the men were joining the party. In honor of that turn of events I drained my third mimosa and nodded to the staff member bringing out more food and alcohol. We were going to need a lot more alcohol.

Anthony sat down next to me and left no space between our bodies. He wrapped his arm around the back of my chair and leaned in to whisper to me. "I wasn't finished with you this morning."

I choked on a bite of bacon and then looked up at him with wide eyes. I didn't know what to say so I just forced yet another slice of bacon into my mouth and chewed it aggressively.

"Don't think you get to hog the maid of honor, Anthony." Zane took the seat next to me and slid his hand over my leg to grip the inside of my thigh. "In case you were wondering, I dominated at volleyball."

Will managed to sit directly across from me and he leaned forward with his elbows on the table and his gaze locked in on me. "Bullshit. He just about cried when the ball slightly bent his fingers backwards."

My glass was refilled and I drained it once more. Zane still had a tight grip on my thigh, Anthony had moved his hand to the back of my neck, and Will was doing his best to undress me with his gaze. I cleared my throat and tried to think of something to say but instead of coming up with anything, I just took another bite of bacon.

Zane laughed even as he let his pinky finger stroke higher up my leg. "My fingers are worth a lot, fire boy. But I didn't almost cry."

Anthony tightened his grip on my neck. "My fingers are worth a lot, too, aren't they, Claire?"

Will's gaze narrowed and moved to Anthony. "Really?"

I was almost grateful to see Madeline as she sat next to Will and leaned into his side. That flare of jealousy popped back up but I stomped it back down. Madeline had been after Will since before he and I were together. If he wanted her, he would've had her already. That thought didn't quite sit right with me, though.

"Wow, Claire. You must really get around. Sophia just told everyone. Three exes at one event?" Madeline laughed and tipped her glass in my direction. "You were with them before they got rich and famous, right?"

Instead of focusing on the insult, I honed in on the number of exes. "Three? What? I don't have three exes here."

Will scowled but kept his lips shut.

"The two sitting beside you and the guy who dumped you but still came for the vacation?" She rolled her eyes. "Surely there aren't so many that even you have lost track?"

Anthony let out a dark sounding laugh. "Careful. People are going to think you're jealous of Claire if you keep prodding at her."

19

Claire

"Turn it up! I want to dance!" Sophia dragged Jake to his feet and as soon as the music was turned higher, she forced him to dance with her. I was thankful for the distraction and would have to hug her later.

"Dance with me?" Zane didn't give me a chance to say no; he slid to his feet and pulled me out of my chair and Anthony's arms. "Remember the first time I got you to dance with me?"

I snapped out of my stunned silence and sucked in a breath of air that I desperately needed. With a clearer head and only one man in front of me, I could almost think clearly. "You called me out in front of the entire campus."

He held me close with both of his hands low on my back. As we moved our hips together, his hands dipped lower. "I saw you sitting on the steps on McConner and I knew you were going home with me. You looked like you'd rather be anywhere else but at that first day celebration. I heard the music and took my chance."

I forget everything around us, much the same way I had that first time, when he dipped me and pulled me back with a snap that took my breath. The man had moves and he used them on me without a care for who was watching or where we were. "You did not know I was coming home with you."

The song changed and Zane changed tactics. He slid his thigh between mine and held me loosely. "That's right, Claire. Move with the music. Just like that. Just like that night on the quad. You shocked me that night, you know? I expected you to move like the shy woman you were but instead you rolled your hips like you'd been dancing for tips your whole life."

I felt him tug my hair free and let it sway behind me as we moved together. "I didn't know what I was doing. I never did with you. I still don't."

He gripped the back of my neck and forced my upper half against his. "And yet you do it so fucking well."

"I'm cutting in, pretty boy." Will took my hand and spun me away from Zane and into his own arms. Before I could look around to see if Sophia was watching, Will growled. "Focus on me just like you did with him. No one is watching us."

I was afraid of what it said about me that I was so easily able to switch my attention from Zane to Will. I stared up at him and told myself that dancing with Will in front of everyone was okay. It didn't mean anything.

Will kept his hands in appropriate places but the look in his eyes was pure sex. The log pressing against my stomach was also pretty inappropriate but I wasn't going to mention it. "It's getting harder and harder to just sit by on the sidelines, C. When I see them touching you so openly, it makes me fucking crazy. I'm about ready to bend you over and claim you in front of everyone."

The idea made me shudder and I hated myself for loving the taboo thought. It was wrong. It didn't matter, though. Not when it was Will saying the words.

"You like that, don't you? You like the thought of me fucking you in front of everyone. You want me to yank up that tiny dress and drive my dick so deep inside of you that you scream while everyone watches and sees just how much I own you?"

I whimpered and clutched at his shoulders desperately, like I'd find my sanity there. He couldn't say those things to me. He was making me want to be a bad friend and I needed to be stronger than that. When I forced myself to look around to find Sophia's face to remind myself of why I couldn't give into my lust I realized that Will had danced me to the side of the patio.

He glanced over his shoulder and then pushed me around the side of the hotel and into the first open door. He shoved it closed shut behind us and then he was on me. He kissed me roughly, our teeth knocking more than once as we went at each other. His hands were everywhere as we kissed and I didn't even consider stopping him when he yanked up my dress and palmed my ass.

I went up on my toes as he slid his hand lower and cupped my core over my panties. His grip was possessive and firm as he held me by my sex and kissed his way across my jaw.

"This was mine first." He drew his hand back and lightly slapped me between my thighs. He swallowed my gasp and kissed me deeper while rubbing me, still through my panties. When he pulled away again, I was shocked by the hunger on his face. "It's going to be mine again, isn't it, Claire?"

I opened my mouth, the answer so sure and ready on the tip of my tongue, but before I could get it out, movement from the corner of my eye caught my attention and I nearly screamed until I saw it was Zane and Anthony who'd slipped into the room with us. I sprung away from Will and looked around desperately for something to hide behind. It was the second time in one day that I'd been caught with one of them by the other two and I was starting to feel like Uncle Sal was dressing me based on the fact that I was running around like a dog in heat.

I realized we'd slipped into the ballroom and that there were a couple of staff members on the other side of the room, pretending to not be there. I was making a mess of things. Alcohol, my personality and need to organize things, and my desire to have things be perfect had words spilling out of my mouth before I could stop them.

"I'm just going to come right out and say it. Obviously, I'm attracted to all three of you. Obviously, I have feelings or something and those feelings are making me act like... Well, I'd rather not say how I feel I've been acting. This is weird and awkward and I'm still not sure I'm not stuck in a nightmare. I have this crazy sexual attraction to each of you and I can't seem to keep it in my pants." I paused. "I regret saying it like that. Oh, man, I regret saying any of this. Or maybe I don't. Maybe I need to say it because I don't want to hurt anyone. I don't know what's happening here but it can't happen."

Zane sighed. "There's the part I hate."

"I'm here to make sure Soph's wedding is perfect and that's what I need to be doing. I need to be focused on Soph, not getting myself off with three of the most insanely sexy men... Shit. I lost my train of thought." I tugged at the ends of my hair and gasped. "Oh, yeah! I can't do this. No matter how much I seem to want to. So we just all have to keep our hands to ourselves."

"Oh?" Will shook his head and smiled. "Just how many mimosas did you have? You didn't seem drunk until you started talking."

"Ignore that. We just have to agree to keep our hands to ourselves. Okay?" I looked at each of them and was confused by how amused they all seemed to be. "What?"

"I'm not going to be able to agree to that, baby." Anthony was the first to deny me.

"I hate to agree with this asshole but I do. I'm not agreeing to stay away from you." Zane shrugged. "Sorry."

Will stepped towards me and tapped the end of my nose. "Never going to happen."

I slowly backed away without saying anything else because I wasn't sure what was happening. I let myself out of the ballroom and rushed back around the corner to rejoin the luncheon with a racing heart and a raging libido.

20

Will

"Well, she's not going anywhere for a while." I went straight to the bar in the living room and poured myself a double of whiskey. "I don't know what she and Soph did today but I've never seen either of them that drunk."

Zane smirked at me from his spot on the massive white couch. Everything in the fucking house was sparkling white. No one else seemed as worried as I was about getting shit dirty. I sat across from the cocky rockstar and frowned. He was still smirking at me and it made me want to open a window and throw him into the ocean.

"*What?*"

"I've seen her that drunk. She went through a wild phase with me. She challenged a biker to a drinking contest at a bar in Miami one night... If she hadn't been so fucking cute with her glasses sliding down her nose the guy might've been tempted to murder us." His smirk turned into a genuine smile. "By the end of the night, the biker was so charmed by her that he pretended to pass out so Claire could win. She probably still thinks she drank a biker under the table."

Anthony leaned against the floor to ceiling windows and stared out at the ocean. "She went through a wild phase or she *had* to be hammered to be with you?"

I snorted. "Funny."

"Not funny." Zane drained the last of his beer and put it on the coffee table between us. When Anthony offered him another, he took it. "I usually stick to just one beer these days but it's a special occasion."

"Good for you." With a deep sigh Anthony sank into the other end of the couch from Zane and then grunted as it tried to inhale him. He struggled to sit upright and swore. "Who the fuck thought these couches were a good idea? It's like sitting in quicksand."

"The owner is a local who I'm pretty sure has never sat on a couch a day in her life. She's a speed walker. Competitively." I drained my whiskey. "What are we doing?"

"Sitting and talking?" Zane nodded at Anthony. "You think he's inhaled a little too much smoke? Or is he leaning into the dumb meathead thing a little too hard?"

"When your music career is over, skip the comedy phase of your mid-life crisis, buddy." I put my glass down and pointed at the ceiling. "I meant what are we doing about Claire."

Anthony leaned forward and rested his elbows on his knees. "I don't know what the two of you are doing but I'm planning on ending this week with her at my side."

I bristled. "You're going to need to rework your plans because she's mine."

"You're both wrong." Zane was back to smirking. "Claire is going to be mine."

"Didn't you ghost her when you went to LA to make it big?" I raised my eyebrows at him. "Why the fuck would she give you another chance?"

That knocked the smirk off of his face. "Things were different back then. I'm not the same person and I'm going to show her that. What we had was intense and...special. That means something."

"You don't think what I had with her was?" Anthony stood up and paced to the windows. "I was going to marry her."

"But you didn't." Feeling stressed suddenly, I went to the bar again and poured myself another. "I was her first. We had something-"

"Secretive and taboo. You had something with Claire that she had to hide." Grabbing his now empty beer bottle, Zane twisted it in his hands. "She's never going to choose you over Sophia."

I wanted to hit him because I was afraid he was right. Claire loved Soph like a sister and that love was what stopped us from being together the first time. I wanted to tell everyone that we were together and she didn't. I'd walked away because my pride hadn't been able to handle staying her secret, especially when she seemed to think we would never be open about who we were to each other.

"Sorry to burst your bubble, fire boy, but I'm not pulling any punches. I'm going home with Claire." Zane stood up so the three of us were facing each other. If we swayed a little, I'd blame it on the sea. "She might be attracted to all three of us but it'll only take one night with me for her to forget about the two of you."

Anthony laughed and the sound was so strange coming from him that Zane and I both took a step back. "She came twice on my fingers this morning and that was a slow morning compared to what we used to do. It won't take her long to make her choice."

"Or maybe she cares a little more about quality over quantity. Claire's coming to me first and we'll deal with the shit with Soph later. None of it will matter in the long run. You two may as well pack your bags and head home."

"How about a friendly wager? Whoever Claire lets fuck her is the winner and the losers learn to keep their hands to themselves? Winner takes all and the losers go home empty handed." Zane stared long and hard at each of us. "I'm confident that I'm leaving with Claire so I'm not worried."

Anthony scowled but he stuck out his hand. "Fine. When I win, you both need to go back to the hotel. I have plans for this house."

I glared at his hand and then at Zane. "If it'll get you two assholes to fuck off, fine. I bet I win Claire and have her screaming my name before the week's over. I want you both to stay in the house and hear it, though. So you know for sure who she belongs to."

"And if she doesn't scream your name, fire boy?" Zane shook his head but then he smiled. "Fine. If she screams one of our names first, there should be another bet. A side bet."

"What will I get when I win?" I could be cocky, too.

"I'm so confident that I'll win that I'll put up a hundred grand." Anthony put his hands on his hips and stared us down.

"Fine. I'm in." Zane looked at me. "Can you afford to play, fire boy?"

I couldn't. That didn't mean I was going to back down. "I'm in."

We shook hands and then settled back into the awful couches. Somehow, with the bets settled, the tension eased and when Zane suggested we turn an old game on, it sounded like a good idea. Being shitfaced had nothing to do with how easily we were getting along. Probably.

21

Claire

I'd planned the snorkeling trip without thinking. I wasn't a big fan of the open ocean, my swimming was adequate at best, and I hadn't been on a boat in years. I'd set myself up for failure and I was suffering because of it. I had a hangover and the constant rocking of the boat had me feeling more seasick than I could ever remember being. Seconds after leaving the marina I'd had my head in a bucket and was vomiting. I was stubborn and refused to stay behind, though. I'd planned the excursion for the bridal party and I wasn't missing it.

After Uncle Sal, who'd somehow wrangled an invite from Sophia, started sharing explicit stories from his past, however, I changed my mind and wished I'd stayed behind. Nothing could dull the horror at hearing my geriatric great-uncle describe his penis as a Bruce Willis movie. *Die Hard* would never be the same.

I tried to glare at him to make him stop talking but with my head in the bucket and Will, Zane, and Anthony shuffling around me to be the one holding my hair back, I couldn't get to him. I had to continue to endure his tales.

"Well, after my dalliance with the senator I went on down to Cuba on a boat with a wealthy Canadian named Dom who loved leather and naughty young men like me. Dom had these huge hands... In all the years since my time with that man, I've never been spanked the same way." Uncle Sal sighed so dramatically, I heard it over the engine of the boat. "It's a shame, really. A good spanking is just what the doctor orders some days. Just ask my sweet little niece over there. I heard spanking sounds coming from her apartment in London during one visit..."

I yanked my head up so fast that whoever had managed to hold my hair ended up ripping out a few strands. "Uncle Sal!"

"You know the quiet ones are always the freakiest." Sophia snorted and winked at me. "Although, I am curious about who was spanking you. I know it wasn't Jordan. You would've murdered him."

Jordan, who'd invited himself on the trip, perked up. "I might've slapped that ass a time or-"

"Stop talking or I'll toss your little ass over the side of the boat." Will's voice promised violence and it shut Jordan right up.

"Move, asshole." Anthony shoved Zane out of the way once he and Will were focused on Jordan. He gently wrapped my hair around his hand and squatted next to me. "Do you need me to throw him overboard?"

"Jordan or Uncle Sal?"

He grinned and brushed his knuckles down the side of my face. "Either one of them for you, baby. Just say the word."

I pressed my face into his palm and then paled as another wave of sickness hit me. I barely made it into the bucket.

"Hey, Will, could you rub sunscreen into my back? After Mom had that skin cancer scare a few years ago, I've been neurotic about being safe." Madeline's sickly sweet voice made the nausea worse.

"Now that you're free, Zane, could you sing for us? It would mean the world!" Lizzie grabbed Zane's arm and pulled him towards the front of the boat but I could still hear her begging him to sing.

"You know, your grandmother was quite the lady in her day, Jake." Uncle Sal whistled. "Back when I swung every way possible, she rocked my world a few times. Did I ever tell you that? She had this trick she'd do with a chandelier and a piece of rope that-"

"Oh, my god." Jake groaned. "Move over, Claire. I need the puke bucket."

"Don't be a prude, Jake." Sophia giggled. "Grandma Grace was young once. She had every right to be wild."

"I'm going to talk over that nightmare for you." Anthony settled next to me. "I took a refresher CPR course when I heard about the snorkeling trip. I figured I'd be prepared in case you forgot how to swim again. The ocean's a lot different than a college pool, though. I did some research and I almost wish I hadn't. Did you know that one milliliter of ocean water can contain millions of viruses? Also, there are over three million ships wrecked at the bottom of the sea."

I lifted my head and frowned. "I didn't forget how to swim. And don't tell me about viruses and shipwrecks right now, please."

Uncle Sal, with the hearing of a bat, decided to give his input. "Oh, Claire told me all about how you two first met. She'd been studying for an exam all night long and she cut through the gym to get to her class faster. Only she caught sight of that one's fine body and fell right into the pool."

Anthony's hand tightened slightly in my hair. "Is that true? You never told me you saw me before you fell in."

"Oh, she definitely saw you. And with all the blood rushing to her lady parts, she couldn't think of how to swim so she just sank." Uncle Sal was having too much fun. "Thankfully, her eye candy also happened to be an excellent swimmer. He saved her. Every time she talked about it, she had hearts in her eyes."

I hugged the bucket tighter. "How about someone throws *me* overboard?"

"Not going to happen. Do you know how many sharks live in the ocean? How many creatures in general? We've only explored around twenty percent of the ocean and we've already found colossal squids. What else do you think is hiding down there?" Anthony rubbed my back in gentle circles. "Besides, I want to hear more about those hearts in your eyes."

"That reminds me of a time-"

"Uncle Sal!" I didn't know what he was going to say next but I didn't want to hear it either way.

His eye roll was so prominent that I could hear it in his voice. "Oh, relax. I'm not going to tell anymore of your secrets. I've got plenty of my own to spill, honey."

"Thanks, Will." Madeline giggled. "Tell us more about Claire, Uncle Sal. Was she totally helpless when it came to men in college like she was in high school?"

The thing about Uncle Sal was that he would embarrass me happily but he'd turn into a fierce guard dog at the drop of a hat if he thought someone was messing with me. I almost felt bad for Madeline.

"Look around you. Between the rockstar and the billionaire, what makes you think Claire is helpless when it comes to men? Of course, there are others that I can't name who'd blow your tiny little mind." Uncle Sal cleared his throat haughtily. "How's your daddy, by the way? I hated rejecting him when he came over a few months ago but I just have never been able to see myself with a man who has kids like… Well, you know."

Anthony leaned down, daringly putting himself closer to my mess, and let out a soft laugh against my neck. "Remind me to send that man on whatever shopping spree he wants."

"Okay, Uncle Sal." Will sounded pained as he spoke up for Madeline. "Play nice."

"That *was* me playing nice. You should see me when I'm a bitch."

"I didn't hear you telling Madeline to play nice." Zane returned to our end of the boat and he sounded as grumpy as I felt about Will standing up for Madeline.

The captain of the boat raised his voice and called out over everyone. "How about we all play nice and hit the water? I'm going to drop anchor here for the day."

22

Claire

Anthony stood at the side of the boat looking over the side with a scowl on his face. He'd stripped down to his trunks and with his arms crossed over his chest, he was enough of a vision to make me forget how sick I felt. "How deep is the water here?"

Lizzie wrapped her arms around her waist and stood next to him. "You're really freaking me out."

"You should be freaked out. Have you ever heard of a vampire squid?" Looking back at me, Anthony shook his head. "I haven't even mentioned the hydrothermal vents that can reach temperatures of seven hundred degrees."

Kinsley stood next to Jake's younger brother, Mark, and took a deep breath. "We came to snorkel. We can't snorkel on the boat. So we should just...jump in. Right?"

Jake inched closer to his boss. "Hey, man, maybe don't give us any more ocean facts."

Anthony shrugged and moved back to my side. "If you don't want to know the shit coming your way, that's on you."

I sat back on the bench and toed my sick bucket away from me. While I still felt like crap, I at least didn't feel like I was going to spew. Sophia had even slipped me a mint, bless her. "I never knew you were afraid of the ocean."

He slung his arm around me and didn't hide that he was trying to look down the t-shirt I'd stolen from Jake to wear over another of Sophia's tiny bikinis. "I'm not afraid. I'm just smart. I like to know the risks before jumping into a situation. It's worked for me in business so why would I throw caution to the wind when sharks are involved?"

Zane whipped his shirt off and stood at the edge of the boat, grinning at me. "Anthony might be too scared but I'm not."

Everyone cheered as he flipped off of the boat and shouted about how cold the water was. I leaned over and smiled when I saw him treading water with a silly grin on his face. He looked like a little boy who'd won a race.

"If you want to come in, Claire, I'll keep you sa-" Zane screamed bloody murder and started splashing around wildly while also trying to get back to the boat. "Shark!"

Uncle Sal leaned over the boat and let out a loud laugh. "That's a goddamn fish and a small one at that! Stop splashing around before you get my hair wet, boy!"

Anthony laughed. "Good one, Zane!"

"You keep talking, brainiac. I'm coming for you." Zane huffed. "Someone else get in the damn water. If a shark does come up I want a chance at being faster than someone."

"Here goes nothing!" Sophia jumped off and dragged Jake with her. He went with a scream.

One by one everyone else dove in, except for me, Anthony, Uncle Sal, and the boat captain. I watched with envy as everyone splashed around and had fun. I especially noticed the way Madeline seemed to be having such a great time swimming next to Will. I stared at them for a few moments too long, wondering if there was something there. I knew that Will had kissed me and seemed to want more and I didn't think he was a player but I didn't know him anymore.

"What's wrong?" Anthony brushed my hair away from my face and followed my gaze. "Oh. She's not exactly subtle, is she?"

The captain saved me from having to admit I was jealous. He stopped in front of me and gently patted my knee. "Are you feeling better? If you're feeling up for getting in the water, I have a float you could use. It might help stabilize you a bit."

I'd talked to the man several times while booking the excursion but I never would've imagined he'd be just a little older than me with a beautiful smile. I'd noticed a few of the other bridesmaids checking him out. "Maybe. I am feeling better but now I'm thinking about viruses and hot spots in the ocean."

He shot Anthony a look and rolled his eyes. "In all the years I've been leading these things I've never had a problem that wasn't caused by a drunken idiot."

"Oh, captain! Would you mind coming over here and telling an old man about how he'd get to be your first mate?" Uncle Sal flicked his wrist and perfectly extended a bright pink fan. He fanned himself while batting his eyes. "If you don't mind."

The captain squeezed my knee and winked at me. "You owe me."

Anthony ran his hands down my thighs after the captain moved away. "He's going to look like a cliche when I rip his hand off and he has to have a hook."

I was so shocked by the jealousy evident in his voice and the imagery that I threw my head back and let out a wild laugh. Anthony had never been the jealous type before but he was different. I felt the way he wanted to claim me in every touch and there was something intoxicating about it.

"Hey! Anthony!"

We both looked over at the sound of Will calling him. He stood up and moved to the side of the boat, trying to find out what Will wanted. Before he could get a word out Zane snuck up behind him and shoved him into the water before jumping in after him.

I gasped and hurried to the side to make sure they were both okay. Zane was grinning up at me, clearly proud of his antics. Anthony was several feet behind him, an evil glint to his eyes. He disappeared under the water and I shook my head in sympathy for Zane. Anthony was a championship swimmer. He'd basically just pushed the human equivalent of a shark into the ocean with himself.

Zane noticed my expression and looked around. "Where'd he go?"

A few seconds passed and then Zane screamed before disappearing under the surface of the water. He came up a few seconds later, sputtering and growling at Anthony who came up looking even prouder than Zane had.

"You want to come in, baby?" Anthony smiled up at me, his concerns over the ocean neutralized for the time being.

Will swam up next to him and looked up at me. "I've got you if you want to come in."

Madeline swam close behind him. "Leave her be, Will. She's been sick all morning. She probably doesn't want to get in, the poor thing."

There was no way I was letting Madeline be fake nice to me to get Will to herself. I held my nose and jumped off the boat. My stomach did a few somersaults on the way down but then I was in the water and strong arms were pulling me back to the surface. I gulped in oxygen as I came up and clung to whoever had me.

"Um, Claire? As much as I love you, I'm going to need you to get your boobs off of me. You're like a sister and this is weird." Jake eased me away and clucked his tongue. "The water turns you weird."

I blinked my eyes open and tried to wipe at them. "I didn't put my boobs on you, jerk. I thought you were someone else."

"Me?" Zane wrapped his arms around me from behind and I could feel his legs kicking to keep us afloat.

I glanced at him over my shoulder and smirked. "I don't know. I've heard you scream twice since getting in and I'm worried we'll both need someone to save us."

23

Claire

Captain Avery came through on his promise and sent a little floating board into the water for me. Grateful that I didn't have to cling to anyone to stay above the water, I happily laid across the board and used my snorkel to stick my head under. I got to watch a few fish swimming around and something about having my head in the cool water actually helped me feel better. I was starting to really feel good about my choice of excursion.

My goggles got a slight leak after I'd been playing around for a while and I awkwardly tried to fix them without coming out of the water since I was watching a school of fish move together so gracefully. Grunting when more water got into the mask, I was just about to give up and lift my head out of the water when a heavy weight hit me from behind and someone yanked me off my float.

Panicking, I swung my elbow back, unsure of what was happening. I felt my bone connect with something and then I heard Will grunt. Gasping, I stopped freaking out and looked back at his bloody nose. "What the hell, Will?!"

He pinched his nose while shoving the float into my hands. "You were flopping around. I thought you were fucking drowning."

I winced. "I am so sorry. My mask was filling up with water. I was okay. You scared me but I didn't mean to hurt you!"

He was breathing through his mouth and he sounded terrible. "I scared you? You scared the shit out of me. I forgot all of my training and I nearly jumped straight on top of you. Don't do that. Don't scare me like that."

I looked away and swallowed. "I'm surprised you noticed with how well things seem to be going with you and Madeline."

"What?" Will swam closer and dropped his hand from his nose, letting it bleed freely. "You're kidding, right?"

I felt my face burn with embarrassment at having shown my jealousy. I lightly pressed my hand to his chest to keep him away as I looked anywhere but at him. "Ignore me. The sun must be getting to me."

"Claire, I-"

"You're bleeding?!" Anthony swam up next to us and his eyes went wide as he looked at Will's face. "Are you trying to get Claire eaten by a shark?! You can't just bleed into the open ocean and not expect a shark to show up! They can smell blood from miles away!"

I shuddered. "Get me out of here."

Anthony grabbed me and swam backwards towards the boat. He all but tossed me onto the boat before crawling on himself. "Are you okay?"

Will was on the boat just as fast. He grabbed me under the arms and picked me up. "You and I need to talk."

Sophia gasped when she looked over and saw Will's face. "Will! What happened?"

"He tried to call the sharks, that's what happened." Anthony wedged his body between mine and Will's and then he led me over to the bench to sit.

Zane appeared in front of me, hands on my knees as he squatted. "You looked like you were having fun out there until the meathead jumped on you."

Madeline moved past Zane and shot me a dirty look. "Way to go, Claire. Now no one can enjoy the water."

"Then how about you get some sun on your pale skin, Madeline, and stop being a-" Uncle Sal saw my expression and cut himself off. "What? I'm not allowed to call the duck a duck? She's being a little bitch."

Zane reached over and fist bumped Uncle Sal. "When you're right you're right."

I lifted my chin and stared at Will, waiting for him to come to her defense again. He wasn't paying attention to her, though. He was staring back at me while Sophia dabbed at his bloody face. My breath caught at the intensity in his gaze.

"*You're* being a little bitch." Madeline huffed at Uncle Sal and crossed her arms under her chest, making sure to shove her chest up. "I was just pointing out that because Claire hurt Will none of us can enjoy the water now."

"Don't try to outbitch this old queen, honey. You won't win and you'll go home crying with nothing to show for it. Be nicer to my Claire or I'll show you my claws." Uncle Sal rolled his eyes and waved her away. "Anyway. Did I ever tell y'all about the time I met Hugh Hefner?"

I tuned him out as Will came over and sat next to me. I was all too aware of his body next to mine as he leaned in, bracing one arm behind me and the other on the bench between my thighs. I sucked in a sharp breath and looked at him with wide eyes. "W-what are you doing?"

He lowered his voice and leaned in even closer. "I had to hear about you getting spanked by some random asshole in London earlier and you're concerned about the way I'm acting with her? The things I want to do to you, Claire... You have no idea."

I searched his face and slowly licked my lips as the promise in his voice set me on fire. "Will... I-"

"You got jealous. If you knew how little space there is in my head for anything else but you, you'd know how ridiculous that is." He leaned in even closer and brushed his mouth over the shell of my ear. "I'm just doing my best to make sure I'm not humping your leg in front of everyone all day long, baby. Watching you with these two assholes, hearing about other men touching you, seeing the fucking captain making eyes at you... I'm close to throwing caution to the wind."

Zane cleared his throat and rolled his lips into his mouth as he struggled to not laugh. "If anyone's going to hump our baby's leg, it's going to be me."

Warmth erupted from my core outwards. Not only was I enjoying stealing away with three different men, the way Zane called me *their* baby had me nearly shaking with desire. The flash of heat scared me, especially if I thought about what it meant. So I wasn't going to. At all. Ever.

Will brushed his thumb up my inner thigh as he pulled away. "I'd pay good money to know where your mind just went."

Anthony trailed his hand down my spine. "I think we all know where her mind just went."

Before they could force me to spontaneously combust I was saved by the captain. He pointed to the food I'd had dropped off before we left the marina and winked at me. "We can go ahead and have lunch now. I want to move to a different location so after we finish up here, we'll head out."

I saw my chance to get some space and got up to pass out the lunches. The t-shirt I had on wasn't drying fast enough and every breeze chilled me to the bone so I peeled it off and settled next to Sophia to eat.

She chewed a giant bite of the specialty sandwich from one of her favorite cafes and wagged her brows at me. "Someone has the hots for you."

I'd worn contacts since I knew we were going to be in the water but I still reached up to push my glasses up my nose, a nervous tick that I couldn't kick. "No one has the hots for me. I just passed out delicious food. If anything, you're seeing the happy glazed expressions of hungry men being given a thick sandwich."

"Captain Avery." Sophia stood up suddenly and motioned for the captain to sit next to me. "I have to do something somewhere else. You two chat."

24

Zane

The captain sat next to Claire and I heard Will growl. Anthony wasn't much better. They both looked like guard dogs on the prowl. I didn't feel much better but I was used to being watched and I knew how to put on a good face. Slapping both of them on the shoulder, I stood up and pushed my hair out of my eyes. "I'll handle it."

Claire had taken off the shirt she'd worn all day and the tiny bikini she had on did nothing to hide her beautiful body. The top had my breath catching every other second because I was sure a breast was going to escape. Her eyes flicked to me when she saw me heading their way and I grinned at the way she bit her lip.

"Sorry to interrupt, Captain, but I need to borrow my girl for a minute." I didn't give either of them time to question my claim. I caught her hand and tugged her up and into my chest. I wrapped my arms around her waist and gently swayed despite the lack of music. "You looked too beautiful for me to stay away."

She was red and I knew she was fighting the embarrassment at being on display but I knew more about Claire than she'd probably ever admitted to anyone else. In her wildest moments, she liked being watched.

"Zane..."

I smiled and pulled out a card I'd been saving for a rainy day. I quietly sang one of our favorite songs to her as we danced. I saw the moment she softened to me and pressed my mouth to her ear, finishing the song early. "Want to really make it feel like old times and sneak into my room tonight?"

She pulled back and laughed, lightly slapping my shoulder. That laugh did funny things to me and I knew she had no idea. "I never snuck into your room. You snuck into mine. I could barely get rid of you."

"You're lucky I let you out of bed for even a minute back then." I slid my hands lower on her back and toyed with the hem of her bikini bottom. "You ruined me for all other women, Claire."

She rolled her eyes. "Sure."

Before I could tell her that I wasn't joking her asshole ex bumped into me. I scowled as I acknowledged to myself that there were three other men on the boat who'd dated her. I only really hated one of them, though. Jordan, the little prick.

He ignored me and grabbed Claire's arm. "Claire. Seriously, vacation you is so much hotter than work you. You tricked me."

I was debating about which of his eyes I was going to black when Claire proved that she didn't need my help. She stepped out of my embrace and glared at him. "Seriously, Jordan, I don't even know why you're here. Since you are, though, just do me a favor and don't talk to me. There are plenty of other people on this boat for you to talk to. Or, you could jump into the ocean and check for sharks. Either way, don't comment on my body."

He'd clearly had a few beers because he waved her off with a laugh. "You'll come crawling back."

"Alright, asshole, I-"

"You're done drinking on my boat. If you can't handle your alcohol, you go dry. Go take a seat and be respectful." The captain cut in and stole my thunder. He rested his hand on Claire's shoulder and squeezed. "We're going to take off for the second location soon. We could always leave him here and pick him up on the way home."

She smiled at the man and my blood ran hot. He was lucky we were in the middle of the ocean and that I'd never learned to drive a boat. I wanted to toss *him* overboard.

"He's not worth the legal trouble." Claire eased herself away from both of us and ducked her head. She was fucking adorable with her random displays of bashfulness. It made me want to corrupt her all over again. She bit her lip and tried to push her glasses up her nose, despite not wearing them. "I have to ask Soph something..."

She hurried to the other side of the boat and I couldn't help smiling as she and Sophia fell into each other and started giggling like they were still little girls. When they both looked over at where I was still standing next to the captain, I got the feeling we were the topic of their conversation.

"She's a beautiful woman." The captain crossed his arms as he watched her.

I stepped into his line of sight and scowled at him. "Not for you."

He just smiled. "Yeah, I noticed the line of men following her around."

"And yet you still thought you'd cut in."

That smug smile stretched wider. "Just thought I'd give her a different option. Don't worry, though, rockstar. I'm not a homewrecker. I don't know what the fuck you three are doing with her but it's obvious she likes it."

I looked back and saw that Anthony was on Claire already, with Will hovering close by. Claire's face was one of pure happiness. She glanced at me and I felt a bolt of heat as she winked at me. I couldn't help elbowing the captain. "See that?"

He groaned. "I'm going back to my boat. She always chooses me."

I tried to cut across the boat to get to Claire but one of Sophia's friends cut me off. I couldn't remember her name but she'd propositioned me at the beginning of the boat ride. "Excuse me."

"Wait a second, stud. Where are you running off to so fast?" She leaned into me, pressing her breasts into my arm. "How about a song? Just one?"

I tried to stay polite but I wasn't in Zane Wilson, rockstar mode. I was just Zane, a guy trying to get his ex-girlfriend back. I didn't want to sing for anyone else. I didn't want to think about work at all. "Sorry, I didn't bring my guitar."

The woman stroked my arm and giggled. "Come on! You can just sing. Your voice is amazing. It's a dream of mine to hear you sing."

I saw Claire look up and watched as her face shuttered when she saw the woman hanging all over me. Probably a little rougher than I needed to be, I pulled my arm away and held up my hands. "Sorry, but no."

I walked over to Claire and nearly screamed when she stiffened. Unwilling to lose the progress I'd made with her, I gripped her hips and tugged her back into my chest. She sighed heavily at me but I wasn't easily deterred.

I pressed my mouth to her neck and whispered. "I can't control what other people do, baby. I can only control what *I* do and I never took my eyes off of you. Don't get all stiff on me now."

Slowly, her body relaxed into mine. She sighed again but it felt like an expulsion of the remaining unhappiness. "This is all so crazy."

Anthony looked away from where he'd been talking with Will and Sophia. His eyes tracked down to where I was holding Claire but instead of scowling at me, he nodded.

Claire looked up at me and then back at him. "What the hell was that?"

There was something changing between us but I had no idea where it was going. I'd already gotten comfortable with Anthony and Will and thoughts were starting to form in my head that I had no business entertaining. Thoughts of how Claire liked being watched and how it'd work if the other guys didn't just watch her.

25

Claire

I was on fire. I was getting vibes from the guys that I didn't understand but my body responded to nonetheless. As soon as Captain Avery dropped anchor at the second location, I jumped off the boat and prayed I didn't drown myself while trying to chill out my vagina. Even if I was the only one who'd know the true cause of my death, it'd be mortifying.

The new location was just off the coast of a small island with a private beach. It took me a few minutes and a lot of effort but I swam over and collapsed on my back in the sand, loving the feel of it. It was warm against my back while the sun warmed my front and I instantly felt like napping. I idly dug my hands into the sand and closed my eyes. For those few seconds I could almost forget everything going on and just breathe.

"You swam out of there like you don't have multiple hot men trying to get into your bikini bottoms." Soph flopped down next to me and intertwined our fingers as she got comfortable. "You planned the best day, C. You should take off your responsible hat and pick one of those hotties to bang."

I turned my head to look at her and had to blink away a sudden wave of emotion at the simple act of holding her hand. I'd missed her so much. I hadn't realized just how much until that moment. "I think I want to move back home."

The words were out before I even had the complete thought but it felt right. I'd loved London for what it was but I was ready to come home. I knew Sophia and Jake wouldn't wait long before starting a family and I didn't want to miss a second of it. I didn't want to miss more of Uncle Sal's life, as stressful as he was at times. I missed the sunshine and the smell of the sea.

Sophia sat up and squeezed my hand. "I'm trying to not scream but if you don't mean that, you better not say it. You don't know how much I miss you and want you back home, Claire. I've been patient but I want you here."

A shadow fell over us, ending our conversation. I looked up and saw that it was Will. "Your almost husband is in a very animated debate with his brother over a football game they played when they were twelve. Looks like it might get ugly."

Soph sighed and stood up. "That game almost tore their family apart. I'd better go flash my tits at Jake to distract him and stop the war."

"Jesus, Soph. I'm your brother. Don't say shit like that to me." Will took her spot next to me and shuddered.

"Grow up, William." She grinned at me. "We'll finish that talk later."

I hugged my knees as I watched her swim back to the boat. She was graceful and looked like a damn mermaid, nothing at all like me.

Resting my chin on my knee, I tilted my head to look at Will and found him already watching me. "What?"

He shook his head. "This has always been my favorite version of you. Sunburnt, all natural, and a little sleepy."

I ducked my face as I blushed. "Why?"

"You were even cuddlier than normal after a morning in the sun back in the day. You were like a kitten, rubbing all over me as you got comfy on my chest and it was both the most painful and best thing to ever happen to me." Will looked back out at the boat and smiled. "And you're so fucking beautiful like this. Pretty sure an afternoon like this was when I knew I loved you."

I closed my eyes as his words warmed me from the inside out. When I opened them again, Will had moved closer and was studying me. I smiled. "Just pretty sure?"

His grin was earth-shattering. "July fourth, the summer I turned eighteen. Everyone else had snuck enough beer to take an afternoon nap. You were sitting on the beach all by yourself and I couldn't make myself stay away. The smile on your face when you saw me made me feel ten-feet-tall. You had on a light pink bathing suit and a toe ring that made me worry that I'd stumbled into a foot fetish. Everything about you felt like happiness to me and I knew I was fucked. I knew I loved you in a way that was going to change my life."

I leaned over to rest my head on his arm. He was killing me. My heart was thumping away violently in my chest, desperate to get closer to him. "Will..."

"My pride got the best of me back then, Claire. When you weren't willing to be with me in front of everyone, I took it badly. I thought it meant you didn't want me enough to face the shit that could've come our way. My feelings got hurt and I sent you away."

"I wanted you more than anything. That was never the problem. I just didn't want to hurt Sophia."

He kissed the side of my head. "I know that now. I also know that I've never felt anything even close to what I felt for you for someone else."

I pressed my face into his arm harder. "I-"

"Come on, losers!" Sophia shouted from the water. "We're playing chicken!"

Will stood up and pulled me to my feet and straight into his chest. With his back to the water no one would be able to see me and he took advantage of that by running his fingers inside my bikini top under the guise of straightening it. "You're on my shoulders, Claire. It's not exactly how I want your thighs around my head but I'll take it."

I grabbed his hand and stretched up on my tiptoes to kiss the corner of his mouth. "I don't know what's happening right now with the three of you but what I feel for you is as real as it ever was."

Ducking around him, I hurried into the water and saw Anthony leaning over the edge of the boat, watching me. I didn't know what was happening to me because I really did have feelings for Will. I also had feelings for Anthony and Zane.

I didn't get to analyze those thoughts, though, because Will grabbed me from behind and hefted me onto his shoulders. I grabbed his head and screamed as I swayed in the air. "I think you're too tall! This feels dangerous!"

He gripped my thighs and laughed. "Don't lose this for us, Claire. Take my sister down!"

"Hey!" Sophia giggled as Jake scooped her onto his shoulders. "You're my brother, asshole! You have to support me."

I gripped Will's head tighter and sent Sophia a panicked look. "Don't come over here! I'm not ready! I have to be like eight feet in the air!"

"I can take your place if you're scared, Claire." Madeline bounced next to Will in the water, her boobs doing a dance that even I had to admit was admirable and eye-catching.

Will tightened his grip on my thighs and grunted. "Claire's doing it. Isn't that right, Claire?"

There was no way I was letting Madeline put her tits on Will's head. I tightened my thighs around his head and loosened my grip. "I'm doing it."

Just as Sophia started to reach for me Uncle Sal's voice cried out from the boat. "*Shark!*"

26

Claire

I frowned at Uncle Sal's back as he finger-waved at me and headed back to his trailer and his man. Crossing my arms over my chest, I scuffed my borrowed flip flop over the sidewalk. "That man is going to kill me one day."

Sophia grinned next to me. "Come on, C. It *was* kind of funny."

"Two of your bridesmaids have black eyes." I turned to face her. "Soph, I planned an event that ended with nearly half of the wedding party wounded! Lizzie and Fiona nearly killed each other trying to get back on the boat. Your wedding photos are going to be full of black eyes thanks to me! I even got Will!"

"Honestly, C, it was a blast. I don't care about the wedding photos being perfect, not as long as we all get to spend the time together and I have proof of it. If Uncle Sal didn't fuck with us, I'd worry he was sick. I'm happy, babe. You should be, too."

I wanted to be. I just felt like I was going to ruin her wedding. I wanted it to be perfect because she deserved the very best. I felt terrible but I didn't want her to worry about it so I forced a smile. "Did you see Zane when Uncle Sal yelled shark?"

She howled with laughter. "I think he walked on water!"

We headed back to the hotel but I stopped outside the main entrance. I knew she had dinner with Jake's parents and I had a date with a giant bowl of mac and cheese. I hugged her a little extra tight. "I love you, Soph."

"I love you, too. Go have a little fun." She thrust her hips at me. "The fun kind of fun, if you know what I mean."

I rolled my eyes and pushed her away. "Get out of here, weirdo. Have fun at dinner."

"Pervert. Not in front of Jake's parents!"

I walked next door and let myself into the massive house Anthony rented. I didn't know where the guys had disappeared to but I didn't care right then. I needed comfort food and I didn't want to gorge in front of the three of them. Not when I was having so many confusing feelings over them.

There was still no sign of my suitcase so I hurried upstairs and changed into the closest thing to lounge clothes that Uncle Sal had given me. A small shorts and chemise set in a pale pink silk wasn't exactly something I'd typically relax in, but it was better than the bikini I'd been wearing all day. I changed out my contacts for my glasses and then headed downstairs to grab the frozen mac and cheese I'd seen in the fridge.

I went through the notes on my phone while I waited for it to cook, wanting to be sure there were no other flaws in my plans. The next day was our big spa day. I'd rented the expensive spa out and paid for services for everyone. It was my big gift to Sophia and Jake and I'd pretty much cleared out my savings to do it but I wanted to give Sophia the world. She meant so much to me that I *needed* it to be perfect.

The guys found me a little while later on the couch with my half-eaten bowl of mac and cheese, staring at the black TV screen. I heard them come inside and felt them stop in the entryway to the living room. I sighed. "I couldn't figure out how to turn the TV on."

Zane was the first to join me on the couch. He looked me over and groaned before dropping his head back and staring at the ceiling. "You look like sin and smell like delicious cheese. I don't know which part of my body is reacting more."

I snorted out a laugh and slapped his knee. "Don't tell me that I smell like cheese."

Will sat on my other side and leaned over to take a bite of my dinner. "For the record, I put this in the freezer for you."

"Really?" I heard the soft, starry-eyed tone of my voice and cleared my throat. "That was really nice of you."

"I still know you."

I smiled. "Then you know I don't like to share."

Anthony came around the couch and sat on the coffee table in front of me. "How are you feeling?"

I shrugged. "I don't know. Fine? Confused? What were y'all doing, by the way?"

He rested his elbows on his knees as he sat forward. "Will can have credit for the mac and cheese but I get credit for knowing you well enough to know that you were going to beat yourself up for those two fools banging their heads together. I knew you'd need a way to relax tonight."

My eyes widened and my cheeks warmed. My filthy mind went to the gutter and stayed there until he pulled out a brand new game of Twister. My lips parted on a gasp as I looked back at Anthony. One of our wildest nights had started with a game of Twister and ended in Anthony taking me in a place no one ever had before.

His eyes drank in my reaction and his lips tipped up in the corners. "We're going to play a nice, relaxing game of Twister. Innocent fun, baby. Just something to force you out of your head."

Zane rested his hand on my thigh and smiled at me just like he had when we'd been together. It was a sweet, pure smile with none of his typical cockiness. "I just spent almost an hour shopping with these two assholes. Don't make it have been for nothing."

I hesitated for a moment but seeing the hopeful looks in their eyes pushed me into saying yes. "Fine! Fine. Just let me go brush my teeth. I refuse to hear that I smell like cheese again."

Will took the bowl and groaned when I stood up. "Maybe put on a potato sack while you're up there."

"Don't you dare." Zane watched me leave and whistled. "I'm going to kiss Sal when I see him again."

I brushed my teeth and took a few seconds to reapply my deodorant and brush my hair. I felt like I was standing on the edge of a massive building. My heart was racing and I couldn't stop the thought that whatever happened next was going to be a big deal. I was teetering on the edge of that building and the wind was blowing. My stomach fluttered wildly.

In the living room, the guys had spread out the Twister mat and they were standing there, all of them with their hands on their hips as they watched me. One by one they smiled at me.

I decided to jump.

27

Claire

"Left foot, green!" Will shouted, face red as he bent forward and twisted sideways to spin the wheel.

Zane swore as he looked around at the mat. "Are you fucking kidding me? Are you cheating? Spin it again!"

"No, asshole! Left foot, green!" Will was practically doing the splits with Zane and Anthony both leaning on him and bitching about the moves they kept getting that put them in more and more twisted positions.

Zane grunted as he shoved his foot towards the only green spot open. It put his face practically in my boobs and his attitude changed instantly. "Oh, never mind. Thanks, man. This is great."

His breath tickled me and I laughed. I was hovering over Anthony and under Will somehow and it was brutal. Not only were my muscles aching in new ways, but constantly rubbing against the three of them was killing me. I'd felt more than one erection so I knew it was hurting them, too. I did, however, feel better about the wedding photos potentially being ruined.

Zane leaned forward a bit and looked down my shirt. "Yeah, you really blessed me, Will. You're the best."

Will spun the wheel aggressively and called out my next move. "Right hand red, baby. Get your tits out of that pervert's face."

I looked back at the red spots and took a deep breath. I had to wedge my body directly between Will and Anthony's to get to my spot and instantly broke out in a fit of giggles at the absurdity of the situation. My body writhing between theirs as I laughed just made everything worse.

"Jesus, Claire!" Anthony growled at me. "Stay still, woman."

"I'm sorry but much like the last time we played Twister, it's a tight fit and it feels a little funny!" As soon as the words were out of my mouth my muscles gave up the fight and I crumpled to the mat, forcing the three of them down, too. I laid there in a pile of limbs and groaned. "I think you three might be a bad influence on me."

"Did you really just say what I think you said?" Zane blew out a deep breath. "I am a grown man playing Twister and I have a boner. This feels like a chargeable offense."

I gasped when Anthony pulled me into his lap. "What are you-?"

He cut me off with his mouth. He gripped my hair to hold me steady as he deepened the kiss and I felt him harden under my ass. My brain exploded with sensations and thoughts. He was kissing me in front of Will and Zane. I was kissing him back. When he nipped my bottom lip I even let out a breathy sound that I knew they'd all heard.

I had no idea how long he'd been kissing me when I pulled back and scooted away from him. I couldn't look at them, afraid of the horror and disgust I'd see on their faces, so I kept my head down. "I'm sorry. I don't... That was..."

Will grabbed me and yanked me into his lap. He cupped my face, forcing me to look at him, and searched my eyes. I didn't know what he was looking for but it seemed like he found what he wanted when he swore and dragged my mouth down to his. He kissed me like he was trying to prove something, like he was trying to erase Anthony. It was aggressive and hard and one more piece of my sanity chipped away.

"That's enough." Zane's hard tone broke me away from Will. He'd never sounded so serious and I expected him to lose it on me. Instead, he finished the trifecta of strange by pulling me to his chest. He cupped my ass and jerked me forward against his erection. "Don't think for a second that you're leaving me out, baby."

I kissed him then and I lost myself in it. If I was going to be mortified by my behavior, I was going to make it worth it, I guessed. I wrapped my arms around his neck and tugged his hair while stroking my tongue past his lips. He groaned and rocked me harder against his hard length.

That was when it occurred to me that I was grinding on him in front of Will and Anthony. I flew off of his lap and sequestered myself to the far corner of the Twister mat. Fucking Twister. It'd gotten me again.

No one said anything. The silence was deafening as I sat there, waiting for what came next. I wanted to run away but I wasn't sure my legs would work after being thoroughly kissed by the three of them. I was about to roll out of there when Will broke the silence.

"Fuck it." He was on his feet and scooping me up in the blink of an eye. He tossed me over his shoulder and started towards the stairs. "Unless someone says no, I'm carrying you upstairs and I'm going to finish this."

"You're fucking insane if you think I'm going to let you take her and leave me out here." Anthony sounded like he was ready for a fight. It was so far from the young man that I'd known and I found myself being turned on by his potential changes even as I was over Will's shoulder.

"I'm taking her to your room." Will's statement brought everything to a stop. He'd taken the wind out of Anthony's sails and once again the silence hit hard.

Zane cleared his throat. "Are you saying...? Claire?"

I lifted my head to look at him. "Yeah?"

His lips twitched as my casual response. "Do you understand what's happening right now?"

I swallowed. "I think I need someone to break it down for me because if I assume one thing and it's something else, I'll be forced to tie bricks to my ankles and dive into the ocean."

Will's big hand slid up the back of my thigh and stopped at the bottom curve of my ass. "I need to fuck you, Claire. I need you enough to understand that you want these assholes, too. I'm going to carry you upstairs to what I'm sure is Anthony's oversized and overstuffed bed and I'm going to strip you naked and spread you out like a goddamn buffet. If they're there with me at least they won't be interrupting me. If I read you wrong, just say so. I'll put you down and we can figure out how to turn the TV on."

I shivered with a healthy amount of desire and nervousness. "All three of you?"

"Well, it's my fucking bedroom." Anthony growled. "I'll take you however I can get you, Claire. You know that."

"Yeah, if you think I'm going to stay down here and just listen, you're out of your mind." Zane started up the stairs. "Claire?"

"This is crazy. I shouldn't.... What kind of woman...?"

"Fuck all of that. Do you want us or not, C?" Will put me down on my feet and cupped my face. "What do you want?"

"Yes. I want this." It was an easy answer and I was sure I'd panic later but if I broke it down to what I wanted... I wanted them. "I don't even know what *this* is or how it works. Have any of you done this before? You know what? Don't answer that."

Will tossed me back over his shoulder and took the stairs two at a time. His hands cupped my ass and squeezed. Once we were in Anthony's room, he put me down by the foot of the bed and whipped my top over my head.

I gasped and covered my bare breasts with my hands. I knew what we were going to do but I still felt like I shouldn't be exposed in front of all three of them at the same time.

Zane moved to stand behind me and rested his chin on my shoulder as he ran his hands up my stomach. "Don't be shy, Claire. Where's that brave woman who let me fuck her in the dark corner of a party because she liked the idea of someone watching?"

I blushed furiously. "Zane!"

"You came so hard I walked out of that party looking like I'd pissed myself, baby."

Anthony moved closer and crossed his arms over his chest. His eyes were dark with desire and something else I couldn't name. The promise in them made me shake. "Drop your hands, Claire."

My stomach clenched and my breath caught at the command in his voice. I immediately dropped my hands and licked my lips. I had to stop myself from saying yes, sir.

Will stepped closer and lightly raked his thumbnail over my nipple. "You like being watched, Claire?"

Zane cupped my breasts from behind and held them out like an offering for Anthony and Will. While I whimpered my answer, Anthony trailed his hand down my stomach.

He slipped his hand inside my shorts and cupped my sex. "No one else gets to see you. I'll share with these two assholes but no one else. You want to feel like you're being watched as we fuck you, I'll build a room with two way mirrors and put it in Times Square."

"I never let anyone see her." Zane ran his nose up the side of my neck. "Not like this. Like this, we're all going to watch you, Claire. You have all of our attention."

I didn't bother telling them I never actually wanted anyone else to see me. I just liked the idea of it. If they thought they were being big and bad, keeping me for themselves, that was fine. Anthony gripped me tighter and I forgot everything else beyond that moment. I was theirs.

28

Anthony

Claire's pussy was dripping, her arousal coating my hand and ruining her tiny little shorts. She looked up at me and batted those long eyelashes the same way she always had when she wanted something from me.

"What is it, Claire? What do you need?"

She pouted and rocked her hips forward. "Touch me. Please."

Will gripped her neck and took her mouth, kissing her hard. It should've felt wrong to see another man kissing her but there was something different with Will and Zane because I could see how she cared for them.

I'd never seen her kiss anyone else. Being removed from it, I could watch the way her body responded, the way her shoulders curled in when he sucked on her bottom lip. It was another study of Claire that I'd never done before. I wanted to, though. I wanted to watch her, maybe even more than she wanted to be watched.

I pulled my hand away and took a step back. Three pairs of eyes turned to me. "I want to watch. Will, keep kissing her. Zane... reach down and feel how wet she is for us."

"Wants to watch and be the boss. Of course." Will wasn't bitter, though. He nodded at me and I knew he'd be okay with me doing things my way. Even if I didn't know what exactly that meant yet.

Zane trailed his mouth over Claire's shoulder as he pushed her shorts down. "He can be the boss. Just as long as I get to explore, I don't care."

Claire's eyes stayed on mine. "Are you sure this is what you want?"

I flashed her a wicked grin and settled in the club chair facing the bed. I crossed my ankle over my knee and leaned back. "I only do what I want, Claire. Show me what I want to see. And when I'm done watching, I'll come for you."

"Shit, Claire. You're soaked." Zane ran his fingers over her pussy lips and brought them to his mouth. Sucking them clean, he groaned and went back for more.

"How long has it been since someone ate that pretty pussy, Claire?" I watched as shock and heat flared in her eyes.

She held my gaze. "I don't know... Months? Maybe longer. Jordan didn't-"

"Don't say his name." Will was a man on the edge. He kissed her and then moved down her throat to her tits. He feasted on her nipples while she clutched his head.

"Zane. Do the honors." My dick throbbed painfully as Zane dropped to his knees and spread her ass so he could wedge his face between her thighs and devour her. The three of us were obsessed with the woman between us, that much was obvious.

"I bet if I asked how long it's been since you sucked a cock, Will's head would explode." I leaned forward and felt a twisted sense of satisfaction at the control I had. "Bend over and give him some relief, baby."

She whimpered and shot me a hungry look before bending forward to free Will's cock. She cried out when her new position gave Zane more room and he delved deeper. "Oh, god!"

Will swore and shoved his jeans down. He stroked his hands through Claire's hair and watched her pull him free. "Fuck, baby. Stroke me."

I balled my hands into fists, waiting for the fury to hit at seeing the woman I thought of as mine take another man's dick in her mouth but it didn't happen. My body was primed and ready but it wasn't for a fight. I rested my elbows on my knees and took in the scene before me with an odd sense of pride.

Zane ran his hands up Claire's thighs and squeezed her ass before leaning back and slipping his fingers between her thighs. "Still the best pussy I've ever tasted. And so tight, baby. We're going to wreck you."

I smiled as she shuddered and moaned around Will's length. I never would've imagined my woman would be so kinky but I loved it and was ready to explore it fully. "Take him deeper, Claire."

Will growled at me. "Trying to make me come as fast as fucking possible?"

Zane whistled through his teeth and worked his fingers faster. "Every time you boss her around, she just gets wetter."

"Is that right, baby? You like being told what to do?" I looked at Will. "Get on the bed on your hands and knees, Claire. Will's going to fuck you while you suck Zane's dick. I want you to keep your eyes on me as you do it."

Zane stroked her just the right way and we all watched as Claire came hard, trembling and moaning before her knees buckled. Zane caught her and moved her to the bed. He peppered kisses up her spine and then moved away so Will could take his place behind her.

While Zane undressed, Will took his time rubbing his hands all over Claire. He leaned down and hugged her to his chest. "You're the most beautiful woman I've ever seen, Claire. Fuck, I've missed you."

Will finished undressing, but hesitated with his jeans in his hand. Like she could hear his thoughts, Claire spoke quietly while looking at me. "I'm clean and on the pill."

I think we all groaned in unison. I met Will's gaze and then Zane's. "I'm clean."

Will nodded. "Same."

Zane cupped Claire's face and lifted it to his. "I've used a condom with every woman but you. Are you sure?"

She nodded and smiled at me. "I trust all of you."

29

Anthony

I felt those words in my chest. I had a feeling she knew it, too, judging by the way her eyes watered. I stood up and walked over, unable to stay away when I felt like I was about to hand her the keys to the rest of my life. Leaning down, I kissed her shoulder. "I want you to come as many times as you can. Let yourself go with the men you trust."

I pulled my chair closer and sat where she'd easily be able to watch me and then, I slowly undressed as Zane and Will took their places. The room was so still that it seemed like we were all holding our breath as Will slowly pushed into Claire. She gripped the bedding beneath her and opened her mouth to take Zane deep. All the while, she kept her eyes on mine.

For four people who'd never done what we were doing, things moved seamlessly. Will and Zane started slow, giving her a chance to adjust, and then slowly increased their pace as they grew more desperate. Claire was pinned between them, her tits bouncing under her. On especially deep thrusts, she'd let out a little whine or a slight gag but when Zane tried to pull back, her hand shot up to stop him. Still, she watched me.

The sounds in the room were pornographic with Claire's cries growing louder as she came for the second time. I stood up and shrugged out of my shirt while Will hurtled towards his own release. Skin slapping skin, he fucked Claire harder and reached under her to play with her clit. That quickly she came again with a muffled scream.

Her eyes fluttered closed but I growled. "Open those eyes, Claire."

She did as I said and watched my hands drop to my pants. While I pushed my pants down, Will powered his hips into her and then came with a shout.

"Zane?" I nodded to where Will was pulling out of Claire to collapse on the bed next to her.

Zane didn't hesitate. He moved to get into place behind her and then thrust deep in one stroke, making her cry out. He gripped her hips tight and drove into her like a man possessed.

I moved closer to the bed and leaned one knee on it so I could grasp Claire's face and hold it steady. Her pupils were blown out, her lips were swollen—she'd never been more beautiful. I ran my thumb over her mouth and she stuck her tongue out to chase it. "Such a pretty girl. Come again for Zane. Come hard, Claire."

She sucked my thumb into her mouth and tried her best to keep her eyes on mine but eventually they squeezed shut as she came. I remembered the way her pussy would clamp down when she came and I knew Zane didn't have a chance of lasting. It wasn't a surprise when he shouted her name and came a few seconds later.

Claire slumped forward on the bed after he pulled out and panted as she came down. "Oh, god."

I turned her over on her back and pulled her hips to the edge of the bed so her ass was hanging off. I wanted to watch her face when I sank deep. She was a feast for my eyes with her nipples pebbled and bright pink and her core open for me. I stared at the mixture of their come decorating her cunt and groaned. There had to be something wrong with me because I wanted to photograph it and hang it on every wall of my house. She was so fucking beautiful.

Claire watched me studying her body and flushed. "Should I clean up first?"

I growled and gripped her thighs tight. I ran my fingers over her lower lips and smeared the mess into her pink flesh. "Fuck no."

Will shifted so he could see what I was looking at and swore. He looked at me and then leaned over and cupped Claire's face. "That's fucking sexy, baby. You're taking us so well."

I fingered her and then used the cream to coat her ass. I teased her until she was breathing harder and narrowing her eyes at me in a silent command to hurry up and do something. "This will be mine again, Claire. Not tonight, though. Tonight, I want this pussy."

I lined my cock up at her entrance and pressed my hand down on her lower stomach with my thumb on her clit as I pushed deep. I remembered every moment with Claire and I could see each of them in my head like a movie. I knew exactly where to touch her and how to get the biggest reactions from her.

"Zane, Will. Hold her legs open." Knowing she liked being watched changed things. I wanted to push every button she had. I kept my hand on her stomach but moved the other up to lightly wrap around her throat. Then I rolled my hips and watched her eyes roll. "That's right. Flutter that pussy for me."

Will and Zane fell into place like we'd been fucking Claire together for decades. They watched her as they spread her open and stroked every part of her that I wasn't touching. They teased her nipples until they were swollen and each pull earned another flutter around my cock.

She felt better than I'd remembered. Her pussy squeezed my dick and sucked me back in each time I pulled out. Her body welcomed each of my thrusts with a little grunt from her throat. I put more pressure on her lower stomach and watched her eyes widen.

Fucking her harder, watching the way her tits bounced with each thrust, I tipped my head back but kept my eyes on hers. I wanted to see every single reaction that crossed her face. It didn't take long for her to scream my name as her first orgasm hit her hard. She jerked against our holds and tugged at her own hair when I didn't let up.

"Anthony! Anthony, I can't! I can't come again!" She pawed at my chest but I shook my head as I leaned over her, still thrusting hard.

"You can. You know what I want. Did you ever show Zane and Will what you can do?" I panted just as hard as her as I fucked her like an animal. "Show them."

She came one more time with a scream and her nails buried in my chest. Her pussy spasmed hard enough to suck my own orgasm out of me before I was ready. I was filling her with my come while her body was shaking and tensing as it forced her own come out, coating my thighs and the bed in her juices.

"Ho-ly fuck." Zane stared on in awe as he watched her squirt.

I fed the last of my come deep against her cervix and then slowly eased out. We all watched as our combined mess leaked out of her swollen pussy with matching sounds of approval. Claire whimpered and tried to close her legs but we kept them spread.

"Don't hide. You're fucking amazing, Claire." Will leaned over her and kissed her softly. "So beautiful."

She looked at each of us and bit her lip. "Now what?"

Zane pressed kisses up her ankle. "Now we pass out. For no less than ten hours. But if you get a little handsy before that ten hour mark, I'll still be available."

I laughed at the confusion bubbling across her face. Deciding to cut her some slack, I moved to the middle of the bed and laid on my back before pulling her on top of my chest. Without needing to be invited Will and Zane settled on either side of us. I'd never slept in the same bed as anyone after Claire so I figured it would take me a while to fall asleep with the guys there, but I was fine with it. Especially because it was clear that as soon as Claire accepted that we were all staying in bed with her she was over the moon. She stretched out so she was partially on top of all three of us and was letting out her signature snore within seconds.

30

Claire

The moment my eyes opened the next morning I was struck with a wave of anxiety over what we'd done. I couldn't regret it because it'd been the most amazing experience of my life but I just... I wasn't sure what came next. I knew that most likely nothing came next but I would've been lying if I said I didn't have feelings for all three of my exes. I couldn't deny it after sleeping with them.

I wasn't sure how they'd react to me after the things we'd done the night before and I was too scared to face them. So I snuck out. Again. All three of them were dead asleep as I crawled out of bed and rushed to my room.

I took the world's fastest shower, skipping my hair, and didn't bother looking through the outfits from Uncle Sal. I just grabbed the one on top and pulled it on. It was surprisingly loose around my body and even though it stopped just above my mid-thigh, it felt a lot more conservative than his other picks. I pulled on a pair of borrowed flip flops and only stopped downstairs to find my phone.

As I silently shut the front door behind me, I admitted to myself that I was being a coward. After the things I'd done the night before

I should've been able to stay and face them. I just couldn't. The what-ifs were too many and too dangerous. My delicate feelings couldn't take a bad response.

When I got to the breakfast buffet in the hotel and saw Jordan standing at the waffle maker, I figured it was my karma for running out on the guys. I still tried to stay away from him as I waited for my turn. I hung out by the eggs until a staff member came over and asked me if I was okay.

Jordan had noticed me by then and motioned me over. His eyes widened as I got closer. "Wow."

I scowled at him and crossed my arms. "What?"

He stared at me until I was shifting in discomfort. "You look different."

I let out a high-pitched laugh. "Me? Different? Nah."

"No, there's definitely something different about you." He stepped closer and inspected me. "Did you change your hair?"

I fanned him away and glared at his waffle in the machine. "That *has* to be burning by now."

"Come on, Claire. Don't leave me hanging. There's something besides the clothes that's different about you."

"There's nothing!"

He cupped my upper arm and smiled. "Fine. Don't tell me. I don't care, I guess. Not as long as you come by the room after breakfast. I have something I want to run by you."

I suddenly wanted to strangle him. "Are you serious?"

He flashed another smile that had originally drawn me to him. "Yeah, of course. I want to talk about your manuscript."

His waffle was definitely burning but I didn't care because I no longer wanted one. I stepped closer to him and lowered my voice, not wanting anyone to overhear me ripping into him. "You gross pig. You don't remember that's how you tricked me into dating you in the first place, do you? You asked me to come by your office so we could talk about my book and then you spent the entire meeting flirting with me and undressing me with your eyes. You were in a higher position than me then! I thought you were going to give me a chance. God! How disgusting are you?!"

Jordan grabbed both of my shoulders and pulled me closer, despite the way I dug my fingers into his side to force him to let me go. "You're being a bit dramatic, don't you think?"

I heard people coming in and forced a smile. I wasn't going to cause a scene in front of the rest of the bridal party. "You're gross. I'm going to talk to Jane and Terry when I get back about ensuring that you no longer have access to an unlimited number of young women who are gullible enough to believe you have any power in the company. Asshole."

I pulled away from him and saw Sophia standing across the room with a mug of coffee in her hand. I hurried across to her and smiled. There were so many things flashing through my head. What I'd done the night before. How scummy Jordan was. How I wanted to crawl back in the bed I'd run from.

"What was that?" She pointed with her mug at where Jordan was removing a blackened waffle under the disapproving gaze of a staff member.

I scowled at his back and shook my head. "He asked me to come by his room so he could run something by me."

She gasped. "No!"

Of course, she knew the whole story. "Yeah. The prick."

"I can see why he decided to shoot his shot, though." She motioned at my body. "This is a look, babe."

"It was on top of the pile."

"Did you look in the mirror before you left?"

A chill went down my back. "No. I was in a hurry. Why?"

She threw back her head and laughed. "Oh, boy."

"What?!"

"I'm just saying it's no surprise that Jordan was practically grinding his dick all over you. The dress is see-through in the light, C." Sophia looked over my shoulder and grinned. "Men, you let your roommate out of the house looking like a whole snack and she was already propositioned."

Oh, no. Oh, no, no, no. I stood perfectly still, hoping Sophia was just messing with me. I knew better, though. Especially when the smell of the ocean hit me just before a big, warm hand cupped the back of my neck. I glanced over my shoulder and saw Will's scowling face.

"I wasn't propositioned." I let out a pained laugh and had to clear my throat. Seeing them standing there, looking like avenging gods, had my body reacting in big ways. The dull ache between my thighs turned into a throbbing need.

Anthony looked down at my dress and his eyes narrowed. "Who propositioned you?"

"Jordan. He's missing what he walked out on right about now." Sophia bumped my hip with hers and then looked over at where Jake had just come in. "I'll be back. I have to tell Jake he can't look at you right now or I'll have to poke his eyeballs out."

I looked down at my dress for what felt like the hundredth time and whined. "It doesn't look see-through from up here!"

Zane shrugged out of the worn t-shirt he had on and pulled it over my head. I was shocked to see the deep frown on his face. He gripped my waist and tugged me close. "You snuck out on us. You went prancing around in what might as well have been your birthday suit. And that asshole came onto you. Did he touch you?"

"Of course, he touched her." Anthony growled. "Would you have been able to look at her in that dress and not touch her?"

Will looked around the room and then his gaze zeroed in on Jordan. "I'm just going to have a little chat with him."

I tried to make myself big enough to block all three of them. "Stop it! What is wrong with y'all? This is your sister's wedding week, Will. You can't start a fight and ruin things. And you!"

Zane grunted when I turned on him. "What about me?"

"Since when do you go all caveman and beat your chest over a woman?"

"Not over a woman, Claire." He flashed me a dark smirk. "Over *you*."

31

Will

Claire had no idea what she'd done to us. We wanted her so desperately that we were willing to share her to make it happen. I was starting to understand that once a man was pushed that far, he just had to accept that he was all in. She'd opened Pandora's box, whether she realized it, or not. Judging by the confused look on her face, she didn't realize it.

Waking up and finding her gone was unacceptable. First of all, I didn't appreciate waking up in a bed alone with two other men. Second of all, I didn't appreciate not being able to check on her to make sure she was okay.

"You shouldn't have snuck out." I crossed my arms and stared down at her. Even with Zane's t-shirt over it, her dress was still distracting as hell.

She blushed and deflated in front of us. Her shoulders slumped and she stared down at her feet. "I was scared…"

"Scared of what?" Anthony pressed in closer to her so we were forming a human shield around her.

"What would happen this morning. I didn't know if you'd still feel the same way or if it would be awkward and I just... I was scared." She looked up at each of us and blew out a long breath. "I was so nervous that I ran out of the house in a see-through dress. I'm going to murder Uncle Sal."

Zane kissed her shoulder. "Come back and let us show you how we feel."

My dick hardened at the idea. "That sounds good. I can beat the shit out of Jordan later."

"It wasn't just a one-time thing?" Claire tugged at the hem of her shirt. "You want more?"

Anthony slid his hand under her dress where no one else would see. "I want everything, Claire. Feels like you do, too."

Her eyes fluttered and her cheeks went rosy but then she snapped out of it and removed herself from our little bubble. Standing a safe, unreachable, distance away from us, she licked her lips and straightened her shoulders. "I have to make sure the wedding week is perfect for Sophia. Today is a big day. I need to make sure everything is set up and that everyone gets on the van on time. I... I like this. God help me, I do. But not today."

The three of us watched her stride away, hips swaying, until she reached the front door of the hotel and paused. She looked back at us, pushed up her glasses, and tugged Zane's shirt down before making a run for it.

"She's going back to the house to change. We could just ambush her." Anthony looked like he was already halfway buried inside her.

I groaned. "No. It's for Sophia. If it wasn't for my sister, I'd say fuck, yeah, but I can't mess up shit for Soph."

Zane raised his eyebrows. "More than sleeping with her best friend might?"

I rubbed my temples and shook my head. "I was just starting to find you tolerable."

"Hey, Will! I was hoping you were already here." Madeline hurried over in a cloud of perfume and hugged me. "I'm so glad you're going today. I just don't know the rest of the girls all that well, besides Soph, of course."

Madeline had been a friend for so long that I could overlook most of her flaws normally. She'd been putting me in a bad spot with Claire, though, and I had a bad feeling I was going to have to talk to her about it. I knew she wasn't interested in me, even if she did hang on a little too tight, but Claire didn't. I wasn't going to chance hurting Claire, not when it felt like things could go good for us.

"You should try to get to know them. You're always talking about not having girlfriends." I eased myself out of her hold and nodded to Anthony and Zane. "Breakfast?"

Anthony looked contemplative as he stared at Madeline, a cold edge to his gaze. I didn't know a lot about the man but I'd heard the rumors of him being a ruthless businessman. Everyone in Florida heard those rumors. "You should try being nicer to Claire."

Zane grunted. "That'd be a good place to start."

Madeline looked at me and pouted. "Do *you* think I've been mean to Claire? I would never try to be mean to her. She's Sophia's best friend and I love Soph. Maybe she just took something I said wrong?"

I had Anthony and Zane on one side, drawing a line in the sand, and Madeline on the other, pleading her case. I knew Madeline better than I knew the guys. It felt wrong to join the guys and leave her feeling shitty. Even if I did think she spoke to Claire more harshly than she did anyone else.

"Jesus, man." Anthony shook his head and walked away.

I opened my mouth to say something when the front door opened again and Claire was back. In an even shorter dress that flowed around her thighs in a pretty pink color, she was just as tempting as she'd been in the see-through dress. She'd even put her hair in a higher ponytail that popped behind her like a vintage Barbie Sophia had worshipped as a kid. Her glasses made her look like a sexy librarian barbie who was getting ready for bed.

Anthony changed directions and went straight at her. She saw him coming, though, and rushed across the room to talk to Jake and Soph.

Zane whistled under his breath and slapped my chest. "Remind me to send Sal the biggest fucking gift basket ever. I love that old bastard."

I felt like a teenager again as I slapped him back and grinned. "I'll chip-"

Madeline cleared her throat and when I looked back at her she was frowning up at me with tears in her eyes. "You do think I'm mean, don't you?"

I inwardly cringed, especially when I looked at Zane for help and found him darting away. Not knowing what else to do, I put my arm around her and patted her shoulder. She molded herself to my chest and let out a few weak sounding sobs. "I don't think you're mean, Madeline."

She gripped my shirt and leaned back to meet my gaze. "It's just so hard, Will. I'm here for you and Soph all the time but I still feel like you'd both dump me in a second if Claire said so."

I sighed. "Madeline, that's not true. You're a friend and I don't just dump friends. What's going on with you today? You doing okay?"

She sniffed and nodded. "I'm okay. I just feel lonely. Do you think you could hang out with me a bit today? It's just one of those days, ya know?"

I pulled away and smiled. "Sure. We're friends, Madeline. You don't ever have to ask me if I'll hang out with you."

I blew out a breath of relief when she said she needed to powder her nose before we left for the spa. That relief turned to dust when I turned and saw that Claire was watching with a deep frown on her pretty face. I swore and started over to her, prepared to tell her something, anything, to get that frown off her face, but before I got a chance, more of the bridal party came in and then it was pure chaos as Claire did her best to round everyone up for the van.

32

Claire

Getting everyone tucked away into the appropriate treatment rooms while avoiding the guys, especially Will, had been stressful. At times it felt like herding cats but all that was over. The spa staff would take care of the rest and I was finally alone in a mud bath. Todd, a super nice guy with a dragon tattoo that peeked out of his salon uniform top, had assisted me into the thick mud and dimmed the lights in the solo room. I didn't have to worry about anything for a while. I just had to sink back in the mud and ignore the thoughts in my head about where the mud came from and if there was a chance of there being worms in it.

Each time my mind tried to conjure up the image of Madeline clinging to Will's chest, the two of them gazing into each other's eyes, I decided thinking about the potential worms would be better. I started to wish I'd brought my cellphone with me after just a few minutes. I had nothing to distract myself with and that was a scary place to be when I had a lot of things I was avoiding.

When I heard the door open and shut, I was so happy that Todd was back to free me from my mud prison that I had the biggest grin on my face. "Thank god, you're here. I was about to lose my mind."

"I'm here, Claire. Don't worry."

My eyes flew open. Instead of Todd, I was staring up at Jordan. I gasped and nearly choked on the thick scent of clay and eucalyptus. "What are you doing in here? Get out, Jordan!"

He dropped his towel and revealed he was only wearing a very small banana hammock. There were untamed hairs sticking out of each side of the hammock and I was horrified as it all came at me. "Coming in, babe."

I surged forward, eager to forgo my mud bath, but nothing happened. I grunted as the thick mud held me captive. "This is not happening."

Jordan lifted his leg and dipped his toe in.

I screamed for Todd like I was being murdered. I couldn't fight against the mud and I was about to be trapped in it with Jordan. "Todd! Todd, get me out of here! Jordan, don't you dare! If you get in here with me, I'm going to make you eat all the mud in this tub, worms and all!"

"There are worms in there?"

"Todd!" I screamed so loud that I knew half the spa had to have heard me. I couldn't even get my arms lifted high enough to shove Jordan's leg away from me. I was just stuck in what quickly felt like quicksand, slowly panicking more and more as Jordan dipped more and more of his foot in next to me.

The door behind Jordan burst open but instead of Todd, it was Will who came to my rescue. He took one look at the situation and charged at Jordan. "You sick son of a bitch!"

Jordan yelped and managed to get his foot out of the mud while I was still stuck, sweating from how hard I was working to get free. Will charged at Jordan and they both slipped in the mud and went down. I watched in horror as Will slammed a fist into Jordan's stomach and Jordan elbowed Will in the face.

Adrenaline made me fight even harder to get free and I managed to get one arm out. I threw a huge clump of mud at Jordan and clung to the side of the tub when the mud tried to suck me back in. "Todd!"

Everything happened in a blur. Will and Jordan wrestled on the tile floor, slinging mud everywhere, and I added to it by screaming for help while simultaneously clawing my way out of the tub like a demon in a horror film. Jordan was taking the worst of the hits but it didn't help that when Will slipped in the mud, Jordan just threw himself on top of Will, elbows first.

"Stay the fuck away from her!" Will pinned Jordan to the mud-covered floor and hit him once, twice, and-

The door flew open again and Todd screamed at the mess he saw. Of course, my screaming had brought more than just Todd to the room to see what was going on. Anthony and Jake ran in to separate Will and Jordan but they slid in the mud, too. Sophia was behind them, her eyes wide as she took in everything.

"Knock it off!" Jake slapped Jordan on the forehead and pried Will off of him. "What the fuck is going on?"

"Help me!" I was half in-half out of the tub and I wasn't a huge fan of everyone converging on the room while my ass was straight up in the air. "I'm stuck!"

Sophia and Todd managed to pull me the rest of the way out with Todd wincing as he apologized. "I don't know why the mud is so thick. I'm so sorry."

"He was trying to climb in the tub with Claire while she was screaming for help and telling him no!" Will was red in the face, in the places where he wasn't brown from the mud, anyway. He was still livid as he stood up and slid his way over to me. He cupped my face and tilted my face up to his. "Are you okay? You scared the shit out of me. Tell me you're okay."

My heart lurched into my throat at the concern on his face. It was easy to forget everything else when he looked at me like that. I nodded and brought my hand up to press his more firmly into my cheek. I just needed a second. "I'm okay. I was just trapped and he tried to get in. I'm okay now, though."

Will bent forward and picked me up, bridal style. I slid against his bare chest and coated him in even more mud but he didn't seem to mind as he carried me out of the mud-covered room and towards the exit. "I could kill that motherfucker. You sounded terrified, baby. I don't ever want to hear you scream like that again. Jesus."

I pressed my face into his neck. "I'm sorry. I just couldn't move and the idea of being stuck in the mud with that jerk was a nightmare. I didn't mean to cause a scene, though. I feel horrible. I should go back and offer to clean the room."

"What the hell is going on?" Sophia's voice sent a chill down my spine. Will stopped just outside of the spa entrance and turned to face his sister. Sophia's face was red and blotchy, the same kind of red and blotchy she always got when she was furious. "Someone better start talking right now."

33

Claire

I made Will let me down and shot a look up at him, hoping he'd understand. "I think I should talk to Sophia alone…"

He looked between the two of us and sighed but then he nodded. "I'll be right inside."

Sophia crossed her arms over her chest, covered in her own fair share of mud from helping me. She followed my lead and sat down on a small metal bench in front of the spa. "I don't like this, C."

I blinked away the tears that wanted to fall and straightened my shoulders. "I love you, Soph. You've always been like a sister to me. You practically adopted me when I showed up on the island with nothing. You kept me from going out in the things Uncle Sal picked for me. You were better to me than I ever deserved."

"Jeez, Claire. What are you about to say?"

I grabbed her hands and forced out a shaky breath. "I… God. I dated Will in high school."

She pulled her hands away. "What? No, you didn't. I would've known. You…"

"We dated for almost two years. I was too afraid to tell you about us so he broke up with me the summer before our freshman year of college." I rubbed at my thighs and stared out at the ocean view in front of us. "Will wanted to tell you. He was better than me. I was just... I didn't want to lose you."

She stood up and paced a few feet away from me. "You dated my brother for two years without ever mentioning it to me."

I nodded. "Yes. I'm sorry, Soph. I hate that I kept it a secret from you. I hate myself for lying to you. It's the only thing I've ever kept from you and I'm so incredibly sorry."

"All that shit in there? Will going after Jordan? Is it still going on? Are you still with my brother?"

I swallowed the lump in my throat. "It wasn't. Not until I got here this week. Being around him... There's something there that makes me careless, Soph."

"God. This is... I don't even know what this is! Why would you choose *him*? You literally have a rockstar and a billionaire on the hook this week and you choose *my brother*?" She glanced inside the spa and then gasped. "You *did* choose my brother, didn't you?"

I held up my hands. "I don't know."

"Fuck. I can't believe you kept this from me for all these years, Claire. I have never hidden anything from you. I didn't think we did that. And now I find out that you've been sleeping with my brother! Do you understand how insane this is?"

I nodded. "Yes. I know it's insane. I am so sorry, Soph. I would do anything to avoid hurting or disappointing you. With Will, I just... I was never strong enough to put you over my own feelings and I'm sorry about that. I feel fucking awful and I am terrified of losing you but I don't want to lie to you anymore."

"That's all great, Claire, but I can't... I need time to process this! You dated my brother for two years! I tried to set you up with other guys back then. We both lost our virginities the same weekend and... Oh, my god. Oh, my god. You lost your virginity to my brother." She gagged and shook her head hard, like she was trying to shake the image out. "That's fucking horrible. I'm going to kill Will."

"It wasn't his fault, Soph." I doubled over on the bench and rested my head in my hands. "Take all the time you need. I know I don't deserve much from you after hiding this for so long. I was a bad friend."

"Just give me this afternoon to think about it. I love you, Claire. I'm horrified and I'm angry but you *are* like my sister. Which makes what you and Will did really weird." She sighed. "We'll talk before the movie tonight."

Jake poked his head out from the spa. "Ladies, we're being asked to leave. Apparently mud fist fights aren't welcomed at this fine establishment. Anthony gave them some cash to get over it but the owner is really uppity. He seems to have an ongoing feud with your uncle, Claire. It's making him a little biased, if you ask me."

I groaned. "I'm so, so sorry, Soph."

She grunted. "It's just as well. It's not like I was going to relax now anyway. I'll go get my things..."

I stood up and watched her slip inside. My insides felt heavy as I glanced at Jake and then down at the ground. I was ashamed of myself for hurting Soph.

"Hey. Chin up. Whatever's going on with you two, it'll pass. My future wife loves only one person more than she loves me and that's you, C. Luckily, I'm okay coming in second place." He came over and patted the top of my head. "That's the one place not covered in mud."

"Thanks, Jake. I think I'm going to take a walk. Don't wait on me to leave."

"You sure?"

I sighed and nodded. "Positive. I should give Soph some space."

"Hold on just a minute. At least let me steal a towel for you." Jake disappeared and reappeared in no time and passed me a plush, sage green towel. "We'll see you tonight. Love you, kid."

I gave him a weak smile. "Love you, too."

I wrapped the towel around my filthy body and headed towards the beach. The strange looks I got on the way made sense. It wasn't super often that a sad, mud-covered woman walked around the island. At least, I hoped. For the island's sake.

Straight into the ocean I went, turning the water muddy until the tide refreshed it. If only it'd refresh me. Through all of my exes, through all of my heart break, through everything, Sophia had remained a rock for me. Sophia was my soulmate, my best friend, and the person who'd saved me from a life of grief and feeling sorry for myself. She was everything to me and I'd hurt her.

There was a deep, deep sorrow weighing me down as I waded deeper into the ocean and let it wash me clean. I went under and blew out a deep breath, letting the bubbles tickle my nose.

When I came up I heard shouting and looked back to see Will coming in after me. His face was a mask of frustration. "If you think you're getting away from me this easily, you're sorely mistaken!"

I rolled my eyes and shook my head. "I'm just...bathing."

He reached me and grabbed my arms, pulling me into his chest. "Our secret's out after all of these years, huh?"

I wrapped my arms around his waist. "I feel horrible for upsetting Sophia, Will."

"I know my sister and how much she loves you, Claire. She's probably already forgiven you." He kissed the side of my head and then sputtered. "I don't think your bath did much. How about you come to my house and we get you a real bath?"

"Your house?"

He smiled. "Yes. I do actually live here on the island, you know?"

I let his body heat seep into my body, bone deep. "Brag."

34

Will

My hands still shook as I held Claire close and led her down the side street to my house. I couldn't stop seeing the panic on her face when her ex tried to climb into the tub with her. I wanted to murder Jordan. I wanted to pulverize him until he was just a fucking stain on the ground. He couldn't touch her. End of story. I didn't even want him to look at her. Ever again.

I looked down at her and blew out a harsh breath. There was something about having her back on the island, being able to touch her again, that had gone straight to my head. I didn't know what I was going to do when she left.

Claire looked up at me, her big eyes still full of sadness. "You okay?"

"Yeah, I'm okay."

"Are you worried about Soph?"

Shaking my head, I led her past my truck and to the front steps of my wraparound porch. "No. She'll be angry at me for a little while but she'll get over it. Once she understands that it wasn't some skeezy thing I did to her friend, she'll forgive me for keeping it from her."

"So it wasn't some skeezy thing?" Claire looked at the rocking chairs on the porch and her mouth hung open. "This is your house? It's so beautiful, Will."

I opened the door for her and guided her inside. The open floor plan, single floor house was decorated sparsely but I'd taken the time to pick each item I brought in. I was proud of my home and proud to show it off to Claire. "This is mine. I bought it a few years ago and have been working on it ever since. It a was a time suck in the beginning but it was worth it."

She did a little circle as she looked at everything. "You really are so impressive. The apartment I rent in London is pathetic. It's the size of a closet and I never bothered to decorate it. It's never felt like home."

"Maybe it's never been home." I took her hand and pulled her with me towards the bathroom. "I know that Soph and Sal would both be over the moon if you decided to move back here."

She hesitated when we reached the bathroom. "And you? Would you be happy if I did?"

I held her gaze as I slowly undressed her. The towel pooled at her feet and the ruined bikini went into the sink. Then she was bare before me, her hands itching to cover herself but she didn't. She stayed perfectly still and let me look at her. "If you came back, you would never say those words again, Claire. You would never stay somewhere that didn't feel like home because I'd make damn sure every place you laid your head was somewhere you knew you belonged."

Her eyes watered before she tucked her face into my chest and sniffed. "I'm not sure what I'm doing anymore, Will. I didn't come back here thinking that I'd feel things again. I especially didn't come back thinking I was going to be thrust into an alternate dimension where my exes all want me. I've never quite understood how I caught one of you, much less all of you now."

I ran my hands down her sides and watched as her eyes went wider than usual and her cheeks flushed a pretty deep red color.

"Not that I've caught you. Or all of you. I'm not saying that. Or even that you all want me. That sounded presumptuous, didn't it?" She groaned. "I'm just going to break my glasses and throw away my contacts. If I can't see the way people look at me when I say things, I'll never know if I should be horrified by the things I say."

Gripping her hips tight, I pulled her flush with my body so she could feel just how much I wanted her. "You caught me. And I want you. You don't need your vision to know that."

I pulled her into the shower with me and took the brunt of the cold water before it turned hot. Claire plastered herself to me and licked water droplets from her lips. One of the things I'd always loved so much about her was the way her eyes hid nothing. She'd never been able to look at me when other people were around because those pretty honey brown eyes would've told everyone just how much she wanted me. I could see her need then, shining up at me like a lighthouse in a dark stormy night. She called me to her in ways she'd never known and would never know. There'd never been another woman who ever came close to making me feel what she did.

"Let me clean you." I grabbed the soap and lathered my hands instead of a cloth. I wanted to touch every part of her. I cupped her full breasts and watched her nipples turn dark pink as blood rushed to them. They pebbled under my attention and I only moved on from them when I was sure she was spotless there.

Her soft stomach and flared hips made me think filthy thoughts about how she'd look swollen with my child. I turned her around and started at her shoulders, working my way back down. I pressed kisses to her spine as I lowered myself to my knees behind her and took special care washing her ass and thighs. I stroked and massaged them until she had to grip the wall in front of her to stay on her feet.

"Spread your legs." Cleaning her sex was an act of restraint. I teased her but never gave her what she needed. I planted wet kisses on her ass and inner thighs but that was all I'd do. Standing again, I took even more time washing her hair. I worked the shampoo into her scalp and smiled as she moaned and let me contort her body any way I needed. "Good girl, Claire. We just need conditioner now and you'll be all clean."

Once I had the conditioner in her hair, she turned on me and glared at me through heavy eyelids. "You need to be cleaned, too, Will."

I held up my hands and braced myself for her revenge. It was worse than I thought possible when she started on her knees and took her time cleaning every inch of my skin from my feet to my thighs. She ignored the way my cock jumped and pulsed in front of her and thoroughly cleaned my balls and ass. I was so damn lost in the feel of her hands that I happily leaned against the cold tile wall and let her take care of my chest and arms.

She turned me around and managed to clean my back with her body pressed as closely as possible. Then she reached around me from behind and cleaned my cock with long, slow strokes. Her lips and tongue made the muscles in my back clench and release while her hand lost its soapiness and still stroked my length. Just when I thought I wouldn't be able to take another second, she froze and snatched her hand away. I groaned in pain and tried to reach around for her but she pressed her fingers into a spot under my ribs on my side and ignored me.

"Will..."

I closed my eyes and pressed my forehead into the wall, unsure of how she was going to react to the tattoo hidden amongst the many others that decorated my skin. I hadn't considered she'd ever see it.

"I figured if you ever saw it, you wouldn't realize what it was." I didn't recognize my own voice or the rawness of it.

"When... When did you get this?"

"The first summer after you left."

Her fingers traced the detailed sun tattoo. "Why here?"

I took her hand and slowly pulled her around so she was pinned between my body and the wall. "In protective gear, that spot under the arm is still vulnerable. At the right angle, a shot to the heart is possible. What better place to put your namesake?"

Her eyes stayed on the tattoo. "You're the only person who ever looked up the meaning of my name... Is that what I was, Will? A shot to the heart?"

I smiled. "Every fucking day."

35

Claire

The tattoo sealed my fate. Hearing Will say he cared about me was one thing but seeing it in ink on his skin made it real. I touched the beautiful sun again and then looked up at the intense expression on his face. The smile had faded as he waited on my response. Words failed me so I chose to show him how I felt with my body. I dropped to my knees and gripped his hips as I opened my mouth and took his length into my mouth. With my head pinned between his body and the shower wall, I didn't have much room to work with but I was determined.

"Fuck. Claire, you don't-" He didn't finish his sentence when I took him deeper.

I breathed through my nose and pushed myself to do more and be better for him. I wanted to make him feel as good as that tattoo made me feel. I wanted him to know how much I cared about him without needing to formulate the words. I looked up at him as I sucked and moaned when I saw the expression on his face. He was holding back and I didn't want him to.

He must've seen the challenge in my gaze because his jaw tightened. "Stop looking at me like you want me to devour you, baby."

I reached up and grabbed his hands where they were pressed into the wall and brought them down to my head. He'd spent months being delicate with me when we were together. He gave me the best introduction to sex I could've ever had. I wanted to give him the best of me in return.

Will tightened his grip on my head and growled. "Tap my thigh if it's too much."

I relaxed my throat and trailed my hand down to my core. Will let himself go and he gave me a taste of the power that radiated off of his body. He pinned my head to the wall by my hair and fucked my mouth through my gags and gargling. He pulled back every few thrusts to let me breathe but then he was back, thrusting deep and fast.

I stroked my clit fast in time with those thrusts and when I felt Will's first jet of come paint the back of my throat, I came hard. I swallowed as much of his come as I could and slumped against the wall when he pulled out and sprayed the last few jets on my chest. Moaning with my hand still between my thighs, I expected a few minutes of recovery time but Will proved that he was a different breed.

He picked me up and entered my aching core with one deep stroke. Then his mouth was on mine as he pressed me into the glass shower door. He kissed me hard and let his come smear all over our chests. He growled when I wrapped my limbs around his hard body.

"I never got to hear you really scream my name before, Claire. I want to hear it."

My head dropped back into the door as he drove his dick into me hard and fast. My nerve endings took a pounding and loved every second of it. I was barely containing my pleasure when he dropped his mouth to my throat and sucked. Giving him what he wanted, I screamed his name as I came.

Will shut off the water and carried me to his bedroom. Dropping me down on it, he followed me, spreading my thighs wide with his body as he continued fucking me with quick, pleasurable snaps of his hips. He dropped his hand between our bodies and teased my clit until I was coming again.

"I need to hear you scream one more time, baby." He pulled out and flipped me over on my stomach. He slammed deep while I was still flat on my stomach and I cried out his name as the new position made him feel even larger inside me.

I twisted my head back to watch him and he grabbed my chin so he could kiss me. He was everywhere, all around and over me, pressing me into the bed, and the sensation of being consumed and controlled by him was enough with the friction of the bedding brushing against my clit to shove me over the edge into one last orgasm. I screamed his name and held on while he drove into me a few more times and then stilled as he unloaded into my sex.

I went limp and he covered my neck and back in kisses before rolling us both over so I was on his chest, my body a sweaty mess. He held me there and reached down between my thighs to play with his seed that was spilling from my core. He pushed it back inside and then used it to paint my ass.

"Having fun?" I yawned and teased his nipple. "I never knew you were into finger painting."

He pushed two fingers deep and curled them until I moaned. "Any excuse to touch you."

"You don't need an excuse."

"In that case..." He grinned and rolled us both over. "I have a lot of lost time to make up for."

I learned that he was insatiable, even more so than when he was a teenager still. By the time we let go of each other and made it back to the rented house, I could hardly keep my eyes open. I'd been showered in affection and orgasms and then actually showered again before making it out of Will's house. I was in heaven.

Seeing the hotel again brought back reality, though, and I felt that impending doom feeling rush back because I knew I had to meet with Sophia before making sure the dinner and movie night went off without a hitch.

Maybe I shouldn't have spent the day in Will's bed before hearing Soph out. I didn't know what to expect from her and I was terrified she'd tell me that she didn't want me anywhere near her brother. I didn't know what I'd do because I was quickly realizing that I was hopeless when it came to Will. And Zane. And Anthony.

I forced Will to stay behind as I left to meet Soph at her room. I'd dressed in the most conservative outfit Uncle Sal had provided, another sheer, silk chemise and short set in black with white lace trim. Even with more of my body being covered than normal in his outfits, I felt like a whore when my body ached in places Will had just touched and with it covered in signs of his attention.

Sophia was waiting on me outside her room with two glasses of wine and a quick shake of her head. "You slut."

Horror and shame slammed down on me and I was seconds from begging her to forgive me when she laughed. I looked up and saw her smiling at me with tears in her eyes.

"Claire, get real. You're my best friend and sister. You think I'd trash our relationship just because you have bad taste in men and dated Will?" She grabbed me and pulled me into a hug, accidentally spilling wine down my back. "Oh, shit! Sorry! I'm sorry! I promise I didn't mean to do that."

I grimaced as wine soaked my panties and trailed down my thighs. "I'd deserve it if you did."

"Shut up. I don't like that you hid it from me for so long but I can understand. I think I knew you had a crush on him. I think I knew he'd always had a thing for you, too. I just never thought it was a good idea because I was terrified of losing you. But you proved to me that you can be with Will and then without Will and it not affect our friendship. Do what you want, C. Just don't make me watch my brother kiss you. God, the idea of it still grosses me out, even if I'm a fully grown adult now."

"I would never chance losing you, Soph. You're my family."

She sniffed and then drained the wine that wasn't dripping down my back. "I'm going to give Will hell, you know?"

I smiled. "Yeah, I know. You always do."

36

Claire

I sat with Sophia for dinner and we were in our own world as we laughed and made sure that we were okay. I ignored the rest of the world around us and poured my heart out to her about what was going on with me. She returned the favor by going into explicit detail about the sex she'd had with Jake that afternoon. Apparently Sophia liked sad sex because Jake worked extra hard to cheer her up. Judging by how easily she'd forgiven me, I'd say he did a great job.

If she was freaked out by the fact that I'd slept with three of my exes at once, she didn't show it. She forced me to leave out Will's name for her sanity and by the end of dinner, she'd practically tackled Jake and forced him into the bathroom at the back of the restaurant.

Anthony took her seat as soon as she left and dragged my chair closer to his so I was sitting between his legs. "I missed you."

I bit my lip and leaned into him. "I missed you, too. I don't really know what we're doing. I'm not sure how it works or if it's bad to spend time alone with each of you."

His smile was sensual and slow. "I expect my own time alone with you, Claire, so I can't say it's bad. It seemed like you needed to spend some time with Will. Everything okay?"

I felt an overwhelming amount of affection for him in that moment and I couldn't stop myself from shifting out of my chair and onto his thigh. I wrapped my arms around his neck and brushed my lips over his. "You were always so careful with my emotions. I was lucky to have you back then, Anthony. You treated me like I was your entire world. I don't think I ever would've been brave enough to go to London if I hadn't spent the year with you telling me how amazing I was."

"I've changed in a lot of ways since that time, Claire, but the way I feel about you hasn't. You're still my world and I'll still spend all my time making sure you see that you *are* amazing. I'd be lying if I said I didn't regret telling you to go." He licked his lips and looked away. "I hated myself for sending you away. I needed time to grow up so I could become the man I am now, the man who can give you anything and everything you could ever want, Claire. But I think if I could go back, I'd beg you to stay. Or tell you I was coming with you. Anything so I didn't have to lose you for all these years."

"Anthony..." With my heart hammering away, I stared into his eyes and saw nothing but the truth. "You're serious."

He slid his hands into my hair and kissed me the way he wanted. He slid his tongue over my lips and groaned when I leaned closer and pressed my thigh into his erection. "I'm very serious."

"I don't want to be in London anymore." I realized Will and Zane had joined us when I heard them both react to my news. I sat up straighter and gripped my shaking hands together. "It feels like a failure but I haven't written anything in a few years. I hate my job now. I hate working with guys like Jordan who use their position to get women into bed with no real intent on ever seeing their potential. I hate being so far away from the only family I have. I want to come back."

"Done." Anthony shrugged. "If you don't want to work while you start writing again, you don't have to."

"I just came into some money, too, so any of us can support you. Or...all of us, I guess? If this is going to be a thing, I mean." Will smiled and took my hands. "Come home. You belong here."

I looked at Zane because I was in a state of shock. I expected him, the rockstar, to talk some sense into them. I figured he'd be all for sending me back to London while he carried on with his career.

"What are you looking at me like that for? I'm with these idiots. Come home. I always loved your writing, Claire, and I think it's a fucking shame that you're not doing it anymore. Fuck that job. Come home." He looked at Anthony and Will. "We'll figure the rest out as we go."

"You're all serious?" I felt my world changing, the things I thought were fact growing murky as other possibilities solidified.

Anthony gripped the back of my neck and pressed his lips to my ear. "It would seem so."

Sophia and Jake came back then, both of them grinning like fools. Jake sat across from us and pulled Soph into his lap. "Well, this has been a hell of a day."

Soph winked at me and then turned on her brother. "There's Captain Perv. I should've known you were panting after Claire. You know I caught you with that picture of her when we were younger."

Will's face turned bright red and I gasped. "No!"

Will crossed his arms and frowned. "I was sixteen. You developed early. What do you want from me?"

Zane patted him on the shoulder. "Man, I get it. I still have a picture of C that-"

"Excuse me?" I shifted on Anthony's lap as I scowled. "What picture?"

Anthony cleared his throat. "Maybe we should compare later. And I'll need to make sure the security on your phones is up to par. A single pixel of Claire gets out and I'll murder each of you."

Sophia raised her eyebrows as she looked at me. "I'm not sure if we should get to the movie or continue watching this."

"The movie." I stood up and put my hands on my hips. "We're going to have a talk about keeping photos of people after a breakup. Or in your case, Zane. a ghosting. After the movie, though."

Sophia tucked her arm through mine and we walked away. "Have you made Zane suffer enough for ghosting you?"

"Hardly." I looked back at him and caught his eyes on my ass. "I'd tell you to take a picture but it seems like the three of you would take it literally. Pervs."

"I told you, C. They're all pervs. There's Captain Perv and CEO Perv and Rocker Perv. You've got a whole set." Soph sighed. "Although, if you added an athlete, you could have Sporty Perv."

"Don't even think about it." I put my hand over her mouth. "I can see you're about to make a joke about Baby Perv and I refuse to even hear it."

37

Claire

The two screen movie theater on Manatee Key was cozy, especially since I'd rented it out so we'd have the place to ourselves. After grabbing popcorn and enough candy to kill someone, I settled in my seat between Zane and Anthony while Will was exiled to sitting with Sophia since he'd spent the day with me. At least that's how Zane and Anthony justified it. We were watching a scary movie, one of Sophia's favorites, and the drinks were already flowing with several of the bridesmaids being terrified of horror films. The open bar had been a nice touch but I'd skipped the liquor to have even more sugar.

Once the movie started, I was in the zone. I watched with my breath and a handful of gummy bears caught in my throat as a woman was chased through her house by a knife-wielding maniac. At the first jumpscare, I screamed like I was the one being chased and nearly gave Anthony a heart attack.

He leaned over and grunted. "I forgot how you act during horror films."

"We never watched any together. What are you talking about?"

"We watched one together. One was all it took for me to learn my lesson." He leaned back again and then took my popcorn from me. "You're going to choke and the only way I want to see you choke is if it's on my cock."

Sophia turned from three rows in front of us. "We *all* heard that!"

I slid lower in my seat as a few of Jake's other friends catcalled and laughed. Glaring at Anthony, I shoved more candy in my mouth and then turned back to the movie.

When Zane moved my candy from my lap I assumed he was just being overprotective like Anthony. I was so caught up in the movie that I gasped dramatically when two hands worked my dress up my thighs. Neither of them stopped, even when a few people glanced back, because we were hidden well enough.

I looked between the two of them and decided to let go and have a little fun. I spread my legs as wide as the theater seat would allow and was rewarded with Anthony's breath against my neck as he moved closer.

"Good girl. You're going to have to stay very quiet for us. Can you do that?"

Zane's quiet voice was a growl when he moved higher up my thighs and didn't find anything blocking his way. "She's not wearing panties."

"So maybe she's not such a good girl, huh?" Anthony kissed down my neck and then bit. "Maybe this need to be watched is getting out of hand, huh? I'm not sure we should reward that type of behavior. What do you think, Zane?"

38

Will

I stood at the bar outside of the theater, doing my best to control my body's reaction to the show I'd just secretly watched. Claire was a goddess when she came, silent or not. I would repay Zane and Anthony for making sure I could see what was happening while not giving me the space to join in. Still, there was a smile on my face that nothing had been able to touch. She was moving back home.

"Just a beer, please." I nodded to the bartender when he looked up from what he was doing and noticed me.

"Well, don't you look happy!" Madeline walked over to stand next to me and motioned to the bartender that she'd take a beer, too. "What's going on with you?"

I ducked my head and let out a small laugh. "I'm just...happy. How are you doing? It's almost time for your big job, huh?"

She'd taken the job of wedding planner for Soph, even though Soph swore up and down that she didn't need anything planned out. I was sure she'd be grateful to have someone else in charge come the wedding day. Madeline was good at what she did, too. No one could deny that.

"This wedding is tiny compared to the ones I normally do. I could handle it in my sleep." She narrowed her eyes and studied me. "I caught part of that show with Claire earlier. Is that why you're happy?"

I hesitated and then felt guilty about it. Madeline had been my friend for a long time. I didn't want to treat her differently and confirm her fears about being ditched. "Yeah. There's been something there for a long time."

"Did Sophia know?"

I shook my head. "No. We were afraid of hurting her. She surprised both of us today with how well she took it. Although, I'm sure she still has something up her sleeve for me as payback."

"I've seen Claire hanging all over Zane and Anthony, too, though." Madeline moved closer and rested her hand on my arm. "Is Claire not serious about you?"

I grabbed the beer when the bartender came back and thanked him. Taking a long pull, I decided that it'd be nice to talk to someone outside of the immediate situation with Claire and the guys. "We all dated her at some point in the past and we all still have feelings for her. She has feelings for us, too. We... Never mind."

She squeezed my arm. "Will, you can talk to me. I'm worried about you. I don't want you to get hurt."

"This is going to sound strange... We were competing for her attention at first. We even made a stupid bet to see who could win her over first." I rolled my eyes. "Things changed, though, and now we're just working together...as a team? That sounds insane, I know. I don't want this getting out to anyone else, Mad, not until I know

Claire is okay with people knowing. I'm only telling you because you're my friend and you've known me and Claire for forever. I'm crazy about her. I always have been. Probably since the day she showed up at our house when she was still just a kid. I'd do anything to be with her. Including sharing her."

Madeline looked like a stiff wind would've blown her away. "Sharing?"

I waved it off. "The details don't matter."

She cleared her throat. "Wow. I'm just shocked, I guess. Do you and the other guys...?"

I choked on my beer and ended up coughing part of it up while the rest shot out of my nose. I grabbed some cocktail napkins and wiped my face while trying not to think about how red I'd gone. I was hoping it'd just fade away. "No. Dear god, no. It's all about Claire for us."

She laughed and pinched my cheek. "I don't think I've ever seen you blush before."

"Thanks for noticing." I shook my head and smiled. "Look, I know it's not conventional. I don't think any of us have thought it all the way through yet. It's only been a few days."

"I'm not judging you, Will. I've been your good friend for years and years. We've seen each other through some odd times before. This is no different."

"It is, though. This is it for me. It's always been Claire and now that she's probably coming back for good... I'm not letting her go."

She nodded and looked down at her beer. "She's coming back?"

"It's not set in stone yet." I took a deep breath and pulled out my wallet. I opened it and turned it to show her the picture of Claire with her cheek pressed to mine when we were just kids. "I've kept this close the entire time she was gone. I kept up with her as much as I dared without killing myself. Honestly, Mad, I'll follow her to London if I have to."

She gasped. "But your job! You love being a firefighter, Will. What would you do in *London*?"

I laughed and shrugged. "I'd figure it out. That stupid bet? I won. Even though I never expected those idiots to pay up, they did. I have enough money to live off of for a while. I could take my time looking and find something perfect. But maybe it won't come to that. I really think she wants to come home."

"Wait. The bet? Explain that a little more. I'm confused how a stupid bet could earn you enough money to live off of."

I groaned and rubbed the back of my neck, more than a little embarrassed by it. "Promise not to judge us?"

Madeline laughed and drained the rest of her beer. "I'm not going to judge you, Will. Promise."

"We were all trying to get Claire and we made this stupid bet that whoever got her first won and got a large sum of money. It was just the three of us guys being idiots and talking shit to each other, really. I never expected them to ante up the money. Lord knows I had no intention of paying them if they'd won. I tried explaining that but they're both as stubborn as a couple of mules." Sighing, I cringed at my own behavior. "That's all in the past, though. What we feel for

Claire is so much more than some stupid bet. What *I* feel for Claire is more than anything I ever expected to feel again."

"How much?" Madeline grinned and then rolled her eyes. "Come on. I'm not judging you but I at least want to know what you fools were willing to bet over Miss Perfect."

That Miss Perfect taunt made my hackles rise. I trusted Madeline and expected her to get on board Team Claire. Just like any other friend would. "Madeline, is there something between you and Claire that I don't know about? You seem a little standoffish with her."

She shook her head so fast that her hair whipped around her face. "No! No, Will. I don't have an issue with Claire. I think I'm just... I mean, I told you that I'm afraid with Claire back that you and Sophia will forget me. I guess I'm just worried. You're so crazy about her, so suddenly, and I know how people can get lost in their relationships. You're one of my best friends, Will, and I'd be really sad to lose you."

I felt like shit when I saw the tears in her eyes. I pulled her in for a hug and then pulled back so I could squeeze her shoulders while looking her in the eye. "You're not going to lose us, Mad. I'd love it if you and Claire became friends. We could all hang out and you could stop worrying about losing us. Who knows? Maybe Zane will bring one of his rich, rockstar friends with him and you'll meet the love of your life. Then it'll be me telling you not to forget me when you run off to LA or New York."

"Maybe." She swallowed and shrugged. "I guess we'll see."

39

Anthony

I was already on the porch waiting for Claire's vanishing act the next morning. After another night of insane sex, I figured she'd be too confused and conflicted to stay and chat. I was ready for her, though. She stepped out on the porch with a pair of heels in her hands and silently closed the door with her face pinched in concentration. Just as she shut it and stepped back, she looked over and saw me.

"Shit!" She dropped her heels and grabbed her chest. "What are you doing?! You scared the hell out of me!"

I stood up and flexed when her eyes drank in my bare chest. "I figured you'd try sneaking away again so I left a note for Zane and Will to let them know that I stole you away for the morning."

"But you didn't..."

I took her hand and pulled her with me towards the beach. "But I did."

I expected her to argue a bit but she didn't. She laced her fingers through mine and smiled up at me. "You knew I'd sneak away, huh?"

"I had no intention of waking up in bed with just Zane and Will again. Neither of them are very pretty first thing in the morning. And Will's morning breath is fucking nightmare fuel." It earned the laugh I'd hoped for. "Want to explain why you're sneaking away?"

She quietly contemplated my question as we walked down the beach, just out of the water. The early morning sun brought out the gold in her eyes when she finally looked up at me again. "I'm scared."

I waited for her to elaborate and when she didn't, I raised my eyebrows and sighed. "Of?"

"You used to be more patient, you know?" She hugged my arm to her chest. "I'm scared of waking up and it being off. I don't know what I'm doing here. I don't know the rules. I guess I'm scared that in the morning light, it'll have just been good sex between old acquaintances."

"It isn't just good sex between old acquaintances, Claire."

She pulled away and walked into the water. The morning waves lapped gently at her ankles as she turned to face me. "How? How is it not just good sex? I don't understand what's happening. How is this happening? I'm not someone who's ever believed that I can have my cake and eat it, too. This is that. This is having my cake, eating it, and then getting a fucking reward for it. Is it just this week? Will we all go our separate ways after the wedding? I know the things we say in the heat of the moment but...it's the morning that scares me, Anthony. It's the morning when I expect reality to dawn."

I walked into the water after her and wrapped my arms around her waist. "I'm not going my separate way. I'm willing to bet my fortune that Will and Zane aren't either. It seems we all need to sit down with our clothes on and have a talk about what this is. I can tell you, for me, this is real. You try to walk away and I'm coming after you. I won't make the same mistake of letting you go twice."

"And you're okay sharing me?" She winced. "I feel so greedy and awful even saying that. I shouldn't want all three of you. I should want one of you. Right? I should feel stronger about one of you and do the right thing. I just…"

"You can't decide, can you?" I smiled and smoothed out the worry lines creasing her forehead. "I don't need you to. I see the way you look at them. I also see the way you look at me. I'm willing to share you with the two idiots still knocked out in my bed because it means I get you. Throw all the things you think you're supposed to do out the window and just be ours. It's enough for me. Especially when I can steal you away for moments like this."

"I would never want to cheat you out of something complete, Anthony."

"You don't think this feels complete? I don't feel cheated. I feel like I have you back in my life finally and that's what's been missing for me." I cupped her face and made her look at me. "I've changed since we were together. I'm not the same man I was then. I don't take no for an answer now and you should know that if I wanted things to happen a different way, I'd make them happen a different way. I like whatever this is. I like seeing you so fucking happy. I also really like watching you get fucked by Zane and Will. This whole thing has shown me a different part of myself that I'm eager to explore more of. With you. And, to a lesser extent, those idiots."

Her eyes were wide as she looked up at me, her glasses slightly askew from my grip. Her voice dropped to a whisper. "What changed?"

I stroked my thumb over her lips. "I let you walk away. I never wanted to be that man again, the man who doesn't fight tooth and nail for what he wants. I won't be that man again, sweetheart. I'll be waiting on the porch every morning for the rest of my life if I need to."

She knocked my hands away and jumped into me, locking her limbs around my body when I caught her. She kissed me like I'd just come home from war. Her hands tugged at my hair as she came up for air long enough to show me that I wasn't the only one who could give orders. "Take me somewhere and fuck me, Anthony."

I gripped her ass and took off at a jog down the beach, farther from the house. There were dunes up ahead that would provide us enough privacy, especially so early in the morning. The way her body bounced against mine had my cock already leaking precum by the time I had us hidden away in the dunes.

"I just need you in me, Anthony. I need to feel you." She kissed across my jaw and over my throat, raking her teeth over my skin as she went. It was sensation overload as I fell into the sand and wasted no time in yanking my pants down and her panties to the side so I could impale her with my cock the way we both needed.

She shuddered and raked her nails over my shoulders while I yanked the top of her dress down so I could bury my face in her tits and suck her nipples the way that made her back arch. Tasting her made me hungry for more, though, and I pulled out so I could sit back on my knees and yank her hips in the air. I feasted on her pussy, using all the tricks I knew to force her into an orgasm fast and hard. When I sucked her clit a little harder than might've been pleasurable, she screamed into her arm and came like a freight train.

I wanted to feel her pussy clamping down on me as she came so I flipped us over and let her sink down on my length. Sitting astride me with her tits free from her dress and her body flushed with her orgasm, she was fucking perfect. I could've come just from the way her cunt milked my cock but I wanted more.

"Play with your nipples and ride me, baby." I stroked her thighs and squeezed her hips. "Put on a show for me. Let me watch you fuck me this time, Claire."

She moaned my name and did as I said. She pinched and twisted her nipples while working herself up and down my cock. Her head bent back and she gasped, creating a truly stunning display.

"One hand on your clit. Give me something to replay in my head a million times while I'm stuck in meetings, baby. Let me watch." I slapped her ass and grunted when she rode me harder. "That's it. Ride me hard. I want to see these tits bounce."

Claire was a work of art as she teased her clit and slammed her body down on me with each stroke. The way her body undulated made me see stars.

"Oh, Anthony! I'm close! God, I'm so close!"

I took over. I held her hips off me and fucked her hard and faster from below. The new angle hit the perfect spot for her and I watched her face and neck turn a deep red shade as her mouth fell open in a silent scream. "Stroke your fucking clit, Claire. Don't you dare stop. Not until you come all over me like the good girl you are."

She was lost in her pleasure and so close to losing her mind that I took over. I flipped her onto her back and drove into her even harder while reaching between our bodies to rub her clit. I took her mouth in a messy kiss and swallowed her screams as she erupted, coming hard and wet. Her body squeezed mine so hard that I lost my rhythm and drove into her a few more times as I spilled everything I had in her.

After we were both spent, lying in the sand in a disheveled heap, it was a few minutes before our breathing returned to normal. I finally realized I was probably crushing her and went to roll off of her but she stopped me.

"No. Just a few more minutes." She was half asleep.

I lifted my head and smiled when I saw her eyes were closed and she had a satisfied look on her face. I gently stroked her cheek as her sleepy smile confirmed what I pretty much already knew. I loved her. I wasn't letting her go again. I didn't care what I had to do.

40

Claire

I was late for the dress fitting. I'd fallen asleep on the beach and Anthony had carried me back but hadn't known to wake me up. I hadn't had time to shower so I was racing across the island on foot, holding my dress in its protective bag over my head, still covered in sand. Oh, the places the sand was rubbing…

When I finally burst through the front door of the dress shop, every head turned and I wondered if it was possible to die from humiliation. I apologized as I walked to the back of the shop and found Sophia with her bridesmaids, all sitting while Madeline modeled her dress in front of them.

"Claire!" Sophia's mouth fell open when she saw me and then she fake gagged. "If you were just with my brother, I don't want to hear a single thing. Oh, god."

I had to be the shade of raw beef. "And if I wasn't with Will?"

"Then you're a bit of a whore." Madeline laughed easily when I gasped. "I'm kidding! Relax!"

Sophia frowned and looked like she was ready to say something but I cut her off. I didn't want her to have to deal with any ugliness on her wedding week. I'd already caused enough trouble.

"Anthony. I fell asleep on the beach and now here I am. I'm so sorry I'm late. I didn't miss you trying on your dress, did I?" I handed my dress off to an older woman who looked at me with concern written all over her face. I winced but forced a smile at her. "This is what happens when you move away from the beach and then come back to it. I was just rolling around in the sand... Remembering it... You know?"

Sophia cackled and waved the woman away. "Oh, my god, C. I love you so much. Especially now that I know this was Anthony and not my brother. Thinking of Anthony doing dirty things to you in the sand is not bad at all. It's kind of nice, actually..."

Lizzie fanned herself. "I agree."

I somehow blushed even deeper. "We are not having this conversation."

"He's a big guy..." Katelyn giggled. "All over?"

They all fell out laughing, everyone except Madeline. Her eyes burned through me like I was the devil and she was going to take out all evil with just one gaze. She crossed her arms and rolled her eyes before looking away from me.

I felt appropriately judged but it was hard to sink into that feeling with the rest of the women around me giddily gossiping about the men they were hooking up with and if they compared to Anthony. I didn't say that I would've bet my life that none of their men compared to Anthony. That felt unnecessarily rude.

"Ladies? It's time for the maid of honor and then the bride." The older woman was back. "I'm aware that you had your dress altered elsewhere, dear. Let's see how they did."

I hesitated. "I'm just going to go outside and shake off real fast. I don't want to get sand all over the dress."

"Sure, dear..."

I shot Soph a wide-eyed look and rushed outside. I cleaned up as much as I could and then let the woman assist me in getting into the dress. It zipped up just as easily as I remembered and a quick tongue click and a nod from the older woman told me the dress was good. I walked out of the dressing area and posed in front of the women with a wide smile on my face.

"Wearing the dress makes it feel so real. Soph, I'm so happy for you. If this is how I react when I put on *my* dress, I'm going to need therapy after I see you in yours." I fanned my face and laughed. "You're getting married!"

She clapped her hands and hurried over to hug me tight. "I'm getting married!"

"Does it need to be let out a little in the middle?" Madeline's cool voice broke the moment and I looked up to see her staring at my stomach with her nose scrunched. "It looks a little...tight."

Ouch. I cleared my throat but I didn't get a chance to defend myself before Sophia did.

"It's perfect. It fits her like a glove." She spun me around and smiled. "You're beautiful, Claire."

"I don't mean it in a rude way." Madeline put on her sticky sweet voice. "I'm so sorry if you took that wrong, Claire. I just want to make sure Soph's wedding pictures are perfect. I already had to hire extra makeup artists since half of the wedding party have black eyes."

Double ouch. "I'll cover the cost of that, of course. Since most of those incidents were my fault."

Fiona, sporting double black eyes, scoffed. "No way. I earned these babies and I won't let you take credit for them."

"She's right, C. You didn't cause anything. Stop beating yourself up." Sophia looked at the older woman. "It's perfect, isn't it?"

Despite looking like she didn't want to agree, the woman nodded. "The seam work is adequate."

"Maybe you could just eat a little less in the next few days then? It could just be bloating." Madeline wasn't going to let me go without getting a few more hits in. "Anyway. Let's get to the real show. Get into your dress, Soph!"

"Madeline,-"

I cut Sophia off. "She's right about getting to the real show. Come back and help me get undressed so we can get you into your dress. I'm ready for an ugly cry."

"Not in the photos, though." Madeline smirked at me and shrugged. "Sophia is just so beautiful. I want her photos to reflect that."

I pulled Sophia into the dressing area with me and shook my head. "Whatever you're thinking, just let it go."

She scowled. "I'm going to talk to her. I don't know what her issue is, but she can't talk to you like that."

I sighed. "I think she has a thing for Will. And if that's the case, I understand her not liking me. I don't appreciate it, but I understand it. No matter what, though, she planned your wedding, Soph. I don't want to upset her and have her go nutty on the wedding plans."

"I don't give a shit about the wedding plans, Claire. You're my best friend and I'm not going to allow her to talk to you like that. I'm going to talk to her. If she can't get her attitude in check, she can go." Shaking her head, Sophia looked so upset that I hated myself a bit in that moment.

"I'm sorry. I didn't want to cause any trouble this week and I've caused a lot. I haven't been the best maid of honor. Please, just let this go with Madeline. At least until after the wedding. You're trying on your dress today and you're upset. You shouldn't be upset, Soph. So, let's just put this behind us and focus on the fact that you're getting married to the man you love and I'm going to be at your side for it."

She sighed. "We need to talk about the way you treat yourself."

"Soph."

"Fine! Fine. I won't say anything right now." She shook out her hands and blew out a breath. "Get me in this giant dress already."

41

Claire

"It looks..." Martha, the seventy-year-old paint instructor I'd hired to lead the wedding party in a paint and sip afternoon, stared down at Will's painting and tilted her head to the side. "Honey, it looks like a big cock. Is that what you were going for?"

Will's cheeks turned red as our table burst out laughing. He launched into a defense of his painting. "No! See, this is the lighthouse and this, that round part there, is the rock it's built out of. It's a lighthouse! Just like the one everyone else painted."

The old woman tapped her finger to the tip of her nose. "Dear, it's a cock."

I was crying from laughing so hard. It was rare to see Will be bad at anything and we were all eating it up. I grasped my sides and ended up snorting. That just made me laugh harder.

"Let's see what you painted then, you brat." Will grabbed my canvas and spun it around to see what was a decent lighthouse and coastal horizon. He scowled at it and then at me. "That's not fair. You planned this. You've probably been practicing. Let me see yours, Anthony."

Anthony turned his around and it was a perfect replica of what Martha had shown us. He grinned at Will and shrugged. "I just have talented hands, man."

Zane proudly showed us that he'd skipped the assignment completely and had instead painted a silhouette of-

"Zane!" I shouted his name as I realized he'd painted my body. I wouldn't have known if not for the exact placement of my birthmark. "You idiot!"

Martha hummed. "I do love a rebel. Good work."

I scoffed. "Don't encourage him!"

Will tossed his painting down on the table. "No one told me I could've painted you, Claire. I would've blown your mind."

"No one was supposed to paint me!" I slapped my palm to my forehead and sighed. "Hide that."

Zane just smirked back at me. "This is going to hang in our bedroom."

My breath caught. *Our* bedroom. It was one more sign that they were serious.

"Oh, god, Will! Why'd you paint a dick?" Sophia had come up behind us and she leaned against my chair while judging her brother. "I'm starting to worry about you."

Will shook his head. "No."

She laughed. "No, what?"

"No, I'm not dealing with the two of you teaming up against me." He got up and pressed a kiss to both of our heads before backing away. "I'm going to sit with Jake. I bet his painting looks like shit, too."

"Hey!"

We ignored Jake's outburst and Sophia took Will's seat so she could lean in and whisper to me. "I might've let it slip to our parents that you and Will are a thing... I think my mom is still crying."

"Sophia!"

"What? It's a good thing. Her and Dad are already planning the wedding." She looked across the room at Will and grinned. "Did you hear that, Will? Mom and Dad are planning your wedding. Since I refused Great Aunt Maggie's ring, Mom's going to want you to take it."

My stomach dropped. "Sophia!"

"We're not going to use that ring. It's cursed." Will winked at me. "Just tell them I'll buy my own."

The entire room erupted in whistles and cheers while I buried my face in my hands and groaned. It was way too early for Sophia to be bringing up rings and marriage. She was going to make me look like a lunatic.

Warm hands pulled my hands away and Zane was there, kneeling beside me with a sweet smile on his face. "How about I steal you away for a while before dinner tonight?"

I nodded. "Yes, please. I would like that very much."

Sophia patted my hand. "Go on. Get out of here. If you think I was bad, you need to prepare for Mom."

Will and Anthony caught us before we slipped away. Anthony pulled me into a hug and kissed me while letting his hands wander and causing an uproar of hoots amongst our friends. Will was next and he bent me backwards and kissed the living daylights out of me.

When he put me back upright, his smile was so wide that it gave me butterflies. He was happy. Because of me. "For the record, I love my Mom and where her head is. I'm going to be the favorite child when I officially bring you into the family."

Zane pushed him away. "My turn, fools. Goodbye and good riddance."

I paused for a moment as I looked around and saw that everyone, including Martha, had watched me kiss two men before leaving with a third and no one seemed plussed. No one but Madeline but I wasn't going to give her any value. I bit my lip and tried to contain my smile as I let Zane pull me away.

"You're happy." Zane led me back to the hotel with my hand held tight in his. "I like it."

I rested my head on his shoulder. "I didn't realize I wasn't before. But I am now, I think."

"Good. Let's keep you that way." He stopped outside of one of the hotel rooms and used a keycard to open it. "I have some ideas about that. Why don't you get comfortable? Take that dress off and stay awhile."

I raised my eyebrow at him. "Zane. I thought you didn't have a room."

He started pulling small bottles of paint from his pockets. He grinned when I laughed and shrugged. "I lied a little and I stole a little. It's all in the name of keeping you happy. And close."

"What are you planning on doing with that paint, Zane Wilson?"

He reached over his shoulder, grabbed his shirt, and pulled it over his head. "We're going to make some art of our own."

42

Zane

I peeled Claire's dress off her slowly and stepped back to appreciate her standing in front of me in a tiny pair of white lace panties. Her full breasts fell in perfect teardrops that I planned on decorating in all the colors of the rainbow. At least the colors that I'd stolen. I slowly ran my knuckle over the tip of one hard nipple and watched her skin pebble with goosebumps.

"And the panties." I'd taken the blanket off the bed and the white sheets were begging to be ruined. I watched her work her panties down her long legs while I unbuttoned my jeans. "In the middle of the bed, baby."

She flashed me a sweet smile and crawled up the bed, ass swaying seductively as she did. By the time she was on her back, completely stretched out and open for me, I had a bottle of paint in my hand and one knee on the bed.

"You're going to make a mess of me, aren't you?"

I opened the black paint and poured a line of it from her ankle to her knee. "Only physically. The rest of you is safe with me this time, Claire."

She pointed her toes and wiggled her hips when I smeared the cold paint down her foot and scooped up enough to write my name across her thigh. "Promise me."

I kissed the bottom of her foot before painting a strip of white over it. "I promise that if I leave this time, I'm coming right back. I promise that I'll take you with me as often as you'll let me."

She gasped when I splattered a handful of hot pink across her upper thighs. "*Zane.*"

"Lie still." I straddled her thighs and used every color I had to paint her chest and stomach. I ran yellow fingers up her sides and tipped her nipples in purple. My handprint in a smear of colors across her throat made me unzip my jeans to relieve some of the pressure I was feeling. I painted her face with red and orange flowers and tasted her mouth before staining it white.

I touched every part of her and had her roll over so I could do the same to her back. My name down the middle of her back in large letters soothed something primal inside me. The sheet was a swirl of colors already when Claire stripped me naked and had me lie on my stomach so she could decorate my body.

The feel of her fingertips and the cold paint tracing lines and patterns over my skin was sweet torture. She straddled my hips as she worked and raked her hands over my skull. Her lips touched just as many places as her fingers. Going down my thighs, she hummed her pleasure.

"Over."

I rolled over and she started the whole process again at my feet. I watched as she dipped her nipples in paint and dragged them over my legs. Up my thighs, she lightly scratched lines through blobs of paint. Then she nearly killed me as she lifted herself over my cock and slowly sank down on it.

Neither of us spoke or moved as she drew lines over my tattoos in pink and red. She left white handprints over my chest and intertwined our fingers before dancing paint up my arms and across my shoulders. My throat enticed her to leave more handprints and there was something about her sitting on my dick with her hand around my throat that made my body pulse.

Her eyes burned with desire as she painted my face with her own flowers. She drew a line of black around my mouth and then leaned forward to kiss me. Our mouths and bodies were slick with the paint and we slid against each other while Claire ground her hips into mine.

With the painting done I flipped her over and pinned her arms over her head. I was already so far gone with need for her that I knew I wouldn't last long. I angled my hips so I could grind into her clit with each stroke and locked gazes with her. She squeezed my hips with her thighs and arched her back.

"Zane." She moaned and worked her hips up to meet mine. "Zane!"

Her body clenching around mine was too much and I came with her name on my lips. I kissed her hungrily before rolling off of her. We both turned our heads so we could still look at each other and I tried to show her everything I was feeling.

She slowly smiled and reached over to trace the line of my nose. "You're different."

My heart lurched. "I am."

She rolled into my side and curled her leg over me. "You scared me before. I never said anything but there was something wild in you that terrified me because I knew you'd leave to chase it. I held parts of myself back, I think, because of that."

I raised up on my elbow and cupped the side of her neck. "And now?"

"And now you don't scare me."

I rolled over her again and pressed my already hardening cock back home. "Good. No holding back. I want everything, Claire."

43

Claire

Zane and I tried to sneak into the dinner that evening but Soph spotted us and shouted a greeting so everyone turned to look. I felt like everyone could see what we'd done, the room we'd ruined, the sheet we'd stained with paint and come. Zane tightened his hold on my hand and led across the room to the table that Will and Anthony were waiting at.

Both men stood up and greeted me with a hug and a kiss in a way that I didn't think would ever get old. I ended up squeezed between the two of them with both of them sliding a hand between my legs to grip my thigh at the same time. I laughed and blushed harder when Jake's brother, Paul, raised his eyebrows at me.

"You have a little paint in your hair..." He pointed to his own temple with a sly grin on his face. "Can't imagine how that happened."

Zane slapped the back of his head playfully. "Mind your own business."

Will gripped the back of my neck and leaned in closer. "Did you have a good time?"

I smiled and nodded. "We made art."

He laughed and tapped his phone sitting on the table. "I saw."

I ducked my face. It'd been my idea to snap a photo and send it to Anthony and Will. I had a problem. "I better start writing again because I'm going to need a backup career when my photos eventually get leaked and I'm fired from all respectable jobs."

He slid the phone into his pocket and shook his head. "Anthony took care of it. No one will ever get these pictures but us, baby. So feel free to send as many as you'd like."

"Is it weird that I like it?"

Anthony's hand squeezed my thigh harder until I turned to look at him. "No. It's something we'll have to delve into a little more when I'm sure everything can be protected."

I shuddered with anticipation. "I'd like that."

Sophia got my attention and waved me over to where she was sitting with Jake and his parents. I didn't want to leave the guys but I made my exit anyway, much to their displeasure.

"Hey, C, come here and tell Jake's parents that I did in fact beat Jake at basketball that time in Miami." Sophia wagged her eyebrows at me. "You've got a little... Right there, yep."

I swatted her arm. "I don't remember you beating Jake. Jake? Do you?"

He high-fived me and laughed at the scowl on Soph's face. "Nope. Not even a little bit."

"Now the party can start! I'm here, everybody!" Uncle Sal swirled into the restaurant in a fully sequined jumpsuit with a matching cape that went all the way to the floor. His platform shoes were neon pink and lit up as he walked. "Oh, babygirl! You look like you rolled around in a bunch of paint! What have you been up to?"

Jake's mom giggled. "Oh, I just love it when Sal shows up."

A man around my age followed Uncle Sal, stopping every so often to straighten his cape. He was dressed in his own sequined jumpsuit and cape and there was another man following him, straightening his cape. It just kept going. I realized what was happening a few seconds before it happened.

"Oh, god."

Uncle Sal and his band of merry men broke into a perfectly choreographed dance. Capes flew, sequins sparkled, shoes lit up the room. There was hip thrusting and twerking. There was music that wasn't loud enough to cover the squeaks of their shoes on the polished wood floor. There was even a muffled counting. It was a lot. A brilliant, messy, horrifyingly beautiful lot. And then it was just…done.

One moment the room was full of flamboyantly gay men and then the next they were gone and the room was silent. It was only broken when Sophia let out a loud snort and then cackled wildly.

"I love that man!" Jake's mom clapped excitedly and slapped her husband's arm. "Don't you just love that man?!"

I wordlessly made my way back over to my seat and screamed when Uncle Sal popped out from nowhere and hugged me. He laughed boisterously and hooked his arm through mine. "Oh, honey. Come on. I need to talk to you about some things I heard."

I blanched. "You don't."

He waved to Sophia. "Happy wedding week, honey!"

I grunted when Uncle Sal proved that he was much stronger than he looked by swirling me around, straight into Anthony's chest. I didn't have to worry about catching myself with Anthony's arms locked around me. "Uncle Sal!"

He pointed at Anthony and then behind him. "All three of you boys are a part of this, too. Come. Come on. All of you."

I'd never felt more like a little kid than in that moment. We somehow ended up in a line, trailing behind Uncle Sal as he led us outside and to a quiet corner of the patio. I started to say something but one finger wag from Uncle Sal shut me up.

He looked at the guys. "You know I'm all for alternative lifestyles. I support loving who you love and fucking who you want to fuck. It's all good in theory but when it comes to my honey, Claire, I feel a little more traditional. So I'm going to ask you boys this one time and one time only. Are the three of you prepared to take care of my niece and stick by her side, no matter what? Unlike the first time around? If she's willing to forgive the three of you, I can, too. If you aren't serious, though, I think you should all pack up your bags, tie them to your ankles, and walk off the pier. Understand?"

It was the most parental thing that Uncle Sal had ever said around me and I wanted to cry. I grabbed him and hugged him tight. "I love you, Uncle Sal."

"I love you, too, honey, but don't wrinkle my cape."

"We're going to take care of her, Sal." Will looked at me as he said it. "It's serious."

Anthony nodded. "She's not going anywhere without us."

Uncle Sal looked at Zane and frowned. "You. Rocker boy. I know what life on the road is like."

Holding up his hands, Zane shook his head. "Not for me. Not anymore. This is what I want. I didn't realize there'd be so many other dicks in the picture, but life is funny that way, I guess."

Uncle Sal smirked. "Baby, there are always more dicks than you expect. That's the joy in life."

"I liked your show?" Anthony cleared his throat when Uncle Sal cut his eyes at him. "I mean it. I liked your show. I think you could steal Jake's mom if you wanted."

"I could steal any woman in there, babe. I'm legendary." He looked at me and then assessed my outfit. "This isn't working. Come over tomorrow morning. I had to dress you like a whore to get you some attention but now that you've got the attention, I need to tweak it a little."

"Can it still be…" Will realized what he was about to ask and shook his head. "You know what? Whatever you pick will be great."

44

Will

"You're dating out of your league, Will." Sophia stared up at me as we danced. Claire had the ballroom turned into something like a prom and I'd stolen Sophia away from Jake so I could make sure she was okay with me. I hadn't made enough time to check in with her. Of course, she happily busted my balls right away.

I nodded. "I know. She's too good for me."

"She is. Which is saying a lot because you're pretty great, too." She smiled and rolled her eyes. "You know I'm fine, William. I love you and Claire. I expect your first child to have my name, though."

Oddly enough, the thought of a little girl running around who looked like Claire with Sophia's name didn't give me hives. "I love you, too. I'm sorry. I should've talked to you before I made a move on Claire all those years ago."

"Will, no. I would've been a bitch about it. I would've accused you of trying to steal my best friend and I might've even done physical damage. I was possessive of her." She glanced over at where

Anthony was dancing with Claire. "I'm kind of surprised you're not feeling more possessive of her."

I followed her gaze and watched as Zane slipped Claire away from Anthony just to have Anthony steal her back. "I am. Not as much as I expected, though. With anyone else, I'm still seeing red... I don't know why it's different with those two."

"If you were ever going to pick two men to share your woman with... I mean... You chose a rock star and a freaking billionaire, Will. If y'all get married, you're set for life."

I scowled at her. "I'm not marrying *them*, Soph. Their money will stay their money."

"I'm just saying, you could've done worse." She stretched up and kissed my cheek. "I love you, Will. More than almost anyone else in the world. I wouldn't have put you and Claire together but now that I see it, I'm glad it's happening. You two both mean so much to me. And now Claire will be my real sister."

I gently pushed her away. "You're a little too focused on weddings right now."

"Don't disappoint me, William. Marry my bestie and make it official." Sophia laughed at my exasperated expression and danced away to Jake.

I was turning to leave the dance floor when Madeline slipped her hand into mine. She smiled up at me. "Dance with me?"

I glanced over and saw that Anthony and Zane were still struggling to win the battle over who would dance with Claire so I nodded. "I don't foresee Claire being open for a dance for a bit. Those two are going to make her sick with all the spinning back and forth."

Madeline frowned but when I loosely wrapped my arms around her, it shifted into something happier and she rested her head on my chest. I wanted to shift away from the embrace but I wasn't sure how without hurting her feelings.

"I'm worried about you, Will." She did lift her head then, thankfully, but it was just to give me a sad look, complete with puppy dog eyes. "The more I think about your situation and the more I see Claire with Anthony and Zane, the more concerned I get."

I shrugged. "You shouldn't be worried."

"What if she hurts you?"

Glancing back at Claire, I felt my lips tipping up. She was standing between Anthony and Zane, hands out, looking a little green. I could tell that she was telling them off for tossing her around and the sheepish looks on the guys' faces were priceless. I pulled out my phone and snapped a quick picture before going back to Madeline. "I'm good, Mad. You don't get to see the way she looks at me when we're all alone. She's as crazy about me as I am about her. And I'm the one who hurt her the first time. I wanted to tell everyone about us. I had these grandiose ideas about running away and getting married. She didn't want to chance hurting Soph and instead of giving her time to come around to the idea, I broke up with her."

She shifted her hands until they rested on my chest. "I'm just...worried."

I looked over at Claire again and saw that she was staring back, her eyes on Madeline's hands on my chest. Her eyes were narrowed and her lips were turned down in a deep frown. That was all it took for me to step away from Madeline.

"What is it?" Madeline followed my gaze and then let out a quiet scoff. "It's already happening, Will. By the time the wedding is over, you and I won't be friends."

I tore my gaze away from Claire and frowned down at Madeline. "That's not true. I decide who I'm friends with, Mad, and as long as you're kind to Claire, I have no reason to stop being friends with you."

"So I have to kiss her ass for you to be my friend?"

"That's enough, Madeline." I crossed my arms and searched her face for a clue about what was going on in her head. "Look, I understand you being worried but we've been friends for long enough that I expect a certain level of courtesy towards *me*. I'm not an asshole. I think you know that. Nothing has changed. We're still friends. You're the one making it feel like I need to choose. I'm going to go dance with my girlfriend now. Have a good night, Mad."

Zane was doing his best to distract Claire but she was still frowning when I reached her. I pulled her into my arms and tight against my chest, just for her to remain stiff.

"You didn't like me dancing with Madeline."

She stared up at me for a few more seconds before she sighed and her body relaxed into mine. "I'm sorry. It's just weird, you know? She hates me. It makes me feel weird to see a woman who so openly insults me touching my boy-... Touching you, I mean."

Despite the seriousness of the conversation, I couldn't help grinning. "You almost called me your boyfriend."

She blushed a deep, deep red. "No, I didn't."

"It's okay. I *am* your boyfriend. More than that, really, but there aren't a lot of words for the middle ground between boyfriend and husband, are there?" I stole a kiss when her mouth popped open. She melted even more into me and kissed me back hungrily. When I pulled back, her eyes stayed closed and the smile on her mouth was one of the sweetest I'd ever seen. "You're it for me, Claire."

She tangled her hands in my hair and pressed her forehead into my chest. "I know. I don't mean to doubt you."

"You really feel like she hates you?"

With a heavy sigh, she pulled back and shrugged before blowing out a breath and forcing her face into something lighter. "It's nothing to worry about. Just dance with me."

I *was* going to worry about it. It could wait until we were finished dancing, though. Especially since I could see Anthony approaching with a shark-like look on his face. I'd found a flaw in sharing our woman. There weren't many ways to share her while we danced and we each seemed to be feeling greedy.

I spun her away just as Anthony reached for her. "No, sir. This is my turn."

Claire rolled her eyes. "The next one of you who spins me is sleeping outside tonight."

45

Claire

I found the first giant flaw with Madeline being the wedding planner the next night during the rehearsal dinner. While she sat at a table with Sophia, Jake, and my three men, I was exiled to a table by the bathroom with Jordan and a few of Jake's distant cousins who'd flown in earlier than they'd been invited. I was literally at a table with people who weren't supposed to be at the dinner. When the guys had spotted the discrepancy, they'd wanted to speak up but I wouldn't let them. I wasn't going to be the cause of any other trouble for Sophia. So I was sitting between Jordan and Jake's cousin, Jerry. Jerry, who was a forty-year-old toddler with the table manners of a toad.

After his third deep burp I actually leaned closer to Jordan because he was the lesser of the two evils. He, of course, took advantage of the situation. He put his arm along the back of my chair and even pulled me closer.

"I'm glad we're getting to spend some time together, babe. I've missed you."

Jerry leaned towards me, lifted his right leg, and let a loud fart rip. He made eye contact with me while he did it and then grinned. "Sorry."

It was too much. I popped up from my chair and excused myself. "I need to ask Sophia something. Be right back."

Before I made it two feet from the table and Jerry's toxic fumes, Madeline was there. With her official clipboard in her hands and a chilly smile on her face, she tilted her head as she looked me over. I wasn't going to let her think she was getting to me so I just smiled back at her.

"Could you stay in your seat until after dinner is served? I don't want to confuse the servers." She tapped her nails on the glittery clipboard and I noticed it read 'Maid of Honor'. She saw me looking at it and her grin turned even chillier. "It's from another wedding. Don't worry. We *all* think you're doing just the best job at being Sophia's maid of honor."

I took a deep breath and counted to ten. It didn't help. I wanted to strangle her. Instead, I took another deep breath and stepped around her. "I just need to run to the bathroom. Excuse me."

She waited until I was almost by her and then she lightly grabbed my upper arm. "I'm really happy for you, Claire. I think it's so great that you're open enough and brave enough to screw three men so openly without worrying about what people are thinking and saying about you."

I didn't manage to form a retort before she'd skirted away to haunt the next person. All my desire to flee from my table vanished so I just plopped back down in my seat and did my best to not breathe in all of Jerry's gases.

Jordan leaned over. "Maybe we should play a game. Every fart or burp from him, we take a shot."

I snorted. "I have no interest in dying of alcohol poisoning."

He laughed and tried to put his arm around me until I pushed it away. "I'm just trying to be friendly, Claire. Give a guy a break."

"You can be friendly without touching me." I squeezed my eyes shut as Jerry farted again. "Nope. I can't do this."

"Here. Change seats with me. It's the least I can do." Jordan stood up and ushered me into his seat, farther from Jerry. "We're together for the rest of the night. I'd much rather us play nice than spend the night being bitter at each other the whole time. Maybe we should pretend we're different people tonight."

I took a deep breath and nearly gagged when I inhaled what smelled like rotten eggs. Turning away, I gripped Jordan's arm tight and shook my head as my eyes watered. "I can't do this. Oh, god. He's not well."

Jordan's face turned green. "Jerry! Bloody hell, man! Either plug yourself or slink back to whatever mud hole you crawled out of!"

Jerry had the decency to look at least a little embarrassed. "Sorry. I'm lactose intolerant."

I watched in horror as he picked up another piece of the cheese that came as our appetizer. I wanted to slap it out of his hand and cry at the same time. The smells he was emitting had no place anywhere near a dinner table. A waiter came our way and then immediately changed direction after inhaling the toxic air surrounding us.

I shook my head and pushed away from the table. "I can't. I just can't!"

Sophia caught me when I was fleeing the table for fresh air. I'd almost escaped the hotel when her fingers latched onto my hand and held firm. "What the hell are you doing way over there? You know damn well you're supposed to be at my table. Maybe even closer to me than Jake so we can put our heads together and talk shit."

I tried to force a smile but my eyes were still watering from Jerry's last fart. Tears ran down my cheeks and when I opened my mouth to try to explain that I wasn't upset I just started cackling. I doubled over and held my sides as my muscles ached. "Oh, my god. I- Jerry- Gas!"

Jordan suddenly pushed past us, nearly knocking me over, on his own search for fresh air. As soon as he opened the door, he sucked in a lung full of the good stuff and let out a loud, shaky breath. "I believe I've smelled hell in the bowels of that man."

Anthony was at my side in a flash, a growl in his throat. "Watch where you're going. You almost knocked Claire over."

I held up my hand and tried to contain my laughter to explain that Jordan's push was excusable under the circumstances. "Couldn't breathe! Jerry! Gas!"

Jake's face appeared in front of mine, even as I was doubled over, and his eyes were wide. "Someone gave Jerry cheese, didn't they?"

I let out a howl of laughter and tried to stand up straight. Anthony had to help me and in the end, he just ended up holding my body against his, my back to his front with his arms around me. I wiped tears from my face as fast as they fell and sagged against Anthony. It took me a while to get control of myself but when I did, I still barely got more than a few sentences out before I cackled again. "I'm sorry! That table needs to be declared a biohazard. I think something's seriously wrong with Jerry, internally. No human should make that smell."

Sophia giggled hard enough that her plunging neckline and bouncing boobs stole Jake's attention. When she saw where he was looking, she slipped her arms around his waist and grinned up at him. "I've still got it, huh?"

"I really, really hate to tell you this, but I think some of the smell is clinging to your hair..." Anthony sniffed me and his entire body stiffened. "Wow..."

Will chose that moment to join us and his eyes widened as he inhaled. I watched his nostrils flare before he took a step back. "Um..."

"This is not happening to me." I pushed away from Anthony and held my hands up as he and Will both tried to reach for me. "No! I stink! I can't believe you told me I stink, Anthony! I can't believe I stink!"

Zane moved around the group of people staring at me and rolled his eyes. "I've got this. You don't spend a few years on a tour bus without losing your ability to smell bad things. Come on, stinky. Let's get you cleaned up."

Madeline appeared with her clipboard. "The meal is about to be served, everyone. If you could all return to your tables..."

"You put Claire at the wrong table, Madeline. When she gets back from her biohazard rinse, she needs a seat at our table." Sophia's tone left no room for argument but Madeline still tried.

"Everything's already planned and organized-"

"I don't care much for weddings but one of the traditions I'm into is the maid of honor sticking close to the bride." Sophia tapped Madeline's clipboard. "I'm sure it was just an oversight, not putting Claire with me, but I'd love it if you could fix that."

I took no joy in the flush that crept up Madeline's neck. I didn't want to cause her problems but I was more than grateful to have Sophia on my side, ready to save me from Jerry. "I can just pull up a chair."

Zane sniffed me and whistled. "Let's let them figure it out. We need to get you hosed down before this funk seeps any deeper."

I made a panicked sound. "Don't even joke about that. I feel like I just survived something traumatic. Look at my hands. They're shaking."

He grinned and easily tossed me over his shoulder. No sooner than I felt the breeze against my asscheeks did I feel his big hand settle over my short dress to cover me. "We'll be right back."

46

Claire

Zane walked us both into the shower in his abandoned hotel room, still fully clothed. He laughed as I sputtered. "Let's get you soaped up."

After a few minutes of scrubbing myself over my dress, Zane peeled it off of me and we repeated the cleansing process over again. As Zane washed my hair, I stood there, mind wandering. "They should bottle Jerry's smells and sell them as libido blockers. You've had your hands all over me and I'm not attempting to climb you. He broke me."

He rinsed my hair and added conditioner before turning me to face him. He looked sexy and rumbled in his wet clothes, with his wet hair hanging down in his eyes. He gave me a slow smile and then laughed when I groaned. "Not broken, baby. I can see that look in your eyes."

I huffed at him. "Don't tease me right now. I don't know if I'll ever be the same. He just kept farting, Zane. It was the grossest version of a horror movie ever. It was so bad that I think Jordan and I might've come to a truce and bonded over it."

He scowled. "No. He's still persona non grata."

For the first time since the gas event, I found myself relaxing. I bit my lip as I studied Zane's unhappy face and even reached up to trace the lines of his furrowed brows. "Are you worried?"

He deepened his scowl and lightly wrapped his hand around my throat. His thumb stroked my sensitive skin as he leaned closer. "Should I be?"

Whatever humor had been hanging around slipped away as I gripped his wet shirt in my fists. "I think I proved my loyalty to you, Zane."

His face pinched tighter. "And I didn't."

I suddenly couldn't meet his intense gaze. We were both silent as he rinsed my hair and then shut the water off. I wasn't sure how the mood had shifted so suddenly but it had and I wasn't sure how to recover.

"It was stupid of me to think we could gloss over what I did." He yanked off his own wet clothes and grabbed a towel to dry us both off. As he worked it roughly over his own body he left red, flushed skin behind. When he moved to me, he was as gentle as ever. "I'm sorry. The way I left you was fucked up. I was fucked up. I spent a lot of years chasing away my feelings and guilt with alcohol and worse things but nothing has ever felt as good as being back in your arms, Claire."

I stared up at him as he rubbed the towel over my hair. "Are you going to do it again?"

His face darkened and he dropped the towel before dragging me into his chest. "Never."

That one word felt like the biggest promise I'd ever been made. The intensity in his voice made my pulse race. "Is it weird to promise you my loyalty when I'm with Will and Anthony, too?"

He ran his hands up and down my back, comforting me. "No. Tell me. I want to hear you tell me that you're going to stay loyal to me, forever."

I felt his erection pressing into my stomach, an angry beast pulsing between us, begging for attention. "I'm going to be loyal to you for the rest of my life, Zane."

"And beyond."

I smiled and leaned forward to rest my head on his chest. "And beyond."

I gasped when he gripped my ass and picked me up. He put me down on the counter and stepped between my thighs, forcing them open wider. His hands slid around to my hips and then one dipped between my thighs to tease my clit. "I need to see you come and then I'll take you back."

My libido was back. I arched my back, offering him my breasts, and reached behind me to steady myself as he stroked my clit in just the right way to make me come hard and fast.

"I'm going to spend the rest of my life making up for walking away from you. Even when I'm old and gray, I'm going to wake up every morning with one thought in my head. You. Making you laugh, making you happy, making you come hard. It'll never be enough, though, and when I die, I'm still going to follow you around like a lovesick teenager."

I gasped as he pushed me higher and higher, with his fingers and his words. "Zane!"

"I love you, Claire." He said it as he pinched my clit and sent me sailing over the edge of my sanity.

I panted and tried to catch my breath while my mind raced. He loved me? When he started to pull away, I grabbed his shoulders and pulled him into me. I wasn't ready to say the words yet but I wanted him to know my feelings were real. I kissed him with everything I could, doing my all to show him what I felt.

The next time he pulled back, I let him. His mouth twisted up on one side. "You're crazy about me."

I laughed because it was so Zane to break the intensity with just the right thing. I realized something right then and decided to tell him instead of holding back. "I don't think I have as much fun without you. Will and Anthony each bring their own thing to this crazy mess but you, Zane... You bring me to life in a way that no one else ever has."

His eyes glowed with emotion that he quickly ducked his head to hide. "I'll never walk away from you again. If you decide you don't want this, Claire, you'll have to fight me tooth and nail to get me to leave."

I lifted his chin so he had to face me again. "Never."

His hands gripped my thighs tight as he struggled with his control. "All I want to do is say fuck that dinner and bury myself as deep in you as I can get."

"After. As soon as dinner's over, you can drag me back to our room by my hair, caveman style, and do whatever you want to me." I loved watching the fire burn in his gaze.

With a tension in his body that promised chaos later he stepped back and wrapped me in a towel. "We have to run to the house next door. Do not let that towel slip or you won't be making it to dinner."

I let out a wild laugh and took off. It was crazy how carefree I felt. Running in just a towel across a very nice, very booked hotel wasn't anything I ever would've done in London. Jordan was right when he said I was different on the island. I just hadn't realized how different or how much I needed that difference to feel like I could breathe again.

47

Claire

We returned to the dinner and I found my new seat between Sophia and Will. I'd changed into one of Uncle Sal's new choice of dresses for me and I couldn't miss the appreciative glances my guys sent my way as I took my place. The white slip dress hugged my figure and stopped mid-thigh, which was reserved compared to some of Uncle Sal's previous choices. I knew what the guys were seeing, though. The material and color of the dress created a magical guessing game of whether or not it was see-through. Every shift had them leaning closer and looking harder. I'd barely gotten out of the house with it on without Zane tearing it off.

My wet hair was piled on top of my head in a bun and my glasses kept sliding down my nose but I felt sexy. I found myself moving differently, even, doing things with more of an exaggerated reach to tease my guys.

Sophia leaned over after the waitstaff had cleared our dinner plates. "Don't take this the wrong way but if you ever made a sex tape with Zane and Anthony, I'd buy a dozen copies and watch it nightly. The energy between y'all is so hot."

Will leaned forward, his expression sour. "Really, Sophia?"

She didn't even blush. "Obviously you agree with me."

Jake raised his eyebrows. "About what?"

"I was saying that if Claire made a sex tape with Anthony and Zane, I'd buy it." Sophia fanned herself. "I'd have to blindfold you before we watched it because you can't see Claire like that but you'd enjoy the benefits of me watching it."

"Soph!" I was as red as a tomato. Shoving my glasses up my nose, I shook my head. "No one is making a sex tape."

"Why not?" Madeline's cold voice was a bucket of ice water, reminding me that she was there. She tilted her head to the side and her pretty face remained blank, despite the aggression I felt coming from her. "You're obviously pretty open sexually."

Will stiffened beside me and I could feel him start to respond but once again I found myself wanting to stop any drama before it started. I grabbed his hand under the table and squeezed.

"Why not make a sex tape?" I laughed, being sure to keep it light. "Probably because the idea of anyone actually watching it would leave me dead from humiliation. Being open with the men I care about is a long way away from strangers watching my body during...that."

"And there's the fact that I'd never let anyone else see what's mine." Anthony met Madeline's gaze with a cold one of his own. "Ours."

Sophia leaned into me and groaned. "So. Hot."

"There are two other men seeing what's *yours* every time you have sex, right? Or am I not understanding how this works?" Madeline waved a dismissive hand around as she said 'this'.

Zane leaned forward and rested his arms on the table. "Doesn't seem like you're all that understanding."

Jake nodded and shot her a stern look, which was wildly out of character. "Seems like you'd be one of the first ones to buy up that tape, Madeline. You're so curious."

I could feel everything going off the rails and started to panic. I grabbed my glass of wine and did the only thing I could think to do. I stood up and cleared my throat. "A toast!"

Everyone looked up at me, including Madeline. She stared at me with a disgruntled look on her face that promised violence if I wasn't careful. Crazy bitch...

"I'm not going to give the long, dramatic speech that I have prepared for tomorrow. I just want to raise a glass to my best friend and her other half. Sophia, you couldn't have found a better man for you. Jake, you couldn't have found a better woman. Period. Sophia is way out of your league." I grinned at him and then captured Sophia's hand. "I'm so happy for you. From the day I met you, you took me in and claimed me as your own. You did the same thing to Jake and I think it has to be said that you're amazing at claiming the people you want and holding onto them. And we're all so lucky to have been claimed by you, Soph. I love you so much and I can't wait to watch you walk down the aisle tomorrow."

Jake popped out of his seat and gave me a tight hug. "You love me, too?"

I let out a watery laugh and hugged him back just as hard. "I do love you, Jakey."

Sophia wedged her way into the hug and we both laughed as we both struggled to fight the tears that wanted to fall. "I love you, C. Tomorrow, it's my turn, but it'll be your turn soon and I can't wait to make emotional speeches to make you cry."

Blushing, I pushed her away and sank back into my seat just as the dessert course was being brought out. Will tugged me closer and then let out a frustrated growl before pulling me into his lap and wrapping his arms around my waist. I tried to slide back into my chair but he held me tight.

"Let me hold you." His voice was rough. "It's the only thing keeping me from spilling my guts right here and now about how much I care about you, Claire."

I let out a soft breath and cupped his face in my hands. "I care about you, too."

"No, not him! I don't want to see you making sex eyes at my brother. Climb on Anthony or Zane! Sophia broke the tension and earned a deep laugh from Will.

Zane perked up. "I'm ready and willing to be climbed on."

Jake's mother happened to be passing by. "Oh?"

Jake groaned. "Mom!"

Zane winked at me and then smirked at Jake. "Let your mom live, man. If she wants to climb on, who am I to stop her?"

"Oh!" The excitement in that one syllable was enough to make Zane's eyes go wide. He'd clearly underestimated Jake's mom.

A few seconds later, the older woman was settling herself on Zane's lap, her arms wrapped around his head while she clutched his head to her ample chest. Zane's arms and legs kind of flailed as he avoided touching her as much as possible and the muffled sounds he made just added to the complete kerfuffle of it all.

"Mom!" Jake looked like he wasn't sure if he wanted to run away or drag his mom off of Zane first.

"Well, this leads nicely into the next events of the night." Madeline cleared her throat and stood up. "The bachelor party will be held down the street at Moe's. The bachelorette party will be held right here, in the smaller ballroom."

"Bachelorette party?" I looked at Sophia and saw she was just as confused as I was.

"I thought we were just going to skip them." Sophia did look a little excited, though. "Are there going to be penis straws?"

48

Claire

Strippers. There were strippers striding into the hotel ballroom, each of them dressed as firefighters, carrying penis balloons and other penis garb. My mouth was hanging open, a dangerous choice considering all the penises, but I wasn't sure I'd ever be able to close it again. Madeline had ordered strippers for Sophia's bachelorette. Firefighter strippers. If I hadn't thought she had the hots for Will before, the firefighters cemented it. She wanted my man.

The ballroom had been transformed into a pink whirlwind in preparation for the party and it just made the strippers look even more masculine and huge. All of them were in the traditional firefighter suits, including the helmets. A few of them had the shields down on those big helmets, blocking their faces. A spark started to burn down deep in my body as I thought of Will in one of those suits getting ready to dance for me. It was something I was going to have to bring up to him because I had to admit, it was working for me.

One of the strippers sidled up to Sophia and she held her hands up and shrieked while bouncing away. "No! You're all dressed like my brother! This is my worst nightmare!"

Jake's mom whirled a penis balloon over her head and hooted at the dancers. "Yes! This is the best night ever!"

The other bridesmaids were already fanning themselves and inching closer to the men. Madeline stood just off to the side, her eyes wide as she watched with a hungry look on her face. It was no surprise that one of the strippers had already set his sights on her. I wished them both well in my head and moved over to Sophia, giggling at the horrified look on her face.

One of the men quickly stripped down to a very small pair of black underwear and grinned at her. "Better, sweetheart?"

I laughed at the hesitation on her face. Before I could poke fun at her too much, one of the firefighters with his shield down approached me and took my hands. I immediately shook my head and turned bright red. "Oh, no! No, I'm okay. Thank you, though. I'm just going to-"

I shrieked as the big man wrapped his hands around my waist and picked me up. He tucked one arm under my ass and held me against his body as he walked towards the small stage. I wasn't exactly struggling because I was shocked at being manhandled by a stranger but I had plans to skirt away as soon as the man put me down.

"Oh!" I gasped as he put me down in a metal folding chair and gripped the back while thrusting his hips at me. I pushed my glasses back up my nose and let out a high-pitched giggle. "Um. That's okay. I'm not the bride or anything. You should dance for her. She's over there. The one getting the lap dance by the naked guy? Oh? Oh! Sir? I-"

My stripper dropped to his knees in front of me and gripped my knees tight. He was still gyrating his hips and rolling his body when he brushed his face over my thighs. By that point, I was shocked stupid. I'd never been danced on like he was dancing on me. I wasn't sure what to do with my hands so I just cupped my face as I stared at the show happening *on* me.

My mind started playing tricks on me, convincing me that the firefighter dancing for me was *my* firefighter. It made it easier to watch as he worked the heavy jacket off and tossed it aside before snapping the red suspenders holding up the heavy pants. The loud snap made me jump and then giggle again. The long-sleeved shirt he wore still hid most of his body but I still blushed at having one less layer between us.

"Um. My boyfriend's a firefighter. A real firefighter. Not that you're not a real firefighter. Your...uniform? Your uniform looks very official. And this is giving me a lot of ideas for my boyfriend but I still think I should-" I lost my breath as he grabbed me again and laid me out on the floor. Before I could make sense of what the hell was happening or get up he was over me, rolling that big body like he was having his wicked way with me. "Oh, wow. Okay, yeah, this is... Um, sir? I don't think my-"

He planted his middle against mine and I felt his hard shaft press into my core through the thick pants. He must've felt me stiffen because he lowered his helmet-covered head and growled at me through the shield. "Relax, baby. I happen to know your boyfriend wants you to enjoy yourself."

It took me a second to make sense of what I was hearing. *Will.* I let out a shocked gasp and grabbed his helmet. Shoving the shield up, I wasn't prepared for his wicked, filthy grin or the barrage of thoughts raging through my head. "You're a stripper?!"

He let out a bark of laughter and lowered his shield before rolling his hips against me again. *Oh.* Knowing it was him made it a little too enjoyable. "You think I was going to let some random guy dressed like a firefighter come in here and touch you? No, baby. You have your own firefighter. If another man was pressing his hard cock into you like this, I'd kill him. So be a good girl and take what I give you."

I was on fire. He slid his body up mine in a way that made me think he was a little *too* good at dancing and then thrust his hips over my face before spinning his big body and working his way down so we were in a sixty-nine position. Ideas lit up my brain like fireworks.

I was just getting used to having his hips thrusting over my head when he somehow twisted around and flipped me onto my stomach. He jerked me up on my hands and knees and grabbed a fistful of my hair while simulating fucking me from behind. I wasn't sure if that was typical behavior but when I managed to open my eyes and look forward my eyes clashed with Sophia's.

She had two mostly naked men gyrating on her but her eyes were horrified and focused on where Will was behind me, pretending to take me like an animal. I realized that there was probably a look of bliss on my face and gasped. Reaching back, I smacked Will's hip and apparently that was his sign to change positions again. I somehow found myself in the air, thighs wrapped around Will's helmeted head, clutching that helmet as he spun in a circle.

I kept seeing Sophia's face on a loop with each spin. It wasn't until the music stopped that Will paused his dancing and put me back on my feet. I looked over and saw Madeline at the sound system, hands on her hips.

"I think you're getting a little carried away, Claire. You're disrespecting Will." She moved closer and glared at me, a disgusted twist to her lips. "Can't you control yourself?"

Sophia had never looked so uncomfortable and disappointed in me. It was too much for me to take so I turned and slapped Will's chest. He grunted and wrapped an arm around my waist while flipping his shield up with his other hand. I watched Sophia's face shift with relief and then she threw her head back and laughed so loud that it made the dancer next to her flinch. Then she froze and glared at Will. "Ew! Will! I just watched you humping my best friend!"

The ballroom doors swung open and the bachelor party came in, arms crossed. I spotted Anthony and Zane before they spotted me and I almost laughed at the cross looks on their faces.

"Let's have a little fun with those two, huh?" Will slid his shield back into place just as one of the clueless dancers turned the music back on. Will, deciding to play with fire, bent me over until I had to press my hands to the floor to hold myself up, and gripped my hips while he thrust against me.

My hair was falling down from all of Will's humping but through the strands I saw the moment Anthony saw me on the stage, bent over in front of a faceless stripper. The man I'd known as such a sweet and kind guy was nowhere to be found as he let out a battle roar and came stomping towards Will.

49

Claire

Anthony was going to kill Will. I was a horrible person, though, because something about the wild rage in Anthony's face turned me on and made me weak in the knees. He looked even larger than normal as he leapt onto the stage and growled. "Get the fuck off of her."

Zane was there a second later, looking every bit the rockstar accused of trashing hotel rooms a decade earlier. He had a dangerous look in his eyes as he came at Will.

I swore and dropped to my knees so I could try to stop the men I loved from killing the other man I loved. I didn't even have time for that thought to solidify because Anthony was there, wrapping his arm around my waist and yanking me up from the ground. I gasped as he held me like a kid, twisting me away from Will.

"Oh, you motherfucker." Zane let out a bark of laughter suddenly and Anthony's body relaxed around me. "You're lucky you flipped that thing up when you did, asshole."

Will's laughter rang out. "I wish I had a picture of your faces."

Anthony's chest still rose and fell faster than normal as he held me close. He brushed his mouth over the side of my head and groaned. "I think someone deserves a spanking for that."

I twisted around so I could look at him over my shoulder. "Will?"

He gave me a dark smile and shook his head. "Oh, no. It's your sweet little ass that's going to be warmed soon. You were enjoying that. You like the idea of your men turning into animals over you, don't you?"

I huffed at him, a sound that wasn't as effective as it might've been since he was still holding me like I was a child. "I don't see how I'm the one in trouble here."

Zane plucked me from his arms and put me on my feet. "You're objecting a lot for a woman who gets soaked when her ass is spanked."

Sophia's loud shriek from directly behind us was the only sign that she'd approached. "Oh, my god! You're wild, Claire! Also, Jake, come here and take some dirty talking notes from Zane. Wow."

I was horrified but when I looked back at the rest of the room and saw Jake dancing between two half naked strippers, I couldn't hold onto that emotion. My laugh was so surprising that I choked on it and ended up with tears leaking down my cheeks as Zane patted my back. I pointed at Jake as my only explanation.

"Well, I was going to take some time to rip my brother a new one for crashing my bachelorette party in the most traumatizing way imaginable but I think I have to go steal my almost husband back from those strippers." Sophia gave me a finger gun as she backed away. "Spanking, huh? You skank."

Will pulled his helmet off and the sight of his sweaty hair sent me right back into a heightened state of arousal. He caught my expression and gave me a teasing grin. "See something you like?"

"I can't believe you snuck away from the bar to do this. How the fuck did you even know about it? Unless…" Zane's eyes widened. "Is this your second gig?"

I put my hands on my hips and narrowed my gaze. "He's too good at it."

Will grabbed my hips and pulled me close. "You're the only person I've ever danced for or ever will dance for. A few guys from the station do moonlight as dancers and they thought it was hilarious that they were going to be dancing at my sister's party. One thing led to another and suddenly I was watching clips from *Magic Mike* before coming in here."

"I think I'm going to require a dance once a week." I considered him. "Actually…. More. And you can teach Zane and Anthony some moves, too, and then the three of you can dance for me. Anthony could be a cop. And Zane… Zane, you'd be a construction worker. Yeah, I like that."

"Why the hell can't I be the cop?" Zane slipped into place behind me and nuzzled my neck. "I'd love to handcuff you and lock you up for being a bad girl."

I shivered and was seconds from dragging the three of them away to have my way with them when one of the other dancers joined us.

"Will, man, you're a natural. You sure you don't want to join us?"

I slipped out from between my guys, still a little too shy to be *so* blatant about our relationship. I looked at the guy and saw that he was in just his tiny underwear. Blushing and looking away, I giggled again. I couldn't help it. There was just something about the strippers that had brought out an almost immature side of me. I felt like covering my eyes and only sneaking a peek or two from between my fingers.

"Well, isn't that just the cutest sound ever. Is that sweet little Claire, all grown up?" The guy put his hands on his hips and flexed. "Remember me?"

Will growled, proving he could be just as jealous as Anthony and Zane. "Put your clothes back on, Randy."

I looked back at the man, shock making me forget his near naked state. "Randy? Randy Faulkner?"

I knew something about Randy that I was willing to bet Will didn't if he was acting threatened by the other man. Randy was as gay as the day was long. He wasn't the scrawny guy he'd been in high school, though. That much was for sure.

"The one and only." He flexed again and then laughed when I rushed over to hug him. "Damn, sweetheart, you are still just as sweet as ever, aren't you?"

I was aware of the three bulldogs behind me growling but I waved them off. "You look so different! I didn't recognize you. Of course, I've never seen you this close to naked before. Nice."

He grinned, flashing twin dimples. "Those three men behind you are all thinking about ripping my head off, honey. Should we tell them I'm not a threat? I'm not in the closet anymore, thank god. I still haven't announced it at the fire station, though. But if it'll save me from having Will swing those big muscles at me in a mean way, I'll let the gay cat out of the bag."

Will, of course, having heard every word, stilled. "Huh. Good for you."

Anthony grumbled. "I guess you can keep your arms."

"You're a very, very lucky girl, Claire. Let's get drinks sometime soon. I'll tell you all about my tryst with your Uncle Sal." He laughed at my horrified expression and hip bumped me before strolling away.

Zane's laughter had me spinning around to glare at him. I crossed my arms. "It's not funny! I'm starting to wonder if there's a gay man in the state that Uncle Sal hasn't been with."

Will moved closer to me again and started dancing to the music. "Cheer up, baby. How about another dance before we get out of here? Anthony and Zane could watch…"

That triggered my body and mind to forget everything else around us. I swallowed and pressed my hips back against Will. "Maybe we-"

"Will!" Madeline was breathless as she stumbled up the stairs and joined us on the stage. She bumped into Zane and then grabbed Will's arm. She hadn't been drunk when she was claiming I couldn't control myself just a few minutes earlier. "The girls all want a dance! I'm first, of course!"

My own jealousy trigger stomped on, I gently pushed her arm off of Will and shook my head. "No. He only dances for me."

Madeline's mask slipped for just a beat, then she was back to playing drunk. She batted my hand away and slid closer to Will, pressing her chest together like some sort of tit offering. "That's silly. He's my best friend. He can dance for me."

I looked up at Will, watching to see how he'd handle her. I trusted him completely and fell even more in love with him when he pulled me closer and turned so I was between the two of them.

"Nope. Like Claire said, I only dance for her." He nodded to the rest of the room. "Plenty of available men out there waiting for a chance to dance with someone other than Jake."

Anthony grunted. "Good luck with that. We're leaving. Our woman was promised a private dance and she's going to get it now."

Zane stepped around Madeline but didn't give her a single look. "Did you eat enough, baby? You're going to need your energy."

Feeling seen and chosen more than I ever had in my life, I bit my lip and turned in Will's arms. All I had to do was wrap my arms around his neck and he picked me up to carry me away. I was so in love with the three of them. Madly in love. "I wouldn't say no to eating cake off of someone's chest."

50

Claire

I had a sex hangover. It was the day of the wedding and I wasn't the only one who looked a little rough around the edges when we filed into the bridal suite the next morning. Lizzie and Fiona looked like their hangovers were from liquor but mine was from having wild sex for hours. I had beard rash in places I couldn't mention in polite company and muscle aches in spots I didn't know could ache. Anthony had even gotten carried away and left a visible bite mark on my neck that I'd silently chastised him for while brushing my teeth that morning.

I was exhausted. I wasn't sure how much sleep I'd gotten but I knew it wasn't much. Every time I thought we were finished, one of the guys would climb over me and it'd all start again. Not that I was complaining. A dozen orgasms or so a night was nothing I'd stick up my nose about, not in a million years.

I moved towards the refreshment table like a zombie, arms outstretched when I spotted the oversized cans of energy drink. Sophia met me there and we both popped open a can at the same time, each taking a long pull before sighing in unison.

She laughed and then groaned while clutching her head. "Oh, god. I drank way too much last night."

"Did y'all party for a while after we left?" I held the cold can up to my face and pressed it into my eye bags. "God. I hope these makeup artists are miracle workers."

"You and me both, girl. These black eyes are no joke." Lizzie joined us with a giant cup of coffee. "Still worth it, though."

Sophia nodded and then groaned again. "I need medicine. Or to be taken out back and shot. Someone just put me out of my misery."

"I've got this. Here I go, stepping into my maid of honor duties." I searched the suite for any sort of pain reliever and then hobbled out of the room and down to the front desk to ask for help.

The woman sitting behind the desk jumped to her feet when she saw me. "How can I help you?"

I read her name tag and forced a smile. "Sara, hi. Please tell me you have pain relievers back there."

She grinned even as she ducked behind the counter to grab something underneath it. "I saw the bride late last night going back to her room and I had a feeling y'all would be feeling rough this morning."

I took the packet of meds and blushed when I saw she was staring at my love bite. Groaning, I covered it and tipped my head back. "I promise that I'm normally a lot more put together."

She waved me off. "I remember you. You were as put together as your uncle was wild. If it's finally your turn to get a little rowdy, I say go for it."

I tilted my head and studied her face. It finally clicked. She'd been a couple of years above me in school and had been intensely goth back then. I shook my head and let out a laugh. "Sorry I didn't recognize you at first. How have you been?"

She looked left, then right, before leaning over the counter. "Great. I've got two kids and a husband that I couldn't get rid of if I left him in the middle of the ocean with a bucket of chum. You've been the talk of the town. You and Will, huh?"

I looked down at my feet as I blushed. "Yeah. It's been a surprise coming home, that's for sure."

She looked around again and then leaned even closer. "I always liked you and Sophia. If I were you, though, I'd watch my back around Madeline. I hate to sound like a gossip but she's still the same mean girl she was back in school. She's had her sights set on Will for a long time and I got the impression she thought this week was going to be her big chance with him."

My stomach dropped even though I pretty much already knew Madeline had the hots for Will. I wasn't sure what to say back to Sara but she just shook her head and waved me off again.

"Go. Ignore me. I was just giving into the gossip. I've seen the way Will has been looking at you this week and no one has a chance with that man."

I forced a smile and held up the pain reliever. "Thank you for this. And for the heads up."

When I got back to the suite I gave the medicine to Sophia and then was ushered into a high-backed chair by a makeup artist. I forced the negative thoughts about Madeline out of my head and focused on the importance of the day. Sophia was getting married. That was the most important thing.

"Oh, god, Claire." Speaking of, Madeline swept into the suite, still clutching her maid of honor clipboard. Her makeup was already perfectly applied and her hair was swept to the side in an old Hollywood wave that made her delicate features look even classier. Dressed in a silk robe that draped gracefully all the way down to the floor, she could've easily been the bride. "What is on your neck?! Does no one care about the pictures?!"

Sophia looked over at my neck and chuckled. "As long as it wasn't from my brother, I say good for you."

The makeup artist clicked her tongue. "I've had to cover way bigger things on wedding days. I've got you, babe."

Madeline mumbled something under her breath that I didn't catch but it made the artist cringe. I frowned after her and then glanced up at the artist. "I'm sorry."

She squeezed my shoulders. "Nothing to be sorry for. Not you, anyway. That one… Now that's another story. Is she a close friend of yours?"

I laughed. "No. Not at all."

"Thank god. I hate to see women keep shitty best friends close by when there are so many good ones out there. Like you two. Y'all are platonic soulmates, aren't you?"

Sophia's eyes filled with tears as she nodded. "Forever."

I reached out and took her hand. "Forever."

The sound of gagging from somewhere else in the suite preceded Fiona sprinting towards the bathroom. Lizzie stood up from her own makeup chair and sighed. "Don't think that our current state of shit show is a reflection of our feelings for you and your big day."

Sophia laughed before grasping her head again. "Oh, god. No more laughing. If Jake thinks he's getting any tonight, he's sorely mistaken. As soon as we get through this thing I'm crawling into a hole and dying for a week straight."

51

Claire

I stood back while Sophia faked her way through posing for the typical getting ready pictures. She was a little green but the photographer promised she could remove any traces of black eyes, hickeys, and green-coloring. Bless her.

Lizzie, Fiona, and Kinsley were all resting on the bed in the suite, their hangovers refusing to let up. The makeup artists had finished up but they were hovering off to the side of the room, waiting for us to need touchups. The bridesmaids had all changed into pretty slips with matching robes for the pictures and my hair was up in massive rollers. I'd already smiled through several hundred photos and I was more than glad to sit back and let Sophia do all the work.

Madeline perched on the edge of a chair next to me, her back stiff and her eyes never moving over to me. She spoke quietly, ensuring that I'd be the only person to hear her. "Ten years you've been gone and you just come back and think you can take everything. You left them here. You left *him* here."

I didn't bother with the pretense. I turned to her and gripped my knees to keep my hands steady. "That's one way to look at things, Madeline."

"I had him. Will was mine, Claire. I know you've seen us together. Those private moments? They're quiet echoes of what we had before, what we'll have again." She turned to me then, her eyes burning bright with unshed tears. "I love him. I understand he needs time to finish this thing with you but as soon as he does, he'll come back to me. All you're doing with him is stopping him from coming home to his happily ever after."

My stomach soured. "You and Will?"

She let out a quiet laugh and dabbed at her eyes. "Yes."

I shook my head, unwilling to believe her. "No."

She stood up and stared down at me with that same burning intensity. For the first time ever, I felt like I was seeing real vulnerability in her eyes and it terrified me. "There's more."

I didn't want to follow her. I wanted to pretend like she wasn't telling me something that made Will out to be a liar. He'd been with her? How? How could he have been with her and not told me? My feet had a mind of their own. I got up and followed her to the bathroom, where she closed us in and then leaned heavily against the door, tears leaking down her face.

"I know I've been cruel to you, Claire, but please understand that you're trying to take the man I've loved for as long as I can remember. You had Zane and Anthony but they weren't enough for you… Still…I feel bad for you." She met my gaze and slightly shook her head. "Even though a part of me hates you, Claire, I still feel bad for the way they acted."

I pressed one hand to the marble countertop and let the cold ground me. "What do you mean?"

"The three of them turned sleeping with you into a game. I'm ashamed that Will participated. I know he needed the money, though, so...I can't be too angry at him. And if he comes back to me and puts that money towards our future, I guess I can't judge him so harshly if I'm willing to use it."

Ice ran through my veins. "What are you talking about?"

"They all made a bet about who'd bag you first. God. Men are fucking assholes sometimes. I couldn't believe they were saying it like that. Bagging you. The three of them bet a hundred thousand dollars to whoever screwed you first." She turned to the mirror and gasped when she saw her reflection. "A hundred thousand dollars just for sleeping with you first. Talk about a magic vagina, I guess."

I couldn't make sense of what she was saying. "You're lying."

"I was there, Claire. It killed me. They were all so drunk that Will didn't even blink twice about making the bet right in front of me. Do you think that I like that the man I love wanted to fuck you? It didn't matter that he tried to convince me it was just about the money. I mean, I know he needs the money, but I know he wanted to screw you, too. I had to just keep my mouth shut and pretend like it wasn't *killing* me when I knew he was with you that way."

I stumbled back a step. No. *No.* "Why would they make a bet like that?"

She let out a bitter laugh. "You're their Moby Dick or something. I don't know. They were salivating at the idea of fucking you. It was disgusting. I might hate you, Claire, but even I felt bad for you after hearing the way they talked about you, like you were just three holes for them to race to. Winner gets the money and the first run. Losers get sloppy seconds. Their words, not mine."

"You're lying." I hissed the words out and moved closer to her, fighting the urge to claw her eyes out of her head. "All of this is bullshit, isn't it?"

"You want to know the truth? Go find the checks. If I know Will, he slipped the checks into his extra shoes."

I was going to vomit. He'd always slipped extra things in his shoes so he didn't lose them or forget them. "And when the checks aren't there?"

She looked at me like she felt sorry for me. "They'll be there."

"They love me." I hated the way my voice shook as I said it. "Whatever you're trying to do, it won't work, Madeline."

"Do they love you or did they make some other fucked up bet? Like who could convince you to move back here first? Or who could get you to admit your feelings first? I don't know. I never would've believed it myself if I hadn't heard it with my own ears. I can't make you believe me. If you think I'm full of shit, that's fine. This does nothing for me. If anything, it puts my relationship with Will in danger. If you tell him that I told you all of this, he could hate me for ruining whatever he's doing."

I already knew that I had to go to the house and check his shoes. It was stupid. I should've just trusted that I knew the guys and that I knew they wouldn't make some stupid bet over me.

I walked towards the door and stopped just inches from Madeline. Leaning into her space, I growled out my words at her. "Even if you're telling the truth, Madeline, you'll never have Will. You'll always be the girl he can talk about fucking other women in front of. Do you think that's how a man talks in front of the woman he'd ever make his wife? Maybe you're being honest but if you are, you should save your pitying looks for the mirror because you're just as big of a loser as me in this whole mess. Good fucking luck."

My entire body shook as I let myself out of the bathroom and slipped around the edge of the room. Sophia was still being posed like a doll, despite her grumbled protests, so I had time. I left the suite and barely managed to walk and not run over to the house.

The guys were all in another suite with Jake getting ready so the house was silent when I let myself in. I raced up the stairs to the room we'd all sort of moved into together. Throwing open the closet, I went to my knees in front of the neat row of their shoes.

It was so domesticated. They stored their shoes together in the closet they shared while I took the one on the other side of the room. They wouldn't organize their lives to be with me, even temporarily, if I was just a bet.

I screamed in my head at my hands to stop reaching for Will's shoes. I didn't need to check. I loved him. I loved all three of them. When I slipped my fingers into the tennis shoes and felt the crinkle of paper, my chest threatened to crack open.

52

Will

I clinked whiskey glasses with Jake and grinned. "I'm happy you made it here, man. I couldn't think of another man I'd rather see marrying Soph today."

He sipped his whiskey and groaned. "Hair of the dog should feel better than this."

Zane slapped him on the back. "And this is why I rarely ever drink these days. Feels like shit, right?"

"I'm just fucking glad that Soph barely cares about the wedding. She'd kick my ass if she was as obsessed with having a perfect wedding because I think I'm going to look more than a little ill in the pictures." Jake made a face that made me think he'd thrown up in his mouth. "Oh, fuck. Remind me to never get drunk with male strippers again."

I laughed. "Sure. It's not something I thought I'd ever have to say to you, but sure."

Anthony looked at Zane and sighed. "You looked like shit and you're not hungover. Fix your tie."

"How are you still this grumpy? You got laid last night. Several times. You'd think it would cheer you up some." Still, Zane fixed his tie.

"I'll cheer up when I see Claire again. On our wedding day, I don't want to do this whole spending the entire day apart shit." Growling, Anthony took over fixing Zane's tie and then turned on me. "Yours looks like shit, too."

Anthony didn't seem to notice that the rest of us had gone silent and still. It was a strange thing to share a moment with a guy you'd just met for the first time less than a week earlier and to know that he was going to be standing next to you when you both married the woman you both loved one day. Looking at him and then at Zane, I let out a low chuckle and shook my head. It was insane that in such a short amount of time I'd come to trust both of them almost as much as I'd ever trusted anyone in my life. Not only that but I felt downright brotherly towards them. I didn't want to get mushy and say that I loved them, but I could no longer imagine my day to day life without them being a part of it somehow.

"On our wedding day?" Zane's smile was so wide that it practically stretched from ear to ear. "You making plans already?"

Jake pretended to fan his eyes with both hands. "Oh, my god. You boys are going to make me cry!"

Anthony reached forward and clapped his hands together loudly next to Jake's head, making Jake back away with his head in his hands. "Of course, I'm making plans. You aren't? Where the fuck do you think this thing with Claire is heading? I always wanted a life with her and now it's a real possibility. If you think I'm letting her slip away, you're fucking nuts. I'm putting a ring on her finger as soon as I can."

"Will?"

I turned and saw Jordan of all people sticking his head in the room. Scowling, I was about to demand he come closer so I could strangle him just a bit when I noticed the panicked look on his face. "What is it? Is it Claire? Did something happen?"

He cringed. "Not Claire. Madeline. I ran into her and she's a mess. I couldn't understand what she was saying but I think it's serious. She asked for you."

Zane whistled. "Of course she did."

Anthony shook his head. "Go on. Go check on your friend. Just know that we're going to sit down with her one day soon to talk to her about how she treats Claire. And with you to talk about how and when you should be fighting for Claire."

I didn't like the implication that I didn't always fight for Claire. I didn't want to fuck up my sister's day, though, so I just glared at Anthony. "Yeah, we're definitely going to talk later."

Jordan stepped back as I passed him. "She's in the lobby. I tried to ask her if she was okay and she just said something about her grandma. At least, that's what I think she said."

My stomach dropped as sympathy rushed forward for Madeline. If something had happened to her grandma, she'd be lost. The woman was everything to Madeline. I felt like an asshole as I quietly wished the timing was better. It was Sophia's big day. Madeline was my friend, though, and I could hear her voice in my head, telling me she was afraid I'd leave her behind because of Claire. I didn't want her to think that.

I found her sitting in the corner of the lobby, her body folded in on itself. "Madeline? What's wrong?"

She got up and threw herself into my arms. "She's gone, Will!"

I hesitated for a moment and then stifled a sigh before wrapping my arms around her in a hug. "I'm so sorry, Mad."

She clung to me, her body pressed a little too tightly to mine for comfort. "I'm sorry for bothering you. I know you're busy and you've got other people to worry about now but I just... I need a minute to lean on you. You know how much she means to me."

Patting her back, I closed my eyes and forced myself to just be her friend for a moment. "Of course. We're friends, Mad. Of course, I'm here for you."

She wound her arms up around my neck and cried into my chest. "Just hold me. Please."

Red flags were waving big time. I reached up and pulled her arms from around my neck because the position was too intimate. Anthony's words were still banging around in my head and I knew I was going to have to analyze my friendship with Madeline.

She pressed even tighter into me and then let out an unhappy grunt when I took her by her shoulders and eased her away. "Will?"

It wasn't the right time. Her grandma had just died and I wasn't going to pile onto her pain by asking her to not touch me so much. "Why don't we sit down? You can tell me what happened."

When she tried to sit in my lap I shot to my feet so fast that she tumbled to the floor. She swore and stared up at me while sniffing.

"I knew this was going to happen. You won't even comfort me now?"

Her eyes were dry. It hit me like a two by four. My head thumped painfully as I frowned down at her. "Madeline..."

She climbed to her feet and dusted her butt off. "What? What do you want from me, Will?"

"The truth. What's going on? You're supposedly falling apart but your eyes are dry, Madeline. Did your grandma die?"

She looked away, the red coloring her face a sign of the lie. "No. I never said she did... My aunt's cat did, though."

I held up my hands and backed away. "I don't have time for this right now. My sister is getting married and you're trying to pull focus. You and I will talk later but I need you to stay away from me today. I can't deal with whatever this is right now."

I jogged away before she could say anything else. I was pissed off and concerned about what all I'd missed with Madeline. Worse even, I had a sinking feeling that everyone else had seen the truth. Including Claire. What did she think of my friendship with Madeline if she'd seen through Madeline's bullshit?

I thought about stopping by the bridal suite to talk to her but I didn't want to create any drama on Sophia's big day. I'd talk to Claire as soon as the wedding was over.

53

Claire

The image of Madeline and Will embracing like long lost lovers wouldn't leave my mind. Seeing them wrapped up in each other in the lobby of the hotel had been the final nail in the coffin of my hope for my relationships with the guys. The two of them had looked so comfortable with each other. Will's arms wrapped so tightly around her waist had looked right, like it was something they were used to doing.

I couldn't fall apart, not on Sophia's day, so I just swallowed everything down and silently changed my flight while the last minute touchups were done on our hair and makeup. I was lucky that Sophia had been sipping steadily at a champagne bottle and was already a little too tipsy to notice any melancholy energy coming from me. Everyone was tipsy and excited to get the ceremony started, everyone but me. Madeline especially looked happy, like she was floating on air or like she'd just gotten the man she loves back.

When it was time for the wedding to start, I lined up behind the other bridesmaids and kept my eyes unfocused. I didn't want to see the guys waiting at the end of the aisle. I wouldn't be able to make it if I looked up and saw them. It was too much like I was walking towards them for another reason and that just broke my heart.

Sophia leaned forward with a giggle and took my hand. "I can't believe this is finally happening!"

I pushed everything down deep and smiled at her. "You're about to be an old married woman and I couldn't be happier for you."

She snickered behind her hand and wagged her brows. "Want to know a secret? Jake and I got married in Vegas after we'd been dating for a month. We never told anyone because we wanted to be able to fix it silently if things went bad between us. Today is twelve years for us."

My mouth fell open and I forgot that I was lost in my own feelings for a moment. "You're kidding."

She grinned and shook her head. "No. It's the only thing I've ever kept from you. So now we're even."

"Thank god." I hugged her tight, careful of her makeup and hair. "I can't believe you two. No wonder you're not all that worried about having the perfect day."

She shrugged. "I already had my perfect day. And a perfect life with that man for the last decade. I'm not greedy. Everything can't be perfect."

The procession music started and my feelings of dread came racing back. I swallowed it down and squeezed her hand. "I'm so happy for you, Soph. I love you more than you know."

"I love you just as much. Now, go! I'm ready to get this ceremony over with so we can get on the plane to Fiji! Did I tell you how much I also love your billionaire man? He gifted us the entire honeymoon."

Madeline, in line ahead of me, hissed at me before I could respond. "Pay attention, Claire! It's time!"

More pain and anger to swallow down. I turned around and started walking down the aisle, my eyes on the pastor. I couldn't look at my guys. I couldn't see them and know they'd made a bet over who would sleep with me first. I couldn't look at Will and know that he'd lied to me about Madeline. I just couldn't handle it.

I took my spot and still kept my eyes away from them. I stared back down the aisle and watched as Sophia walked forward with her dad. Tears filled my eyes and I let them fall since they could be blamed on my happiness at seeing Soph. My hands shook when she handed me her bouquet. My entire body vibrated with a hum of anxiety. I could feel the guys' eyes on me. I knew they were watching me, trying to get my attention to share a moment.

My stomach twisted and my heart ached as the pastor led Sophia and Jake in their vows. It was sweet and special, something perfectly them. I was barely holding on by the time it ended. I knew I was minutes from climbing into a car from the airport and running. Between my heart being broken and my luggage still being missing, I was leaving with a lot less than I'd arrived with. None of it mattered.

"I now pronounce you man and wife. You may kiss your bride."

Cheers rang out as Jake swept Sophia into his arms and kissed the hell out of her. When they parted even more cheers went up in the ballroom. Sophia took her bouquet back from me and flashed me a brilliant smile before going down the aisle with Jake. I hesitated a moment before Jake's brother held out his arm to escort me out behind them. As Jake's best man we were paired up. It didn't slip my notice that Will and Madeline were paired, as well.

By some miracle, Uncle Sal was waiting at the end of the aisle with a sly smile on his face. He gently pulled me to the side just outside of the ballroom and held up his finger. "I've just got to steal you for one minute."

Will's fingertips just brushed my arm as I slipped farther away. "Hurry back."

I didn't look back. I just wanted to get away.

Uncle Sal led me out of the hotel and over to a sleek sports car. "Get in."

I frowned. "You have a car? You can drive?"

He sighed. "Just get in, honey. I know you well enough to know that you're seconds from sobbing. Get in, tell me what happened, and I'll decide what my next steps are."

"A car from the airport is coming to pick me up soon." I looked around and ran my hands over my hair. "I have to go, Uncle Sal."

"Get in the damn car, Claire." He waited until I'd slid inside and buckled the seatbelt. He spun the tires pulling out of the parking lot, letting out a happy growl when I screamed and grabbed at the dash to stabilize myself. "I happen to have a friend at the airport who was looking into your missing stuff for me. He called and said he saw your flight change. The only thing that I can imagine sending you running back to London while also giving you those sad eyes is your men. And considering how thoroughly you avoided looking at them during the ceremony, I'd say they did something stupid."

I leaned my head back and closed my eyes. "I don't want to talk about it."

"Well, we've got a two-hour drive to Miami. You're going to have to talk about something." He sped down the highway leading off the island. "I canceled your car, by the way. It really does pay to have friends all over the place."

I took a deep breath and blew it out slowly. "Thank you for taking me, Uncle Sal."

"Do I need to kill them?"

I let out a quiet laugh. "No. I don't think so… I just want to get away. I don't want to have to face them right now."

"You've got two hours to cry and spill your guts, honey, so get started. It's the least you can do after making me think you were moving back home and then ripping that dream away. I need all the details." He laughed. "Especially the details about penis shape and size."

54

ANTHONY

I leaned against the makeshift bar with my eyes on the doorway into the smaller ballroom. Nursing a whiskey wasn't helping my mood. Where the fuck was Claire? Something was wrong. I could feel it in my bones. She hadn't looked at me once during the ceremony. She hadn't looked at any of us. "I have a bad feeling."

Zane twisted his neck from side to side and then nodded. "She looked upset."

I drained my whiskey and set the glass down with a heavy *thud*. "Goddammit. Where is she?"

Will was quiet, lost in his own thoughts. When Zane elbowed him, he actually jumped. "What?"

"Any clue about Claire?"

I frowned at the pinched look on Will's face, concerned about the cause of it. "Did something happen?"

He scrubbed his hands down his face and stared down at his shoes. "With Claire? No. I didn't get to spend any time with her today. Did you see how she flinched when I tried to touch her?"

"Fuck. I'm going to call her." I dialed her number and then swore when her phone went straight to voicemail. Looking around the room for someone who might know where she disappeared to, my gaze clashed with Madeline's. She was on the other side of the room, watching us with a smirk on her face. "What are the chances that Madeline has an idea about where Claire is?"

Will's gaze jerked up and he frowned. It was the harshest look he'd given Madeline since I'd met him.

I swore louder and grabbed his shoulder. "Something happened. Spit it the fuck out, Will."

He shoved me away and then held up his hands. "Shit. Sorry. I'm... I think I've been avoiding seeing the truth right under my nose for a while."

"Start talking, man." Zane looked around and then swore. "Actually. I have to go perform a song for Jake and Sophia before they leave. Fuck me. I don't feel like doing the dog and pony show right now. If one of you figures out where Claire went, come find me."

I watched him leave and then turned on Will. "Come on. You and I are going to go somewhere else so you can tell me why the sinking feeling in my stomach has your name all over it."

He scowled at me but followed me out of the ballroom and into a small hallway the staff used. "Madeline. I don't even know where to start to unpack that. She let me think her grandma died. She asked me to comfort her and I did because I'm not an asshole and because I thought we were fucking friends."

"Any of us could've told you that she's a manipulative bitch." I shrugged at his surprised expression. "It takes a lot for me to call a woman that but...she is. What did she do?"

"She was just...clinging. And when I tried to sit down to create some space between us she just plopped down on my lap." He shuddered. "She wasn't even fucking crying. The motions were all there but her eyes were dry."

I stilled. "Clinging?"

"All over me. I was uncomfortable but I thought her grandma had died so I didn't immediately push her away. It was just a hug but it was enough to make me want to shove her away."

"Was it something that would've upset Claire if she'd seen it?" I asked the question as calmly as I could manage but I was feeling pretty volatile.

Will looked horrified, as if the thought hadn't crossed his mind. "You think Claire saw Madeline hugging me like that?"

"I think Claire saw *you* hugging Madeline like that." I growled the words and roughly patted the side of his face. "You and the nice guy bullshit needs to end right here and now. You've been so afraid of hurting Madeline's feelings this whole fucking time that you've ignored the way she treats Claire. She's rude to Claire. She stakes a claim on you in Claire's face. And you let her. So, yeah, I think if Claire saw anything, it was *you* hugging the woman who treats her like shit."

His face paled. "I... I've been friends with Madeline for most of my life. She's been a good friend. She said she was worried that with Claire back, Sophia and I would replace her. It...-"

"She manipulated you. And if you can't see the way she eye-fucks you, you're really embodying the whole stupid buff guy trope."

"Fuck." Jerking to his full height, Will scowled. "First, we need to find Claire and make sure we're not just thinking the worst. After all, if she did see that and think the worst, she wouldn't need to hide from you and Zane. Just me. I'm the only fucking idiot here, apparently."

"You said it."

"After we find Claire and fix whatever I might've damaged, I find Madeline and end her games." He looked so furious that I would've felt bad for Madeline if she wasn't so god-awful.

"Do you have Sal's number? I haven't seen him since the end of the wedding, either."

"Yeah, I have it. I'll call him." Will pulled out his phone and after a few seconds he frowned. "He's not answering, either."

"Call him again."

Another few seconds passed and then I heard Sal pick up. Will put him on speaker phone and we both leaned in. "Sal? It's Will. Where are you? Is Claire with you?"

The older man, who I'd liked before those next few moments, let out his own version of a growl. "Yep. And that's all I'm going to say to you. Now we're trying to listen to a podcast about women murdering men and your calls keep interrupting it. Take a hint."

I pressed my palms into my eyes and groaned. "Jesus."

Will shoved his phone back into his pocket and tugged at his hair. "We know that she's with Sal. That's something. Let's go over to his trailer so I can start begging her to forgive me for being a fucking idiot."

I hesitated and replayed the short call with Sal. "Were those car noises?"

Will swore. "I think so. The trailer is probably a pointless place to look. He could be driving her anywhere. Let's go over to the house and see if she grabbed her stuff. If she packed, that narrows the distance they could've gotten by now."

"We'll go as soon as Zane finishes. If she's having second thoughts about us, we'll just have him sing a love song or something." Still, the sinking feeling in my stomach made me feel like a love song wouldn't be enough.

55

Zane

I saw Madeline trying to slip away after I finished up my song for Jake and Sophia and I made a beeline for her. Shifting away from the reaching hands of the other wedding guests, I followed her back into the hotel and caught her arm just before she slipped into the bathroom.

She swung around and frowned when she saw it was me. "Zane? What is it?"

"Claire is missing. Can you think of any reason she'd be missing, Madeline?" I was doing everything I could to not snarl at the woman. I had nothing more than a hunch that she was somehow involved with Claire being gone but it was a strong hunch.

To her credit, Madeline kept her face perfectly blank in the face of my obvious ire. That was the giveaway, though. She'd never once looked at Claire or talked about Claire without a slight scowl on her face. "What are you talking about? Claire's missing?"

"Don't bullshit me, Madeline. You've had your sights on Claire since the day she got here. She was more than happy when she left our bed this morning so what happened?"

"I haven't seen Jordan lately, either, you know. Maybe she decided three men was just one too short. Have you checked behind all the dumpsters and in all the dirty alleys on the island?" Her lips lifted in a mean smirk. "I don't know where she went and I don't care. Now leave me alone."

I growled at her. "It's big of you to insult Claire while following Will around like a sad little pet. Everyone sees your pathetic games and everyone sees Will look right past you, Madeline. Say what you want about her but that woman is loved by the man you're desperate for."

Her face flared red and her hands fisted at her side. "Fuck you. You should've seen the look on her face when I told her about your little bet with Will and Anthony over who would fuck her first. I can't lie; it was everything to see her realize that she's just a whore to the three of you."

I slammed my fist into the wall next to her. "What the fuck did you do?"

She didn't even flinch. "I gave her some information and then let her see what Will and I share. He may want to fuck her but he cares about me. Deeply. Lust fades. Friendship like mine and Will's lasts. It *will* last. Whatever Claire did with that information, I don't know."

"You're fucking nuts. Fully fucking *Single White Female* nuts." I scowled at her and backed away, needing to find Claire more than ever. "If you've seen the way Will looks at Claire and still think there's a chance for you, you need help. You'll never have him and after this? You won't even have his friendship. You fucked yourself, Madeline."

I turned and ran back to the ballroom, searching for Will and Anthony. There was no telling what exactly Madeline had told Claire but the mention of the stupid bet was boggling my mind. How did Madeline even know about it?

The moment I saw Will coming towards me with Anthony, I knew. Hitting him was a gut-deep reaction. Of course, the second my fist connected with his rock hard face, pain radiated up my arm and I swore, swinging away and shaking it out.

Will stumbled back several steps and then froze, his reaction telling. "Did I deserve that?"

I paused and looked back at him. "What do you think?"

He rubbed his jaw and sighed. "I have a feeling I did. That's your one free hit, though, asshole. Touch me again and I'll make sure you never play guitar again."

Ignoring his threat, I stared him down. "Tell me something, Will. How does Madeline know about that stupid bet we made?"

Anthony's body seemed to turn into stone. He froze solid. "What?"

"Yeah. I just had an interesting conversation with Madeline. She mentioned that while she doesn't know where Claire is, she did have a talk with her earlier. About how we made a bet about who could fuck her first. And about how she just showed Claire what you and she shared. So? What the fuck, Will? You told her about that fucking drunken bet?"

His face had paled so much that I almost worried he was going to pass out. Just not enough to be tempted to catch him if he did. "It... It was just a throw away comment. I was just saying that if Claire decided to go back to London, I'd follow her and be able to live off of the winnings for a while. It was nothing. I made it clear that we were drunk and it was stupid."

Anthony turned and stomped away. "Great fucking job, Will."

We both followed after him. Will's face was so devastated that I almost felt bad for him. Almost. Unfortunately for him, I was too worried about where Claire was and how she was to worry about him.

"I have a few connections that I can tap into but some of them aren't quite...legal. If you two would rather be safe, I'll take care of it and then meet back up with you when I know where she is." Anthony jogged towards the house next door, not bothering to wait on us.

Will and I both followed him, unbothered by his warning. I'd have that little tidbit to question it more later but none of that mattered at the moment. I felt like a part of my chest was being torn out and the legalities of *how* we found Claire were beyond my concern.

Anthony settled at the island with his laptop and his cell, tapping away at both as soon as he sat down. "Someone check to see if she packed her stuff."

Will ran off and I stood with my hands braced on the island while I waited. My heart hammered away painfully and it triggered a memory of the last time I'd felt the exact feeling.

I'd just gotten the call that I'd been waiting years for. An agent had heard a track I'd sent out blindly and he wanted me in LA right away. It was a swing while the iron was hot situation. I'd been standing outside of Claire's dorm and I looked up at her window and saw her sitting at her desk, head down. She loved sitting in the window when she wrote because of the view. She could turn her head and do the best people watching, according to her.

Back then, she'd wanted to be a writer. She kept her words close to her chest but when she turned in something for class, I devoured it. I'd been embarrassed the first time because there was something about reading her work that made me feel like crying. She had a voice that deserved to be heard. She was on the right track to getting her voice out there in the world but I knew if she joined me in LA, she'd lose that window seat and her chance of making her own dreams come true. I knew enough about the life I wanted in the music scene to know it wasn't a quiet window seat looking out over a pretty landscape.

I'd walked away thinking I was doing her a favor. At least, that's what I told myself to be able to do it. After several years of feeling like a fucking martyr for giving the love of my life up, I realized I'd been selfish and hungry for the life I'd always thought I'd have. Staying with Claire had meant settling down with kids because there was no other way to live with her but doing everything I could to tie her to me. Marriage, kids, a fucking dog. If I stayed, I'd never do what I'd promised myself I'd do before I met and fell for Claire. I still didn't know for sure if a part of me believed I'd be able to go back again in the beginning.

The night I'd walked away and ran away to LA with just a parting text to Claire to make it seem like if I didn't go that very second, I'd lose my chance, my heart had hammered away in my chest the same way it was right then as I stood next to Anthony, not knowing where she was. It was like I was standing on the edge of a cliff and my toes were slipping over the edge. I knew if I didn't find a way to hold on that I was going to fall over that edge and lose everything all over again. It was terror mixed with desperation.

After living a lifetime without Claire, I knew that I couldn't do it again. No matter what it took, I couldn't give up. I wasn't going to give her the same release she eventually gave me when I stopped answering her calls. I was going to follow her wherever she ran and bring her back to us.

"Everything's still here. She left straight from the ceremony, looks like." Will rubbed his face and looked up at the ceiling. "I'm sorry. I swear to god that I'll make it right. I'll make sure she knows that you two didn't do a fucking thing wrong. If she's going to hate someone and run from them, it should only be me. I was stupid and fucking blind about Madeline and I let this happen."

Anthony looked up from his laptop. "Are you going to walk away if she tells you to? Would you let her be with just me and Zane?"

Will turned away from us and raised his arms, locking his hands together and resting them on top of his head. The silence was heavy and when he finally turned back to us, his expression was dark. "How could I? I let her go once. Doing it again will fucking kill me. I *can't* let her go. I love her. But... If she can't forgive me, I'll do whatever I have to make her happy. If that means she just wants you two, I'll crawl back here with the knowledge that she at least has two men who love her and who will take care of her."

I rubbed at my chest as the ache deepened. It was like looking into a mirror, seeing the pain on his face and knowing he was facing down the same loss. There would never be another person in the world who would, or could, understand exactly what it felt like to have life with Claire dangling at the tips of our fingers.

"I have a feeling losing one of us would hurt her enough to make her walk away from everything. It's been all of us from the beginning and I think it's the only way it works." Anthony growled. "But you're on my shit list. And Madeline? She fucked with the wrong people. She won't come out of this unscathed so whatever obligation or responsibility to her needs to end now. You won't like however I decide to handle her, I guarantee you."

Will's face hardened. "Do whatever you want. I'll be there to help."

With a nod, Anthony closed his laptop and stood up. "She changed her flight to London. She's boarding in half an hour. We'll meet her in London."

I frowned. "How'd you...?"

"Don't ask questions." He dialed someone on his phone and spoke quickly. "Barry. Have the jet fueled and waiting. I'll be taking it to London with two friends. Send Michael with the helicopter to whatever parking lot will accommodate a landing to pick us up."

I gaped at Will. I was loaded from years in the business and smart investments by a really fucking decent manager and accountant but I wasn't personal jet loaded. The friends I did have with personal jets shared them to make it more economical and it would take a little more than one short call to have the jet ready.

Will shook his head. "We're a long way from Kansas..."

Anthony looked between the two of us and shrugged. "This way we'll beat her to London and be there waiting on her by the time her commercial flight lands. And then we'll bring her back here, where she belongs."

I winced. "And if she's not excited about coming with us?"

His smirk was dark. "Another benefit of the jet. No one in my employ is going to stop the plane because of an angry little woman."

56

Claire

Flying in a bridesmaid dress with tear-streaked makeup was only slightly less attention-grabbing than running across the airport in a broken bra and stained shirt. I at least had the benefit of my tits not bouncing all over the place, thanks to the structure of the dress. I was exhausted after catching a layover and having to sprint across yet another airport. There'd been no direct flights from Miami to London and there'd been no one to secretly upgrade my seat to first class. By the time I landed in London I was more exhausted than I was human.

After waiting to get off the plane and waiting in baggage claim for ten minutes before remembering I didn't have any luggage, I slowly made my way towards the cab pickup. I was so tired that the idea of telling a driver my address even felt like too much.

My heart hurt, I missed the same guys who'd broken it, and I couldn't get the image of Madeline and Will embracing out of my head. The worst part of it all was knowing I was going home to my empty apartment in a place I didn't want to be anymore when what I really wanted was to be in the Keys with Will, Anthony, and

Zane. My dream of moving back to Manatee Key was dying right in front of my eyes. There was no way I'd be able to move back there, chancing seeing Will and Madeline living their lives together.

I wrapped my arms around myself as I thought about just how lonely London felt after being home. The idea of returning to work like I hadn't been irrevocably changed seemed impossible. How could I?

Tears blurred my eyes for what felt like the hundredth time that day and I didn't notice someone stepping into my path until it was too late. I collided with a rock-hard body and would've bounced back on my ass if two strong arms didn't lock around my back.

"You're in a lot of trouble, sweetheart."

I jerked my eyes up and gasped when I saw Anthony gazing down at me. Shock did its best to convince me that I was hallucinating. "Anthony?"

His arms tightened. "Mm-hmm. You ran away from us, Claire."

Us. I glanced over and saw that Zane and Will were there, too. "What...? How...?"

"You don't get to run away from us. Did we not make that clear?" There was a bite to Anthony's voice, one I'd never heard when he spoke to me.

My brain was struggling to catch up but that tone in his voice kicked up a little fight in me. I pressed my hands to his chest and pushed until he let me go. "How are you here?"

"We took Anthony's jet." Zane's hesitant smile didn't feel right on his face. "You can't leave a guy with a private jet, Claire."

"You flew here to...what?" I looked between the three of them but my gaze stayed on Will. Everything came raging to the surface in a breath. "Did you bring Madeline?"

He flinched and looked down at his feet. "I deserve that."

"Why are y'all here?"

Anthony growled and gripped my upper arms. "I already told you. You don't get to run away from us. You have an issue, you come talk to us. You get mad, sad, heartbroken, you come talk to us. Do you understand that you're not getting away from us?"

I frowned up at him. "You're mad."

He lightly shook me. "Yeah, I fucking am. I just spent hours worried about you, not knowing if you're okay or stuck somewhere, if you were safe. And then we find you and you're walking through the airport like a fucking ghost, crying, Claire. *Crying*. The only time I want to see you crying is from happiness or because you've come too many times."

I flushed and brushed his hands away. "No. No, you don't get to be angry at me. I'm angry at you. At all of you. More than angry."

"It's my fault." Will's ears went red as he stepped closer to me and I held out my hands to stop him. "I'd like a chance to talk to you somewhere away from here, if you're willing. If not, I'll just do it right here."

"I don't want to hear anything from you. I saw you today. I saw you holding Madeline like she was everything to you. She told me the truth. You were *with* her. Why didn't you just tell me that?" I cursed the emotion filling my voice. "And you made that awful bet about me in front of her! She told me all about it and then I found the checks so don't try to deny it, Will. Why did you do this? If you wanted Madeline this whole time, you could've had her. Why hurt me?"

His eyes flashed angrily. "Madeline said *what*?"

"She was more than happy to tell me everything."

Anthony looked at his watch and cleared his throat. "We're not doing this here. We have to get back to the states. I have a meeting that I can't miss."

Pain scorched me. "Fine. Go."

He laughed bitterly. "You're coming with us, sweetheart."

I frowned. "No. No, I'm not. I just spent half a day flying here and I'm staying."

"I'll give you one chance to go with us willingly."

"Anthony, you can't-" I yelped when he bent forward and tossed me over his shoulder. "Anthony!"

He landed one sharp slap over my ass and left his hand there. "There isn't a you without us anymore, baby. You're coming with us and you're going to listen to what we have to say, even if I have to tie you down and stuff your mouth to shut you up."

I gasped and kicked my legs, hurt and angry enough to make a scene. "I'm not going back with y'all! You had your fun! Now let me go! I'm going back to my apartment and I'm going back to work and I'm going to pretend like none of this happened!"

"Sir? Is everything okay?"

The twisting emotions warring in me when I saw the security agent approaching us made me angrier. The small part of me that was sad that they'd been caught trying to haul me off was stupid.

I should've been thrilled that the agent would help get me out of Anthony's grip.

"We're heading back to my private jet. This is our girlfriend and she's mad at us right now but once she stops throwing a fit and listens, she's going to feel really silly about this. How about an escort?" Anthony shifted his hand over my ass and cupped the back of my thigh with his other hand. "An escort would be greatly appreciated."

I twisted around and saw the security agent fawning over Anthony. Groaning, I knew he wasn't going to be a help.

"Oh, yes! Yes, sir! Follow me."

I let out a little huff of frustration and let my body go limp. I didn't stand a chance of getting out of his grip. Especially when he seemed even larger than normal while angry at me.

That thought lit a secondary fire in me, though. I jerked my upper body upright and braced my hands against his lower back. "You have no right to be angry at me or throw me around to do your bidding. I left for a good reason and I'd like to stay here, away from the three of you."

"No." Anthony's fingers flexed on my ass and I got the distinct impression that he wanted to spank me again.

"Anthony! You can't just take me!"

"That's not what you said last night." Zane groaned at his own sad attempt at a joke. "Ignore me. I'm still having a hard time breathing since finding out you'd vanished."

57

Claire

"Phuck eww!" I growled out the muffled words around the actual gag one of them had put in my mouth during take-off. Apparently my shouting was worrying some of Anthony's staff and he didn't want them bothered. So they'd fucking gagged me with a cloth napkin that probably cost more than all of my bedding together.

I wanted to scream and stomp. They'd used who knew what to tie me to my chair with my hands bound by Anthony's tie. I could tell that the three of them had thrown caution and common sense out the window by that point. They were kidnapping me. I knew crossing state lines during a kidnapping was a big deal but they'd crossed the fucking ocean!

As angry as I was, there was a part of me, a part of me that I wanted to kick, that was thrilled at the way they'd tied me up. The weight of their desire to keep me was almost intoxicating. Not that I'd ever admit it.

Anthony's flight attendant came down the aisle with a bottle of water and a pair of scissors. "Sir."

Anthony grabbed the two things and gently pulled the gag from my mouth. "Before you start screaming, take a drink of water."

I wanted to headbutt him. Instead, I lifted my mouth to the water he offered and gulped it down. As soon as my mouth wasn't a desert, I turned my head from him and huffed. "Leave me alone."

He made quick work of cutting through my bindings and tossing everything away from me. Kneeling in front of me, he was tall enough that we were still almost eye to eye. "I'm sorry for that. If we'd hit turbulence and you weren't in your seat, buckled in, you could've been hurt."

"Can we talk now, Claire?" Will sat across from me in an identical oversized, cream leather chair. He'd looked like a kicked puppy the entire time and I wanted to actually kick him for it.

I crossed my arms and stared out the window on my right. "What's there to talk about? Why are you even here? Shouldn't you be wrapped up with Madeline by now?"

"Tell me what all she told you." He took a deep breath. "Please."

I took an identical deep breath and blew it out slowly. It was going to be a long flight, no matter what. With the ache in my chest worsening with each repeated word, I told him everything she'd said. I couldn't help watching his face as I did and the horror I saw there felt real. The anger that came next was definitely real. I'd never seen Will's face contort with so much rage. He was normally a laid back guy.

"I've never fucking touched Madeline a day in my life. Not one time, Claire. She was a friend and I treated her like one, with respect. What you saw today was me hugging her because I was under the impression that her grandma died. I was blind before. I should've drawn clearer boundaries with her but I didn't think I had to. We've always just been friends. Now I know that I was wrong. She's a fucking asshole."

"And the bet? Is she still the fucking asshole when you three are the ones who made the bet?"

He winced and looked away. "No. That was all us."

Zane sat next to me and leaned forward with his elbows on his knees. "It was just the three of us. Madeline is full of shit. She wasn't there and it wasn't anything like she made it seem. Not to say that it wasn't stupid, because it was, but it wasn't quite as awful as she made it sound. We were drunk, arguing about which one of us was going to win you over, and it was me who suggested the bet. It was one of the few times I've allowed myself to consume alcohol recently and it took over the dumb alpha part of my brain that wanted to prove that I was a better mate to claim you then them. I'm sorry. I'm stupid. You have to know that it wasn't meant to be hurtful. It was just the three of us trying to deal with our competing feelings for you."

I looked back at Will. "You told Madeline about it."

He ran his hands over his hair. "I thought I was talking to my friend. I was telling her about things being good with you and how I thought you might be coming back to the island. I mentioned that even if you didn't want to move back home, I'd quit my job and move to London to be with you. I mentioned that I had the money from the bet so I'd be able to support myself until I found a job I'd like. It wasn't a brag or anything, Claire. And I'm going to rip up those damn checks as soon as I get back. I just said too much without thinking about it. But the bet wasn't meant to be anything gross. I think it was the three of us just trying to come to terms with all of us wanting you and knowing it. It was strange at first."

"Claire, look at us. We flew to a different country to kidnap you and bring you back home to us. If this thing between us was just about some stupid fucking bet, do you think we'd risk kidnapping charges for you?" Anthony gripped my knees. "Each of us loved you in our own way in the past. Now... We love you in our own way but also...together. We love you enough to share you, enough to make sure you're getting everything you want and deserve. We messed up. God knows Will fucked up more than a few times. Is that enough to ignore the love we're trying to give you?"

I blinked away tears and looked out the window again. I wasn't sure what to say. My heart was racing. They were saying everything I wanted to hear but I was still scared. They'd walked away from me before. How was I supposed to believe they wouldn't again? How could I trust their maturity and loyalty after something like this?

It was like Will could read my mind. "I'm sorry, Claire. I'm horrified that I allowed Madeline to hurt you. I'm horrified that *I* hurt you. I'm not walking away, though. I let you go once before and I lost a decade of time with you. I'm not asshole enough to think I deserve you but I'm fucking taking you anyway. I'm not losing you again."

A thrill went down my spine at the way his face shifted through his speech. By the end it was a mask of furious determination. Gone was the kicked puppy.

Zane reached over and gripped my chin to turn my face to his. "Will's right. None of us are walking away. This is not the life I expected, I'll say that much, but it's the life I'm demanding now. It's the four of us against the world, or whatever. So...be mad but eventually you're going to have to forgive us for being stupid and accept that you belong with us."

I sighed and rubbed my temples. I was so tired and, more than that, I was worn out. It'd been just over a week since I left London the first time and I felt like I'd lived a lifetime in that week. So much had changed, even down to the things I wanted in my career. Spending the last sixteen hours or so mourning my heart hadn't helped.

"There's a bedroom in the back of the plane. Why don't you go lay down?" Anthony sighed and stood up. "We've got the rest of our lives for you to forgive us. A nap won't kill us."

I looked over my shoulder towards the door that was apparently hiding a bedroom. A nap sounded like exactly what I needed. I looked back at the three of them and blew out a deep breath. "Just a small nap..."

"Go on. We'll be out here if you need us."

I stood on shaky legs and edged past Anthony. Looking at them for a few more seconds, I wondered if I wasn't making a mistake in not immediately forgiving them. Because I already knew I was going to. I just needed a nap first.

58

Claire

"Come on, sweetheart. Time to buckle in again." Will's voice was soft as he spoke next to my ear while picking me up. "We're almost home, baby."

I wrapped my arms around his neck and pressed my face into his neck. I wasn't ready to wake up. I'd forgiven them in my sleep and things had been great again. I wasn't sure I was ready for it while I was awake. One strange thought kept bouncing around my head, though. "She told you her grandma died?"

Will stopped and snorted. "No, but she had Jordan imply it. And then she was crying about someone dying. When I finally asked her about it, she admitted it was her aunt's cat who'd died."

I let out a strangled laugh. "No."

"Yeah." He sighed a bone deep sigh. "I'm sorry, Claire. I love you. Then, now, and forever. You're the only person I want to hold."

I wasn't ready to say anything but I tightened my arms around his neck and pressed my cheek into his neck again. It seemed good enough for him because he kissed the side of my head and let out a grunt before moving to the seats.

He loved me. They all loved me. I was in love with them. They'd flown over an ocean to get me. My heart pummeled my chest and my breathing hitched. It was exactly what I'd wanted from all of them the first time around. I'd stayed awake for what felt like days waiting for them to show up and sweep me off my feet and tell me they loved me a decade earlier. They were giving me exactly what I'd wanted and needed. There was something inside me still holding back, though.

Will put me down and buckled me in before taking the seat next to me. "When we get back to the island, I have to find Madeline and set this straight. I'd like you to come with me."

That woke me right up. "Why?"

"I need you to know for sure that nothing happened with her. I need you to hear me end the friendship. So you know that I'm serious about this, Claire."

I wanted to tell him that he didn't need to end the friendship but I wasn't stupid, or a saint. I wasn't great at forgiveness and no part of me believed that Madeline deserved it. So instead of pretending like I was a better person than I was, I just nodded. I wanted to see him end the friendship. I wanted to see Madeline suffer the way she'd made me suffer.

"We'll all go. It wasn't just you that she hurt, Will." Anthony sat across from me with a hard look on his face.

I tilted my head as I studied him. "I thought you had a meeting you couldn't miss."

A small smirk lifted one side of his mouth and it made him look devilishly handsome. "So I lied. I just wanted to get you back on our home turf. This way it'll be harder for you to get away from us."

I gaped at him. "Are you serious?"

"Yep."

"You lied."

"Yep."

I sighed. "You're not even sorry."

He shook his head. "Nope."

"Whatever."

Zane laughed. "Don't leave us to deal with his billionaire bullshit by ourselves ever again, Claire. He's impossible when you're not here."

"I'm great all the time. I'm just better with you around, Claire. Maybe it was wrong for me to lie to get you back here but I also kidnapped you, so... I don't think I should start looking too closely at my morals where you're concerned." Anthony glanced out the window as the plane eased onto the runway. "I'll just say this now so we're all clear. If you're thinking of running once you get off this plane, I will chase you down. I'm not losing you. If you need me to keep my hands to myself and my mouth shut until you're ready to forgive us, that's fine, but I'm not letting you go. Ever. I love you. We all love you. Maybe alone we didn't deserve you but there are three of us and *you* deserve this much love and care. Okay?"

My breathing sped up as my heart raced. Maybe I wasn't ready to let everything go but I could concede that much. "Okay."

"Okay?"

I nodded. "I won't run away. Being kidnapped one time is enough for me. Plus, after taking the longest nap in a luxury bed on a private jet, I'm afraid to admit that I never want to fly economy ever again. Just this morning... Yesterday...? Whenever I was on that flight alone to London, I think someone sneezed on the back of my neck from two rows back. And I definitely caught a guy trying to take a picture of my ass while I tried to get to the bathroom."

"So you'll stay for my plane?" Anthony said it without any hint of malice. He sent me a soft smile after. "Whatever it takes. Whatever I have is yours, sweetheart."

The pilot came over the clear intercom to announce we'd landed and spouted off the temperature and weather before going silent again. I stood up and realized the three of them were watching me with tension clear on their faces.

I rubbed my eyes and looked down at my feet. "I'm not ready to say things are fine just yet but I'm not crazy. Even just the few hours I was away from y'all I felt like my chest was cracking open. You each love me. I'm not ready to say *that* back yet, either. I'm not going anywhere, though. I should've stayed here and talked everything out. So that's what we'll do now. After we find Madeline."

Will interlaced our fingers and his big body shuddered as he exhaled. "I'll make it right."

I believed him. I also felt like a fool for letting Madeline trick me. One thing about Will that I should've known down to my bones was that he was a good man. He wasn't an asshole who would've done anything to hurt me. On purpose, anyway. He was the same man who'd taken my virginity so sweetly and patiently that when other friends told me their horror stories later in life, I'd had to look away guiltily because mine had been perfect. Because of him.

Zane cupped my chin and tipped my face up to his. Before I knew what he was doing, he stole a kiss and then sent me a devilish wink. "If Anthony can be heavy-handed and unapologetic I can, too."

I followed them out of the plane, a smile trying to fight through my stoic expression.

59

Claire

They'd taken me to the rental house so I could shower and change into clean clothes before Will led us across the island to Madeline's apartment. I tugged the hem of my dress down my thighs but it did nothing to make the outfit any longer, or more appropriate for what we were going to do. The bubblegum pink color and bouncy material felt way too happy and fun for the occasion.

Will still held my hand tight as we walked, his eyes moving over me every few moments. "Are you sure you want to be there?"

I huffed. "She hurt us. The things she said... I need to see her face when she realizes she failed. I need to see her understand that she can't have you."

He tightened his grip. "She never had a chance."

Zane spoke up. "And what are you going to do and say if she claims her last living relative died?"

Will growled. "It won't trick me twice, asshole."

"We need to hear it. You're too goddamn nice for your own good and it's up to us to asshole you up." Zane pitched his voice higher. "But, Will, my godmother's brother's ex-girlfriend's dog got his rejection letter from Harvard. Hold me!"

I giggled at the ridiculousness of it all.

"Did the dog not have backup schools?" Will flashed me a grin. "I'm sorry for his loss but there are plenty of great state schools."

Anthony groaned. "Why do I like you idiots?"

Zane continued. "Will, I just miss you. Be my friend! Ignore all the bad things I've done and will continue to do!"

That hardened Will's jaw. "No."

"Again!" Zane grabbed his shoulders from behind and shook him. "Tell her to take a hike!"

Will let go of my hand to turn around and lunge at Zane. "Alright, asshole, I don't need your coaching."

I watched as the two of them went down in the sand and then popped right back up. Both of them bounced around while dusting the molten sand off of their skin.

"Jesus. That can't be safe for kids." Zane growled at the sand like he was considering fighting it. "Are your feet okay, Claire?"

I looked down at my wedges and rolled my eyes. "No. They're melting into the sidewalk and I'm silently screaming like Satan himself is trying to drag me down to hell."

He growled and tossed me over his shoulder. "Smartass."

"We're here." Will sighed. "Her car's here. Come on. Let's get this over with so we can get back to enjoying ourselves."

Anthony snorted. "Is that what we were doing?"

Will ignored him and led our little band of fools up a set of stairs to the first apartment on the right on the stairs. Without waiting to see if we were ready he lifted his hand and knocked on the door.

My stomach twisted as I listened to someone coming closer to the door and then the sound of the lock turning. When the door opened, it wasn't Madeline who opened the door, though. It was a shirtless Jordan. He was looking over his shoulder into the apartment and scratching his belly so when he turned to us, we'd already had a moment to adjust our faces and hide our surprise.

Jordan choked and took a giant step back. "What-? Um, Madeline?"

And then Madeline was there, standing in the doorway in a tiny piece of silk, her hair and makeup done to make her look like a movie star. She was stunning. Beyond stunning and it made my body buzz with nerves, like her looks would somehow lure Will over to the dark side. Her glossy lips popped open when she spotted Will but it tightened to a firm line when she saw me standing next to him with Anthony and Zane at our backs.

"What are you doing here?" She crossed her arms and pushed her tits nearly up to her chin. It was another practiced move, I was sure.

I meant to let Will start the conversation but I couldn't. "You lied. You told me you and Will were lovers and would be again. Say it again. Say it with him standing right here with us."

Her face turned an unpleasant shade of red. "I think you misunderstood-"

"Enough." Will's hard voice surprised everyone. All traces of the sweetheart were gone. "You went too far."

Jordan stepped forward again and made eyes at me. "Hey, Claire."

Zane wrapped his arm around me from behind, his forearm locked under my chest. "Fuck off, you human shaped bag of farts."

That pulled everyone's attention for a moment. Will shot a befuddled look at Zane and then had to shake his head and clear his throat to get back to what he was trying to do. I just smiled at Zane over my shoulder, loving that his version of possessive protection involved calling someone a bag of farts.

"Will, let me explain. I just-" Madeline reached for Will and before I could claw her arm, he twisted away so she couldn't touch him. "Will, please. I don't know what she told you but-"

"She told me the truth. Something that you seem to be disconnected with. I told you how much I care about her and you decided to lie to her in some misguided attempt to split us up. I have never touched you with anything other than friendship as a motive, Madeline. I thought we were friends. I was happy with our friendship. I thought I could talk to you and trust you but it was all bullshit. You've done everything in your power to hurt Claire."

"Will, please. Please, please, please, just listen to me." Madeline's eyes filled with tears. "Alright, I did lie. I just wanted her to go away. I've been here for you all along, Will. She left you! She left and when she did decide to come back, she can't even choose just you. You deserve better. I just wanted to take care of you. I-... I love you, Will. I always have. Can't you see that?"

Jordan grunted from beside her. "That's news to me. Did you love him while you were riding me fifteen minutes ago?"

It was almost enough to make me feel bad for her. I knew from personal experience how disappointing Jordan was in bed.

"There is no one better than Claire!" Will shouted, his hands balled into fists at his sides. "I don't deserve her but she's mine somehow and I'm never going to take that lightly. I love *her*. I love Claire and that's never going to change. What is going to change is our friendship. You lied and you manipulated me. You pushed past every boundary. We can't be friends, Madeline. You don't respect me or my relationship enough to be a decent person, much less a decent friend. I hope things work out for you but I won't be there to cheer you on."

She practically melted into the doorframe, using it to hold her up. "Will, please."

I reached over and took his hand, worried about him. He was a sensitive guy. When he looked back at me, though, he didn't look distraught. He actually looked a little relieved.

"Your plan didn't work, Madeline." Zane growled the words out. "But you still caused our woman pain and that's unacceptable. There's a good chance we're going to be on the island a lot and if I were you, I'd think about moving somewhere new where no one knew the awful things I'd done. Who's going to book a wedding planner who tried to destroy a happy home?"

60

Will

I stretched out on the couch across from Zane and Anthony as we waited for Claire to come back down after changing. I kept waiting for some kind of shift in my emotions, like the anger would change into sadness at the loss of a friend, but it didn't happen. I kept thinking of all the times I'd changed plans and missed things I'd wanted to do because Madeline called and needed something. She'd been demanding my time and attention for years but I'd always been clear that we were just friends. I thought we were good friends. It pissed me off to know that she had ulterior motives the entire time.

I was angry at myself, too, for being dumb enough to fall for her bullshit. I'd hurt Claire and every time she looked at me I worried she'd see Madeline. I'd told her I loved her but she hadn't said it back. It wasn't fair to expect her to after everything that had gone down but it was killing me.

"You did the right thing." Anthony leaned forward and rubbed his temples. "Ending the friendship, I mean."

Zane nodded. "She would've never left you alone."

I let out a bitter laugh. "I'm not upset about ending the friendship. I'm pissed about the years I spent being her friend. I'm pissed that she hurt Claire. I'm pissed that I was stupid enough to let it all happen the way it did. I should've known better."

"Anything else?" Anthony smirked.

"Yeah, actually." I tugged at my hair. "I'm a little pissed that Claire left and still hasn't clarified how she feels about us. Not at her, but just... I don't know. Maybe I am pissed at her. We're each twisting ourselves into something new to be with her. You think I ever imagined being with the woman I love would include sharing her with two other assholes? Two other assholes who make a fuck ton more money than me? I'm fighting all kinds of shit to be with her. Insecurities I didn't even know I had are showing up. I fucking checked out my ass a few days ago, wondering if it looked good enough to stand up next to a rockstar and a man who owns his own private jet.

"I fucked up. I know it. I'll never forget how easily I hurt her and I'll work for the rest of my life to make sure I treat her like she deserves. I just want a little bit in return. Some fucking sign that she's here with us, that she's not biding her time to get rid of me."

Anthony blew out a deep breath. "I'm a giant fucking nerd."

Zane and I just stared at him, waiting to see where he was going.

"I mean... I've always been the odd man out. I was a virgin until Claire. And now that I have money I'm still a nerd but I'm a nerd with money and it's brought out plenty of unsavory people wanting a bit of what I have. It took me a little longer than I'd like to admit to learn that not everyone who says they care actually gives a shit. I used to be a nice guy. Now, I don't even know if my face still has the muscles to smile most days. Until coming here, anyway. I'm an asshole now. A cold asshole." He shrugged. "I've got my own shit that I'm insecure about, man. She has just as much reason to get rid of me as she does to get rid of you. I'm the one who fucking kidnapped her and tied her up."

We both looked at Zane and he stared back at us with a blank expression. "What? You want me to tell you everything that's wrong with me now? I'm perfect. Keep waiting."

I tossed a pillow at his head and he knocked it away. "Asshole."

His smile faded slowly. "Honestly? You want to know everything wrong with me? Just look at any tabloid for the last decade. Drugs, drinking, arrests... I've been a fucking loser with a good voice for a long time now. Just because I'm clean and don't party the way I used to doesn't mean I don't still get that itch once in a blue moon. I don't tour anymore. When I do shows I practically run to hide by myself when it's over. The band hates me because they think I think I'm better than them. A few weeks ago a woman threw her dirty panties at me and I cringed away from them so hard that I threw my back out. My body is tired from living like an asshole and all I want to do is curl up with Claire and a book, or something. I don't know. I feel like I'm an old man already and I'm not sure I'm a catch."

I grunted. "What I'm hearing is that maybe Claire is right to not commit to us. We're all fucked up."

"I'm an asshole enough to not care that we don't deserve her. We'll work at it. There's three of us. Put us together and that has to equal one good and decent man." Anthony shook his head. "Surely."

Zane snorted. "Between the three of us, we'll make sure we get enough things right to win Claire over every day."

"Where is she?" I rolled my neck from side to side. "This is cruel. I need to know what she's thinking."

"I'm here." Claire slowly walked into the living room wearing one of my t-shirts like a dress with tears in her eyes.

My stomach twisted violently. "Claire?"

She held up her hands and took a deep breath. "I'm sorry. I was angry before but I should've told each of you how I feel so you weren't just wondering. I guess I thought it was obvious. I... I never thought you'd be worried that I was going to turn you away. I look at the three of you and I see strong, confident men who don't need reassuring but you do. I thought I was the only one who felt insecure and lacking in this relationship. I'm sorry I didn't look deeper."

I wanted to grab her and shake her. I needed to hear the words.

"The bet was stupid. I'm still not happy about it but now that I know no one else was there to witness it, it takes the air out of my angry sails. Everything else was just Madeline playing games, I guess. I know your heart, Will, and I know you'd give anyone a dozen chances before cutting them off. Of course, Madeline was able to prey on your goodness." She looked down and when she looked back at me, she did it through her lashes. "But you cut her off for me. That shows me way more than some fake dead grandma comfort hug."

I leaned closer. She still hadn't said the words.

"I quit my job. I sent in my resignation letter upstairs. I don't know if I even want to go back to clean out my apartment. I'm ready for that part of my life to be over. I want this. I want the three of you. I'm sorry I made you wait. I think I needed to see how you handled Madeline before I could tell you how I really feel. Because, despite what the three of you seem to think, I'm far from perfect. I'm jobless and I don't think I want to go back to a typical job. I want to write again. I can live off of my savings for a while but then I'm potentially going to be a mooch living in your home and eating your food while giving nothing back to the household. I'm great at cleaning but my cooking could use some work. I tend to run away from hard situations. And I'm a chicken. I'm still terrified to tell the three of you that I love you because I'm convinced you'll disappear.

"But I do. I love each of you and I want to spend the rest of my life with you. I'm sorry for running. I should've stayed and confronted everything head on. It's something I'd like to work on." She'd turned bright red as she confessed her love. "If it's possible, I want to keep all three of you as mine. It's greedy but it's what I want. I think this only works if we're all together. So I think we should all have sex together. Together, together."

All the blood drained from my head. I shot a horrified look at Anthony and Zane, hoping I was misunderstanding, but they each looked as appalled as I did.

Claire grinned. "Gotcha."

61

Claire

I laughed at the relief that seemed to make each of my men weak. They slumped back on their couches and I even saw Zane wipe sweat from his forehead. Maybe it was mean to joke at such a serious moment but I needed them to focus on something besides what they considered their failures. Listening to them list out things as some sort of proof that they weren't good men was painful. I wanted to prove to them that they were good and decent and everything I needed. I was the lucky one. I had three men who loved me and wanted to spend their lives with me.

"That wasn't very nice, Claire." Anthony slowly stood up and put his hands on his hips. "It's been a very long couple of days and I think that little tease is going to cost you. First, I need to hear you say it again."

I shivered with need for them. It'd been hardly any time since we were last together but it felt like a lifetime had passed. "What do you need me to say?"

Will stood up and slowly moved towards me. "How you feel about us."

"I-" A knock on the front door interrupted me.

Zane growled and proved that he could be just as moody as Anthony as he stormed over to the door and yanked it open. "What?"

I heard Jordan's voice, of all people's, and winced. What the hell did he want? I walked over and saw him standing on the other side of the doorway with his suitcase. "What are you doing here?"

He looked relieved when he saw me. "Claire! Thank god. I was supposed to stay with Madeline for a few more days but that didn't work out, obviously. I already checked out of the hotel and they're saying they're booked up. My flight doesn't leave for another few days."

Zane laughed. It wasn't a small laugh, either. It was a deep, deep belly laugh that rang out through the house and sent Jordan stepping back a foot or two. I found myself smiling at the sound, unable to resist the pure joy in it. When he finally got himself under control he had to wipe tears from his eyes. "Please tell me that you're not asking to stay here."

"I don't have anywhere else to go." Jordan made a face at me that I supposed was meant to convince me. "Come on, Claire. Maybe we can work it out so we get the same flight back home. I won't get in the way."

Will growled from behind me. "You're already getting in the way."

I leaned into his chest and shook my head at Jordan. "This is my home now. Well, not this house, but the island. I'm not going back to London. I already quit. And considering you helped Madeline manipulate Will, the thought of you staying here with us is laughable. As Zane made clear. Call a ride to take you to Miami. There are plenty of hotels around the airport you can stay at. You're not welcome here."

"Claire! Come on!"

Zane waved as he slammed the door shut. "Good riddance."

Will spun me in his arms and held my hips. "Now tell me."

I cupped his face. "I love you, Will."

He shuddered. "Again."

"I love you." I gasped when he spun me around to face Zane. "I love you, Zane. And I love you, Anthony. I love each of you so much. I love you each individually and I love you together."

"Not sexually together, though." Zane scowled and then slowly let his face shift into a grin. "I love you, Claire."

Will spoke against my neck. "I love you, Claire."

Anthony pulled me away from Will and into his arms. "And I love you the most."

I laughed and then squealed when he threw me over his shoulder and took off at a sprint for the stairs. "Anthony?! What are you doing?"

"I'm claiming you first!" He sounded almost as carefree as his younger self. "You're mine, sweetheart. Now and forever."

I lifted my head and saw Will and Zane chasing after us, hungry grins on their faces. I suddenly felt very much like a helpless bunny caught between three big, bad wolves. When Anthony cleared the bedroom doorway and tossed me on the bed, the image shifted, though, because I didn't think there was a bunny alive who was as excited as I was about being eaten.

Before I could even fully settle on the bed Anthony was on me. He kissed me like he'd been away at war and was starving for me. I moaned as he stroked his tongue past my lips and deepened the kiss until I was breathless. I gripped his sides, wishing he was naked, and lifted my legs to wrap them around his waist.

He sat back on his haunches and stared down at me, his eyes roaming over my body moments before his hands traced the same lines. Running his hands up my arms, he lifted them both over my head and held me there. "I do have a meeting with the board tomorrow. One I can't miss."

Why was he talking about meetings? I lifted my hips to rub against the hard bulge in his pants and reached up to kiss his throat. "That's cool."

He let out a quiet laugh that turned into a groan. "I'm retiring. I couldn't imagine being gone for work when you're here, so soft and warm and *eager*."

It took a moment for his words to register. When they did, I dropped my head and stared up at him. "What?"

"Don't worry. I have plenty of money for you to mooch off of, if that's what you decide to do. I can support our weird little family for a few lifetimes. I don't want to miss even a day with you, though." He nuzzled his nose into my neck and groaned. "I want to wake up like this every day for the rest of my life."

Zane sat on the bed next to us. "I already found a potential studio space on the island. I like it here."

Will let out a dramatic sigh while kneeling next to us. "I'm happy to keep doing the same job for the next twenty years or so. I love my job. And I love this island."

I hadn't fully thought everything through but what they were saying meant we'd be staying on the island. Near Uncle Sal. Near Sophia and Jake.

Will saw the wonder in my eyes and smiled. "Sophia's going to lose her shit. She's always talked about you moving into a house next door to hers so you can raise your kids together."

Anthony groaned and dipped his hips. "Kids?"

I held my breath as I looked up at him. "Do you...want them?"

"Only a dozen or so. Only with you." He sat up again and yanked his shirt over his head and tossed it away. Looking at Will and then Zane, he questioned them. "Kids? Kids?"

Will nodded. Zane just grinned. "Twelve might be a lot but I guess there's four of us to share the load."

I was on cloud nine. I was getting everything I'd never known I wanted and more. I was ready to get back to the kissing, though. "That's decided, then. Twelve kids, a house next to Soph, and we're all retired or something. Now touch me."

62

Anthony

Feeling happier than I could remember being since the last time I'd been wrapped up in Claire, I dipped my face and lightly raked my teeth over her throat. "You're wearing too many clothes."

Claire sat up, nearly headbutting me, and wiggled out of the massive shirt she had on. It left her in just a tiny pair of panties with a noticeable wet spot. She reached to shove them down but I stopped her. Pressing her down, I kissed her while running my hand down her side and over her thigh. I curled my hand inwards and teased my fingers over that wet spot.

"Oh, god." She broke away from my kiss to moan. "More, please."

I pressed the panties into her clit and rubbed her harder. "I did some shopping. I was going to surprise you after the wedding with them but this is just as good."

Her eyes widened with excitement even as her mouth fell open in a silent moan. She pressed her thighs together, trapping my hand between them, and then whimpered when I didn't slow down. I watched her body and stopped just before she came. The little angry sound she made at me was almost enough to make me give in.

"I'm going to go get your gifts. I want you to be a good girl and treat Zane and Will to your sweet mouth while I'm gone. I want your ass in the air, swaying for me when I get back." I pressed a kiss to her mouth and smiled. "Leave this pretty pussy alone. Your pleasure is ours tonight, baby."

I stopped at the doorway and looked back in time to see Zane and Will settling on the same side of the bed after stripping at the speed of light. Our good girl already had that sweet ass in the air for me.

She looked at me over her shoulder and spread her knees open wider. "Hurry back."

I took the stairs two at a time going down and back up after grabbing the package I'd had delivered from the kitchen island. I stopped in the bathroom next to my room and took the time to clean everything thoroughly before returning to the room. The sounds that greeted me were fucking delicious.

Will and Zane both moaned and growled under Claire's attention. She had her mouth on Zane and her hand on Will and she was putting her all into it. She was taking Zane deep with every stroke, letting his dick choke her slightly before pulling back. And her ass? Swaying beautifully.

I positioned myself behind her on the bed and Zane automatically caught her head when she tried to turn around to see what I was doing. He gripped her hair and used it to pull her mouth back down on his shaft. I nodded at him and put my new toys down beside us.

Leaning forward, I spread her cheeks and flicked my tongue over her asshole.

Zane swore viciously. "Goddamn. Do that again. She just turned the suction up to fucking twenty."

Who was I to argue? I took my time teasing her with my tongue before sitting back. Her pussy was slick and swollen and it called to me. I pushed two fingers in deep and curled them towards the bed to rub the special spot behind her clit. Immediately, her hips bucked against me. Going back to eating her ass, I shoved her towards yet another orgasm and pulled back just before she came.

I sat back and grabbed the anal plug I'd bought to loosen her ass for us. Covering it with lube, I pressed the tip against her tight little hole and slowly forced it deeper. The noises Claire made were music to my ears as the toy breached that tight ring of muscles and settled inside. I didn't give her a chance to recover before tapping the end of the toy and turning it on. It vibrated to life and Claire threw her head back, the cocks she was servicing forgotten as she cried out.

"Keep worshipping those cocks, baby. You can do it." I grabbed the other toy and smiled to myself. The wand was powerful and the instant buzz it made when I turned it on promised to throttle Claire to the moon.

The first touch of the wand against her clit turned her body to stone. She stiffened and let out a muffled scream as an orgasm hit her immediately. I didn't let up. I braced my knees on either side of hers so she couldn't get away from the pleasure slamming through her. With the wand steady against her clit, I slid my fingers back inside and stroked her g-spot again and again.

Claire's body flushed a deep red as she came again, even more powerfully. Her body shook wildly as she rode it out with Will's dick deep in her mouth.

I couldn't wait any longer. I tossed the wand aside and gripped her hips, lining my body up with hers before thrusting deep. Her pulsing core clamped down on my length and the muscles fluttered until my eyes nearly rolled back in my head. I had to freeze to keep from coming embarrassingly fast.

Will and Zane took turns until Claire pulled Will closer while Zane was already in her mouth. I watched their faces shift to bliss when she took both of them in her mouth at the same time. It was intoxicating to watch.

"This isn't going to last long tonight. Jesus." I could feel the vibrator in her ass and it was driving me to thrust hard and fast as I chased my own pleasure.

Will swore and pulled back. "Fuck. I'm too close already."

Zane pulled away and stroked Claire's cheek. "So fucking beautiful. And fucking talented with that mouth."

I fought the urge to come and pulled out against my base desire. "I need to come in your mouth, sweetheart. I want to see those big eyes go even bigger as you swallow me down."

In what felt like a choreographed dance, we all shifted places. Will laid flat on the bed with Claire on top of him while Zane took his position behind her. I squeezed the base of my cock as I watched. Claire sank onto Will's dick and paused there while Zane fucked her ass with the plug before pulling it out and tossing it aside. As he slowly pushed his dick into her ass, Claire called out our names and dug her nails into Will's chest as her back arched.

They moved slowly at first, getting her used to taking them both at the same time. Will pulled Claire down for a deep kiss while Zane cupped her tits from behind and pinched her nipples until she was uselessly shifting her hips to get more. She wasn't moving until they wanted her to, though.

I waited until the three of them were moving faster, all three of them hurtling towards their releases, to pull Claire's to the side. She met my gaze and opened her mouth for my cock to sink deep. She cried out around my girth and sucked hard as Zane and Will both fucked her harder and faster.

Skin slapping against skin, the sound of panting and growling filled the room until everything boiled over. Zane came with a shout, pumping so much come into Claire's ass that it leaked out as he continued to fuck her deep. Will came next, his mouth locked around one of Claire's nipples as he did. Claire's scream vibrated my dick and triggered my own orgasm. I watched her come apart while still managing to swallow every drop of come I spilled.

I came so hard my vision darkened around the edges and I had to fall back on the bed and just lay there while I caught my breath. Zane collapsed on Will's other side and then Claire slumped flat on Will's chest. We all sounded like we'd just run a marathon and it took several minutes before any of us could speak.

When I could think normally again, I let out a laugh and threw my arm over my eyes. "You'd think sex with so many people would take a little longer…"

Claire groaned. "Any longer and I'd be dead."

"We get to do this forever." Will's arm flopped across my face as he stretched out. He didn't move it right away and then grunted when I shoved it back to his side. "Who's going to buy the custom bed? I need space to stretch out, especially since this is going to be a nightly thing."

"Do you think we'll still be able to do this when we're seventy?" Claire yawned and stretched out, arms going across all three of us. No one complained about her arms.

"We're this wiped at our age now? No chance we're making it to seventy with these aerobics. Thankfully I like your personality, too." Zane made a noise like he was thinking it through. "I'm not opposed to Viagra, though."

Claire's giggle was sweet. "Y'all are going to be such grumpy old men."

I grunted. "Already there, baby."

She crawled off of Will and over me. "You're not old."

"But I *am* grumpy?"

She grinned. "You're not old."

I let out a happy laugh and wrapped my arms around her. "I love you."

"I love you, too." She reached over and patted Will and then Zane. "I love y'all, too. Always."

63

Epilogue

Two Years Later

I rested between Will's legs with my back against his chest. My swollen stomach stuck out in front of me, glowing in the bright sun from all the sunscreen Anthony had rubbed into it. "Who thought it would be a good idea to take two massively pregnant women out on a boat?"

Sophia sat across from us, her own stomach just as swollen as mine. We were both eight months pregnant and stuck that way in the middle of the summer. One of the two of us had decided being on the water was a great plan, forgetting completely about how the boat trip out might make us feel. Bad. It'd made us feel bad.

Uncle Sal pranced down the middle of the boat, his new boyfriend following him to keep the sweeping duster he wore from catching on something and taking the old man out. "The worst of it's over now, honey."

"There's still the trip back." I pouted and looked over my shoulder at Will. "Think I could convince Anthony to get his helicopter pilot to pick me up from here?"

Anthony swept by me with a gentle kiss to my forehead. "The helicopter makes you feel sick, too, sweetheart."

Sophia stood up and waddled over to me. "Fuck it. Let's get in the water and let whatever happens happen. If a shark eats my big ass, I'm not going to complain."

Jake winced and moved behind Sophia not completely unlike Uncle Sal's boyfriend had to Uncle Sal. "Please don't hope to be eaten by a shark, babe."

"I'm not hoping, Jake. I'm just saying, if it happens, I'm not going to fight it. Your kid is stomping on my spleen or something in there and it's miserable." She held out her hand to me. "Come on. We're in this together."

I shrugged and took her hand. "I don't want to be eaten by a shark but I get the sentiment."

Zane helped me up and then hesitated to help me into the water. "Your bestie is sounding a little crazy. Are you sure you want to be in the open ocean with her?"

"No shark is going to come near the gas twins." Uncle Sal perched at the end of the boat and crossed his legs. "Before you two I was under the impression that pregnancy was a beautiful event."

Anthony growled at him as he came to help Zane lower me into the water. "My wife is a beautiful pregnant woman and we don't talk about the gas."

I looked over at Sophia and sighed. "You let one little toot out and suddenly you're one half of the gas twins."

As if it was written into a scene, a group of bubbles came up from behind Sophia. "Oops."

I giggled. "It's shark repellant. You're doing a good thing."

Zane's face was red from holding in a laugh. "Who let these two get pregnant at the same time?"

Will jumped into the water behind me and then came up to help me ease my way into the water. "God, Soph. What the hell did you eat?"

Jake sighed. "Don't bring up food, man."

Uncle Sal leaned forward so he could smirk at me. "Imagine the hell these men would go through if I yelled 'shark' right now? They've taken fifteen minutes to get you in the water."

"Not funny, Sal." Anthony glanced around, always on the lookout for sharks or other ocean creatures.

Once we were in the water, Sophia and I floated next to each other, our fingers linked to keep each other close. Lowering her voice, she informed me of what she'd found out at the beauty salon the day before. "Steve left Madeline."

I squeezed her fingers. "No!"

She sounded gleeful. "Yep. Steve's mom was getting a perm while I was getting my nails done. She said he found out that Madeline was cheating and left her ass. They had a prenup, too. She's not getting shit from him."

I couldn't find it in me to feel bad for her. "She'll find someone else to latch onto soon. That's one thing I'll say about her; she's determined."

"Determined to ruin her life and everyone else's, too." Grunting, Sophia moved on. "Do you want to come over and help me with the nursery this week? Since you finished your book early and hopefully have the time to help a lady who stupidly married one man instead of three?"

"It has been handy to have three men around. Although, I thought they were going to come to blows over building the crib." I gasped when hands grabbed my ass from below and then swore when Will's face popped out of the water next to me. "William! Don't scare a pregnant woman! This is not the water birth I want!"

He pulled me into his arms and pushed Sophia towards the boat. "Scram, brat."

She splashed us but spotted Jake and swam over to him.

"You look so beautiful." Will gently kissed me. "How are my girls?"

I smiled at the mention of our daughter. "We're good. She likes the water. I swear it's the only time she stops kicking me these days."

"Shark!" Uncle Sal's voice rang out, loud and clear, but Will and I just rolled our eyes.

"He's a pain. I think we should prank him after-"

"Get the fuck out of the water! Now!" Anthony took a running leap off the boat and we watched in horror as it looked as if he was immediately trying to fist fight the water.

Will dragged me to the boat and all but threw me aboard before doing the same to Sophia. Uncle Sal helped us both up and we all stood there watching as Anthony swam back to the boat. Zane and Will dragged him up and I watched with tears in my eyes as they both quickly hugged Anthony before shoving him towards me.

He was pale and looked freaked out but there was a boyish smile on his lips. "I fought a shark for you."

"There was a real shark?!" I was screeching. Full on screeching. "Anthony! No! You dove into the water to fight a shark?! What the hell?!"

Uncle Sal sank heavily into his chair. "Well, hell. That was enough excitement for this old man."

I jabbed my finger in his direction. "This is why you shouldn't cry wolf!"

"Goddammit." Jake groaned. "I already lose because there's only one of me to do shit around our house and now you just fucking fought a shark for your woman."

Zane looked a little shaken himself as he gripped Anthony's shoulder. "Shit."

"I need to sit down." I found myself immediately being carried to the bench seat. Anthony curled his big body around mine and held me tight. I could feel a tremor go through him every few seconds. "Thank you. Never do that again, though. If something happened to you... Just no more fighting sharks, okay?"

He let go of me and twisted around to throw up over the side of the boat. After he was done he wiped his mouth and let out a shaky laugh. "When we tell our grandchildren this story, we'll leave that part out."

I rested my head on his shoulder and took a deep breath. "That's fair. Um... Guys?"

Everyone looked at me expectantly.

"I think our daughter got a little excited about the idea of seeing a shark..." I took another deep breath. "My water broke."

All hell broke loose.

Ten hours later we welcomed our first daughter to the world and despite being a little early, she was perfectly healthy. Sophia couldn't be bested, however, and that same day she went into labor and gave birth to her son.

By the end of the day no one remembered Anthony threw up. Especially not when Jake passed out at the sight of his son coming into the world.

64

FREE PREVIEW OF MY EX'S ROOMMATES

*H**oly penis*! My mouth dropped open in shock as I stood in the bathroom doorway, where I'd just walked in on my boyfriends' roommate, Silas Turner. *Close your mouth, you idiot, there's a penis just hanging around.* No matter how much my brain screamed at my body to turn around and leave, I was frozen with no idea how to delicately remove myself from the situation. *It's huge.* I meant to slap my hands over my eyes but I covered my mouth instead. It was probably for the best because I didn't trust myself to not repeat my thoughts out loud.

"What the fuck, Harper?!" His angry voice was cold enough to chill the steam filling the room.

I jerked my gaze up his body, stumbling over a lot of abs and two very hard pecs, until I met his hard gaze. He was fuming. His face was twisted with his anger and not even the water droplets rolling down his bare chest could distract from the storm in his eyes.

"I'm so-" Sorry. I was going to say I was so sorry but movement from down below caught my attention and my jaw just about unhinged itself from the shock and awe of watching Silas Turner's huge penis grow stiff in front of me.

Time stood still as it reached towards me, an angry red at the tip and so veiny that I thought I could hear the pulse in it. *Oh. So, that's what a penis is supposed to look like.* That thought sent guilt flushing through my system and I jerked my gaze back up to Silas'.

Too late, I realized he was even more pissed off than before. "It's bad enough that you've been here for days, *Princess*, the least you could do is learn to fucking knock!"

Okay, even with a giant, distracting penis, he didn't get to talk to me like that. "I did knock! No one answered so I came in. Why don't you put a towel on?!"

"Because I'm in *my* bathroom! Fuck! Jake needs to get back here and get you out of here. I can only be around a gold-digging pain in the ass for so long before I lose my shit." He'd riled himself up, it seemed. "You've been nothing but a distraction since you showed up. Jake's a fucking fool for doing this with you."

Buttons pushed. I straightened to my full height and glared at him. "Jake broke records last season, while dating me, so how's that for a distraction? Asshole. For a kicker, you sure do think you're god's gift, don't you?"

Carter Hayes, another of Jake's roommates, joined us, much to my continued horror. He looked at Silas and then grinned at me. "Ah. I was wondering what all the shouting was about but I see that Jake's *baby* has finally seen what Jake's not playing with. It really isn't fair, is it?"

His stupid joke was worse because I'd just been thinking something similar. I scowled at him and then back at Silas. "Thank god we're leaving this hellhole."

Jake's third and final roommate, Dylan Cooper, walked by at the moment and shot me a hard glare. He shook his head and kept walking, not even bothering with a rude comment which was almost more offensive, like I wasn't even worth his time.

"Sure you don't want to take a picture before you leave?" Carter really was an asshole.

I pushed past him and stomped back to Jake's room. Slamming the door, I leaned against it and covered my face with my hands. I couldn't live with them for one more day. Seeing Silas naked was just the icing on the cake.

Jake had been gone for a week, visiting family, and I was ready for him to be home. Living alone with his roommates without him for even just that small amount of time was too much. I told myself over and over again that I just had one more night. Jake would be home that evening and we would attend the beginning of the year banquet for the football team and then we'd move out together in the morning. It was all planned out. I'd packed Jake's things for him while he was away and my stuff was already ready and waiting.

One more night. Just one more night. I groaned heavily as I pushed away from the door and sat on the bed next to my black garment bag. I'd kept one special dress out to wear to the banquet and if I dug down deep, under all the stress of moving and living with three cavemen, I'd find my excitement again. The banquet was a big deal and getting to dress up was nice. A few of the people in my sports medicine program would be there so I'd get to see friendly faces.

I didn't want to let Silas ruin my night. I still felt hot with embarrassment and the idea of facing any of them after I'd stared at his penis was humiliating, but Jake was coming home and I'd spend the night in his arms, forgetting about his roommates.

My dress would be perfect for dancing and I was going to make sure Jake and I danced. I needed something, anything, to get over the mood I was in.

When I knew the coast was clear, I snuck into the bathroom and took a quick shower, taking care to not mess up my hair. I wanted to be perfect for Jake so I did an everything shower, scrubbing and shaving every part of me until I was shiny, smooth, and smelled like his favorite fruit, strawberries. I did my makeup to perfection, making sure my eyes were dramatic but still classy. I let my hair down and it fell in big waves, the dark auburn color shining against the emerald green dress I'd chosen. I'd worn it before but I didn't think anyone would notice. It was an off the shoulder gown with a slit up to my thigh that only showed when I took an exaggerated step or crossed my legs. It was sophisticated and sexy and it made me feel like a goddess.

I'd just struggled to zip up the back by myself when the bedroom door swung open and Jake walked in. I straightened and posed for him, a bright smile on my face. "Hey, babe so glad you're back! What do you think?"

He dropped his duffel bag at his feet and pinched the bridge of his nose. "It's not a pageant, Harper. It's been a long fucking day already and I just need a minute, okay?"

I swallowed down my hurt feelings and gestured to the bed. "Sit down and I'll massage your shoulders."

He finally walked over and stopped just an inch away as he stared down at me. "Your tits look fantastic."

"Jake!" I laughed and pushed him down on the bed. "I have your suit out and ready for you. I'll massage you and then you can take a shower. Just a few hours and we'll be back here for one more night before we move into our new place tomorrow. Then you can take a few days off to just relax. I know you're tired."

His phone vibrated where he'd put it on the bed and I glanced down as he grabbed it and silently tapped away at it before putting it down again. "My right shoulder, Harper. Jesus."

It was fine. He was just stressed and needed a break. I dug my fingers in just the right spot and was rewarded with a deep, satisfied groan. I had a fleeting thought of how much I'd loved massaging him in the beginning of our relationship and how much that moan would've turned me on back then.

Another text came in and he practically dove for the phone again. My nerves were probably shot from everything going on, all the changes we were going through, but I felt uneasy about the way he was acting with his phone. "Who's messaging you?"

Jake scoffed and stood up, nearly knocking me to the floor in his haste. "Jesus, Harper. You're not going to turn into some clingy type now, are you? It's nothing. I just got back, I'm not looking forward to this shit tonight, and I just need some peace for once. I'm going to take a shower. Try to find a different dress. That material looks cheap."

Read "My Ex's Roommates" for $3.99 or FREE with Kindle Unlimited: https://www.amazon.com/dp/B0D3CYQLZK

Printed in Dunstable, United Kingdom